BLOOD FICTION

BLOOD FICTION

DIANE ELLIOTT

NEXT CENTURY
PUBLISHING

Blood Fiction

Cover design by Linda Griffith

Published by Next Century Publishing
Austin, TX
www.NextCenturyPublishing

ISBN: 978-1-68102-497-4

Printed in the United States of America

Books published by Diane Elliott:

Nonfiction
Art & Inspiration, co-author
Sunshine Soil and Short Seasons

Fiction
Strength of Stone

Poetry
Shattering Porcelain Images
When Volcanoes wake
Songs of Bernie Bjorn (a verse novel)

Strength of Stone won the WILLA Literary Award for History and was short listed for the Saroyan award for international fiction in 2003.

Songs of Bernie Bjorn: "These songs of the ardent title character sing like wildfire; readers should be singed and ravished by her burning."

–Kirkus Reviews,
Named to Kirkus Reviews' Best Indie Books of 2016

BLOOD FICTION

CHAPTER 1

Franniemarie Hanks slapped and squeaked a sponge of whole wheat bread to the rhythm of Jean Pierre Rampal's flute (compliments of NPR). Cricket Hanks, smelling of earth and oil, strode into the kitchen on a crisp early morning draft. Flipping the radio to country western, he plunked himself down at the counter and poured coffee into his cup. "Franniebaby, whatcha got to nibble on?"

"Raisin pie or oatmeal cookies," Franniemarie sighed, slipping the sponge into a bowl and covering it.

"Christ-sake, Frannie, can't a man get something to eat around here without tripping over your lower lip? What the hell's the big sigh for?"

"You want the pie or the cookies?"

"I'll take the pie and I deserve a decent answer. Thirty years I been taking care of you an' the kids. Got complaints, spit 'em out. But none of this long face shit."

If there was one thing the years living with Cricket taught Franniemarie, it was to keep her mouth shut.

No matter how she couched her discontent, the ensuing dialogue was bound to blow into a full scale confrontation that could last for days and would end with her on the sofa nursing a migraine.

As she set Cricket's pie in front of him, the phone rang. In one smooth motion Cricket swung around in his chair, turned down the radio—tucked the receiver between his shoulder and ear. Franniemarie didn't realize she was holding her breath till she heard him chuckle, "Charlie! How's she hanging?" Charlie was Cricket's cousin, bonded, so the family story went, first time they crawled together.

Franniemarie ran water into the kitchen sink. Beyond the window above her sink, Nebraska's prairie stretched flat to eternity. Cricket told his bride he'd plant trees outside the window, and had been puzzled when Franniemarie made him promise not to. Even now she did not have words to explain her need to gaze on this uncluttered space—this uncluttered backdrop on which she played snippets of her history, reinvented her present, and experimented with the possibilities of her future.

I could kill him. Might be worth it to never hear another country western whine. Next time he goes to artificially inseminate the cows, I could partner him. When he asks me to hold the nitrogen cartridge, I'll spray him with the liquid, freeze him where he stands, then, just give a little push. On her prairie screen she watched him fall and shatter, watched herself drop the cartridge, and walk back to the house.

Shaking cleanser into the sink, she told herself, *Don't forget to wear gloves. Don't want your prints on anything of his. Freak accident.*

"Charlie's got his planter torn t'hell. Thought I'd go help him with it tomorrow. You hear me Franniemarie? I'm going to Char…"

"I heard you."

"Don't forget to post those bills when you get the mail."

"I won't forget."

"Better do it soon's you're done there, so's you don't…"

"I said, I won't forget."

"All right then. I'm outta here."

The door slammed behind him. She dried her hands and switched the radio back to NPR, the Rampal piece finished, the magic gone.

At the mailbox, she traded outgoing mail for a handful of advertisements and three rejection notices. Walking back to the house, she read the editorial comments. "Not what we're looking for right now … Nice writing, but too strong for our audience … We are sorry to inform our contributors, but due to lack of funding we have been forced to suspend publication."

Franniemarie tossed the junk mail on the counter—then hid the rejects behind a row of cookbooks. She could hide the rejected poetry, but she couldn't hide from the sound of Cricket's witticisms echoing in her mind. "Mailing yourself letters again, I see. If a person were any good at a thing they wouldn't be rejected ninety-nine percent of the time. Time you spend scribbling's time robbed from me." She grabbed her head as if to squeeze the inner voice out. "I'll freeze you stiff and watch you shatter," she shouted. Had her nature allowed, she would have cried.

She punched down the bread, began to peel potatoes, *Maybe I really am crazy.* The way the family told it, her grandfather died in a mental institution, her aunt Dorien was strictly loony tunes, living somewhere in the Bay Area in a house that hadn't seen running water or electricity in over thirty years, and then there was her mother. *No one need tell me mother's not quite square.*

Mother! If she hadn't left the Bay Area, what would have life been like? Guess I wouldn't be. I'll probably never know why she brought me out here—back to Grand's—back to the place where her mother was born. But I do know I wouldn't have survived if it hadn't been for Grand.

Before she could take the thought further, Franniemarie's mind flipped to the last time her mother called. Nannette called to ask her to lunch in Lincoln. To be exact, she called from her Arizona home and said, "Oh, Frannie, I do so miss the people at the Federal Reserve. They always treated me so good, not like these dumb chippies here in Mesa."

When Franniemarie protested, "For heaven's sake Mama, we're right in the middle of harvesting. Look, we haven't seen you in years. Brooks hardly remembers you. If you're going to go flying around the country why don't you come out here?"

Her mother had responded indignantly. "Why would I want to do that? After all, I was just asking you to lunch!"

Franniemarie, long past the anger she once felt toward her mother, giggled. *The woman was nuts. Yep, that was the day I realized she was nuts and nothing I did or could do was going to change it. That's when I first saw the humor in the things she said.* It had been sixteen years since that call came, and she hadn't heard from Nannette since. It still felt like yesterday.

I'm sure as hell not going to call her. Franniemarie snorted and tossed the potatoes into the water. *Fool that I am, and stuck with Cricket—I'll be damned if I'll invite that piece of negative baggage back into my life.* If there were two things that could raise a migraine in Franniemarie, one was Cricket, the other her mother—and her mother was long gone from her life.

By the time Cricket came tromping in for lunch, Franniemarie had swallowed her anger. Lathering his hands at the sink, he sniffed the air. "Smells good, Frannie, what's for lunch?"

"Mashed potatoes and gravy, leftover meatloaf, cabbage salad, and pie."

Cricket beamed. "You do know the way to a man's heart, Franniemarie. If there's another in all of Furnas County can match your cooking, it's one I haven't met." It was an indisputable fact, Cricket did like his food.

Franniemarie was barely seated when the phone rang. Cricket answered, passed it to her, then tackled his lunch.

"Franniemarie Hanks?"

"Yes."

"You be the niece of Mrs. Dorien Weaver?"

"Yes."

"Well, then, I'm Becca Smith, Mrs. Rebecca Smith, with the Oakland Welfare Department. I got your name from Mrs. Weaver's aunt, Prudence Ellen Silverton. I'm callin a'cause we are very concerned for Mrs. Weaver. You familiar with the conditions she's living in?"

"Her poverty?"

"Not only that. She's living in a house should'a been condemned years ago. It's a fire trap and a health hazard. The neighbors are worried 'bout what would happen if a fire broke out. Dry as a bone it's been these last seven years, the whole neighborhood could go up in flames. I want you to know we tried and tried to help her, but she won't hardly talk to us. When she do, she says, 'don't worry 'bout this ole house. I sold it, and I'm buying that piece of property for sale cross from the library. I just need to get the paperwork done. You know how long ever' thing takes.' So we wait and wait. Course nothing ever happens."

"I've always heard she was the family crazy."

"Well, now, we don't go so far as that. Eccentric, very eccentric, that's how we refer to her, but don't doubt this here woman needs care. What we need is to find a family member to take charge—to become a guardian and conservator of her estate. I understand the estate's worth quite a sum of money."

"Have you talked to my mother?"

"Matter of fact, we have. Your mother says, so long's her sister's no threat to anybody, how she lives is nobody's business."

"What about their sister Annamarie?"

"We tried and tried to get aholta her—left a lotta messages and she never called back. And your mother refuses to do one thing. Keeps sayin, 'way Dorien wants to live isn't any of her business'."

"Frankly, Mrs. Smith, that's about my attitude."

"Mrs. Hanks, you cannot conceive how this woman's living. It's not like she's in any mental condition to be making her own decisions. She has NO power, NO running water, NO heat. The roof's falling in on her head. Let me send you some pictures of her house. I mean, you cannot imagine. In spite of the shape the house is in, I understand the lot is worth quite a sum of money."

"Rubbish. Aunt Dorien never paid a cent to anyone after her daughter died. The bank has paid her taxes and not foreclosed—though Lord knows why. At any rate, the bank basically owns the place. If there is any money left, when she dies it will go to her sisters."

"All I can say is we need, she needs, someone to take charge. This just can't go on like this. I have statements from the neighbors I'd like to pass on to you. Will you let me do that? Just look at this stuff afore you say no."

"You can send it, but for the life of me I don't know what good it's going to do." Franniemarie rolled her eyes and handed Cricket the receiver.

Cricket cocked his eyebrow, then cradled the receiver.

"Oakland Welfare Department. Some woman who can't speak the English language. Seems they want someone to commit Aunt Dorien."

Figures." Cricket ran the word around a mouthful of meatloaf. "That's affirmative action for you." Cricket swallowed. "Thought you never met her. How come they're calling you?"

"I guess they tried to get ahold of Aunt Annamarie first, but they haven't been able to get in touch with her. When they called Mother, she basically told them to go soak their heads. Then she called Aunt Pru."

"Figures."

"Aunt Pru gave them our number."

"Why didn't they call your cousin—what's her name?"

"Lilianna? I don't know. Didn't even think about her. Don't know if she even lives in the Bay Area."

Cricket turned his attention back to his meal. Absent-mindedly, Franniemarie spooned mashed potatoes over the slab of meatloaf swimming in a sea of congealed gravy on her plate. *Snowcapped mountains. I've never seen mountains. Never seen the ocean. Or the desert. The Grand Canyon. The*

Great Salt Lake, forests, sequoias. Hell! I've never met any of my family. Well hardly any. Only my mother Nanette, my beloved great-grandmother Anna who will always be Grand to me, and Grand's youngest daughter Pru. My grandmother Lilian died long before I was born. I never met her husband, my grandfather, Francis. And now Grand's dead, and Mother's good as dead to me.

Cricket snapped his fingers in her face. "Where in hell are you, Lady? I said I'm going out."

"Oh, Cricket! I do wish I could meet Aunt Dorien."

"You crazy, or what? Little I've heard, they're all nuts. Not one packin' a full deck—not since your great-grandparents. Look at your mother. Who'd want a bigger dose of that?" Cricket rolled his eyes in exasperation.

"That's not fair. No one has ever said anything nasty about Aunt Annamarie, and she's a movie star. Guess if she were crazy we'd have heard of it."

"Frannie, you've never even met her." The door bounced behind him.

Franniemarie scraped her plate into Dog's dish. *If I could just see my aunt. Maybe—maybe what? Mother always said Aunt Dorien was the writer in the family, wrote plays and poetry when she was a kid. Maybe I just want to reassure myself that I don't have to end up like her. That's silly. So long as I'm anchored to Cricket I'm safe.* She cleared the table, felt a headache coming on, climbed the stairs to their bedroom and pulled back the patchwork comforter Grand had stitched in commemoration of her marriage to Cricket.

Tracing the tulip pattern with her fingers, she felt her great-grandmother Anna Freeman's fingers near—felt the embrace of her arms, took solace in the memory of her voice, and drifted into the bedroom they had shared in her house—a house not twelve miles from this bedroom where her husband's conception had taken place. A child again, she snuggled under Grand's patchwork quilt, taking in the smells and sounds of the kitchen where her grandparents and their hired hand were eating and planning the day. Back to the present, she wondered how she would have survived had Grand not held her close—held her safe when she, Franniemarie, was a small child. *How I wish my mother had left me there longer. I remember those days, before she took a job in Lincoln, steno-clerk for the Union Pacific. They were dream-like, secure, safe. I wish she hadn't retrieved me and brought me to town so that I could attend kindergarten. At least she let me spend summers back on Grand's farm. That is, until Pru Ellen and Al had the farm transferred into their name. That was the summer I was eight. I didn't see the farm for another eight years—not until I'd saved enough for a bus ticket and spent Christmas with them. When I married Cricket, our renewed relationship became cemented.*

We are not all crazy! My Grandmother Lilian wasn't crazy! **I'm not crazy.** *Everyone says, if she'd lived, our lives would have been different. Grand always said, "Altogether different if Lilian hadn't died when your mother, Nanette, was a toddler—Annamarie but a babe." No. The craziness didn't start there. Perhaps it started with their father, my grandfather Francis Tourneau.*

Franniemarie knelt on the floor by the bed and pulled a large cardboard letter file from under it. She wiped a thick layer of dust off the file with her sweatshirt sleeve, then pulled the shirt over her head and tossed it on the floor. Running her fingers over the edges of the double row of envelopes, worn soft as flannel, her fingers unleashed voices recorded on fine old parchment, linen, and cheap rag: her Grandmother

Lilian's voice announcing the births of her daughters Dorien, Nannette, and Annamarie; the price of eggs in San Francisco; a car-men's strike; her take on the elections of the day; the sounds and smells of the tuberculosis sanitarium where she, Lilian, died before her youngest, Annamarie, had celebrated her third birthday; soft exchanges between great-grandparents Anna and Spencer Freeman, sometimes half a continent apart, working their way through the sorrow of survival; notes from a long succession of Grandfather Francis Tourneau's housekeepers gossiping about the state of the Church and reassuring Anna Freeman that her granddaughters were doing fine; Francis Tourneau's voice sometimes courtly, kind and wise, sometimes blunt, brutal and accusatory. *The crazies started there. Had to have. The crazies started with my grandfather Francis.*

"For Christsake Frannie! I been looking all over for you." Startled, she dropped the grayed letter. "What the hell you doing—lollygagging in your underwear in the middle of the day? I come in, bread dough's rising out of the pan, slopping all over the counter." Franniemarie scrambled up, scattering letters across the bed. "What you get outta reading that old stuff, I'll never know. Water over the dam."

Mute, Franniemarie pulled on a fresh shirt. Long ago, she'd given up any attempt to make him understand her contention that somewhere in her family's past were buried keys that could unlock the confusion of her present.

"It's not like those bits and snippets are enough to piece anything together." Cricket stomped down the stairs.

While Franniemarie scooped dough off the counter and shaped it into loaves, Cricket drank his mid-afternoon coffee and read the newspaper. *Sonofabitch has no right to judge me.*

Bastard's never in his life been caught in an introspective thought. Just lives day to day sure in the notion he's all a man can be. Sanctimonious asshole.

Without a word, Cricket finished his coffee, left the house, and tore up the drive in his Chevy S10. *Way he drives I could suck out the brake fluid in that truck and he'd go spinning off the road, down an embankment, over a cliff. Only, there aren't any cliffs around here. He'd shoot over the crossing at Furnace Creek and land in Anderson's corn field, thinking, "Holy Shit! I should have checked the brake fluid."* She giggled at the image of the red battered truck landing in the field—the look of surprise on Cricket's face.

Franniemarie followed her stubborn chin back up the stairs and into their bedroom. Methodically, she gathered the letters and began refiling them according to date. Absentmindedly, she unfolded the one loose note and read:

Arroyo Sanitarium

12 February 1920

Dear Papa,

This note is for your eyes only. Mama, being sheltered as she has been by you and her folks, would never understand. I've prayed and prayed, and I know that if I get out of this place alive, I must collect Dorien and come home. Francis' temper is not good for any of us. Papa dearest, you've been in this world and you know how it can be. If it comes to this, please make her understand for me.

The only thing that gives me courage is that I know the kiddies are safe with you, and God sees that everything works out for the best.

Lilian

Was it best she died six months later? Was it best grandmother Lilian split her daughters? Dorien to live with her mother-in-law—Nannette, and Annamarie to her own mother, my beloved Grand? And how did Grand's husband Spencer take his daughter's easy reference to God? Everyone, my mother, his last born Pru Ellen, his wife Grand—acknowledged he was a confirmed atheist who carried his beliefs to the grave.

And how did this note find its way into the collection? How could Lilian have sent it to her father without Grand knowing? At some point Grand had to have read this note. Would it have been after Lilian died? Perhaps she didn't know about it until after Grandpa died—or could Pru Ellen have found it and filed it with the letters? Pru always spoke of her sister and nieces as the beauties her parents doted on, herself the only ugly one in the bunch. If Aunt Pru placed the letter with the others, did she do it for spite, for the record, or both?

All night Franniemarie's mind swam in shadows tinted sometimes red, sometimes smoky shades of gray. The shadows became smoke stacks spewing flames, moist stalactites dripping fluorescent water, then turned into overstuffed furniture behind which Franniemarie hid with Brooks, her youngest, while Nannette smothered Jacob, her second. To keep Brooks from crying out, she pinched his nose and felt her heart throbbing in her finger tips, her heart's blood pulsing in her mouth. Sacrificing her second-born, she saved the first, only to run through fetid tunnels filled with sweating pipes.

Now all three sons, Preston, Jacob, and Brooks were running with her, and the putrid smell became the smell of rotting flesh; the flesh of Jacob, his eyes poked out by the force behind her mother's knitting needle. Then came fresh air and they followed it to light, into a garden where Nannette sat on a stone bench knitting.

Nannette, aware of Franniemarie's presence, gracefully freed a length of yarn from her basket. Franniemarie stood like a stalagmite pillar at the edge of her mother's garden. Nannette looked toward Franniemarie and smiled. "You know you can't win. Now, if you'd been a son, I might have let you. You chose woman. Big mistake."

Silver needles flashed. Franniemarie and her boys, chased by a knife, raced through a cavern dodging stalagmites, slipping on wet stone. Brooks kept falling. Franniemarie picked him up, stumbling she tried to catch up to her first-born, who ran hand-in-hand with Jacob.

And then Franniemarie lay awake, listening to the sound of Cricket's breathing, staring into the familiar shadows of their bedroom. The dream was a variation on an old night theme that haunted her in the years after she'd lost Jacob. By some strange quirk of shock, they'd stopped five years later when Preston died. Franniemarie thought the dream had spun out of her life. She repeatedly swallowed as if she could vanish the old dream by eating it.

In the safe dark next to Cricket, Franniemarie contemplated her mother. Petite, self-contained, smug, Nannette cocked her left eyebrow and looked toward her. "For God's sake, Franniemarie, it's as easy to fall in love with a man with money as a pauper. Don't be a fool, money always outlasts love."

Nannette knew all the moves, never missed a trick—secured her old age pension long before her body saw middle age.

But had she ever loved? Have I ever seen her cry? No. All I ever saw were two emotions, rage and some giddy high she filled with melodic laughter.

Franniemarie shivered, pushed the image out, and folded herself against the safety of Cricket's strong back.

Tomorrow. Tomorrow I'll go see Aunt Pru Ellen. I may not be able to see the rest of my family—at least I have my aunt—my great aunt.

CHAPTER 2

A T SEVEN IN the morning, Franniemarie strode across the familiar old farm house porch, the porch built by her great grandfather, the house—her childhood haven. She knocked on the weathered door, let herself in and called. "Pru! Pru Ellen! You home?"

"Where else, in God's name, would I be this time of the morning?" Pru Ellen shouted back. "I'm in the bathroom. Come on in."

"Aunt Pru. Sorry to bother you so early, but I got the strangest call yesterday, and I wanted to catch you before you and Val took off for—where's your show tonight?"

"Lincoln Senior Center." Pru Ellen hummed a melody while she smudged a touch of shadow on her eye lids, a bit of rouge on her cheeks, tugged her synthetic wig into place, and smiled at the new face in her mirror. "Who would have guessed I would get myself up like this at seventy-five? My nieces may have been the beauties. Age is one hell of a leveler.

Now, they're not so pretty; I've found Max Factor, and I'm the one on stage."

Franniemarie followed her into the bedroom. "There was this lady. She called from the Oakland welfare office." Franniemarie watched her aunt, her great aunt, as if for the first time. Pru Ellen sat on her bench at the foot of her bed and stretched black fishnet stockings the length of her long athletic legs. She slipped into tap shoes, stood, spun around facing Franniemarie, and then burst into a joyous tap dance and ditty of her own making. "These legs will do the walkin / long after you've stopped talkin / cause this song is mine, all mine. / Perhaps you did not love me / like I wanted you to love me / but now this song is mine, all mine.

"I may not have been the beauty in this family but these legs are gonna keep on going till the energizer bunny's long gone." Pulling on a pair of slacks over the fishnets she asked, "So what brings you here, my little kitten?"

Franniemarie took a deep breath. "This lady from the Oakland Welfare Department called about Aunt Dorien. Said you gave her my number."

"Oh, that. I meant to tell you, but then Val called and we spent the afternoon in rehearsal. To tell the truth, I just forgot. Sorry, 'bout that."

Franniemarie stifled a gasp. *How bizarre, my great aunt speaking in the flip style of my son. Brooks' wife sounds the same. What is this world coming to, when the generations get it all mixed up.* "Why'd you give them my number?"

"Well, if your mother or her sister won't do anything for her, it just seems to me that you would be the next logical person to work with them. After all, you are her niece. And, Franniemarie, you wouldn't believe how she's living. When

I was out there last year I saw her place with my own eyes. Believe me, it's not much better than living under a bridge. Like I told you then, I wished I could have done something for her. After all, I've been her aunt since a time before I was born. Did I tell you I saw her when I was there?"

"Something about meeting her in a coffee shop."

"The welfare people told me that at ten each morning she goes for coffee at this little doughnut shop. The girls there all know her and they seem to like her. She doesn't bother anybody, you know.

"Sure enough she comes in at ten and sits right down beside me. I pretended to be a tourist and not someone who had lived there for two years just before the war. Asked her some questions about the history of the area. She's smart, you know. She can talk about anything—history, astronomy, geology, you name it. Your grandfather always said she was the family brain. She seemed almost normal, except for the way she was dressed. Way she was dressed, you could see crazy coming down the street half a mile off. We had a good talk about the changes down in Long Beach since the war. But when I said, 'Dorien, you do know who I am, don't you? I'm your Aunt Prudence Ellen, your mother, Lilian's sister.' Well, I hope to tell you she just jumped off her stool and she started cursing. I wouldn't use the words she used, but she said, 'you're no relative of mine. I haven't any relatives north of the Mason Dixon Line.' Still, I do feel sorry for her, and I wish you'd commit her."

And why don't you? Out of long habit, Franniemarie bit her tongue. In the years she lived with her mother, she learned that a personal question would be taken as an attack. "Mom seems to think, so long's her sister's no threat to anybody, how she lives isn't anyone's business."

"What do you expect from your mother? She's hardly an angel of compassion."

"But, I couldn't do that to her either. At least not from here. It's weird; I do wish I could see her." Franniemarie sighed, "But you know Cricket, he'd never let me go."

"Now, don't you start on Cricket. Believe me, Franniemarie, when he's gone you'll be singing another tune. You can't imagine how much I miss my Al. This old house is so silent now he's gone."

"Oh, Pru, don't start. He damn near drank himself to death, and …"

"That's just it! I hated it then. Now I'd be glad to put up with it. I miss him that much, Frannie. Oh, my God, just look at the time! Supposed to meet Val at nine. We're taking her car. Gotta book."

Gotta book? Franniemarie pushed the key into her ignition. *Aunt Pru, bedrock solid Aunt Pru, is getting stranger and stranger.*

The car started as a light sprinkle of rain began. By the time she'd reached home and pulled off her jacket, a torrent of rain was cascading down her kitchen window. She was glad she was no longer traveling. The refrigerator motor turned over, reminding her to search for the source of the noxious odor that wafted into the kitchen each time she opened its door. Methodically, she began to empty its contents onto the floor, sorting as she worked; compost, condiment, and not yet perished. *I wonder if Lilianna married. Would she have kept her mother's maiden name? Why did Aunt Annamarie never marry? Or did she? She might have and just kept Tourneau as her stage name. Lilianna's about as common a name as Franniemarie. How hard would it be to find her? Perhaps, if a person knew where to start looking. I know! The Salvation Army. Ann Landers—what was it? Something about they'll do a search for missing relatives.*

Franniemarie cleared a space on the floor, kicked the refrigerator door shut, pulled a Lincoln phone directory from under a stack of newspapers, and thumbed the yellow pages till she found the number for the Salvation Army headquarters.

A week later her reply came, Lilianna Tourneau … San Francisco … Shaking, Franniemarie dialed the number, listened to a recorded message, "You have reached … " She cleared her throat. "I'm Franniemarie Hanks, daughter of Nannette Tourneau Martin. I'd like very much to talk to you …" Franniemarie left her number, poured a cup of coffee, and sat down. *What if she doesn't want to talk to me? Okay, so what? I don't even know what I want from her.* Resting her elbows on the table, Franniemarie ran her fingers over her eyelids, stretching them towards her temples. Automatically, she dialed Aunt Pru's number.

"Who's calling?" Her aunt's abrupt delivery always startled Franniemarie, making her wonder why she had called, making her temporarily forget that Pru Ellen was her only connection with her past.

"Franniemarie."

"What's up?"

"I just got Lilianna's number. Got it through the Salvation Army."

"So, what's her take on Dorien?"

"Haven't talked to her. Called and just got her answering machine."

"About time the two of you did something about your aunt."

"I don't think there's anything we can do about Aunt Dorien. It's just, oh, you know, she's always fascinated me. I wish I knew the family history better."

"Well, you got all Mama's letters. What more do you want?"

"Guess I'd like to just talk to her."

Pru Ellen snorted. "She won't talk to anyone claims kin to her."

"That doesn't stop me from wishing I knew her. In her letters to Grand, she was always asking questions about her mother. What did she like? What did she believe? Was she spiritual? Things her father wouldn't talk about, the same sort of things I wonder about family. What happened to my father? Who lived when, and how did they live? How did they feel about that world?"

"Frannie, you ask too damn many questions!"

"Aunt Dorien asked the same questions."

"Yeah, and look where that got her."

The kitchen door slammed behind Cricket, punctuating Aunt Pru's statement. "Coffee time, Frannie."

"Gotta go. Cricket just came in."

"Give the boy a kiss for me."

When Franniemarie hung up the phone, Cricket had already poured himself a cup of coffee. As she filled a plate with cookies, she wondered how to tell Cricket she'd made contact with her cousin. Tell him in such a way as not to bring down sarcasm and ridicule.

Franniemarie jumped when the phone rang.

"Hello. Yes. Yes. Just having a cup of coffee." *Shower? Oh, my! I forgot it's two hours earlier here!* Franniemarie could almost smell the shower in Lilianna's hair as, half a continent apart, they became acquainted.

Lilianna answered the marriage question, "Never married. Don't much like men. If I'da married, first time he crossed me I'da probably hadta kill the son of a bitch."

Franniemarie said she'd married, and wished she could add that she thought about killing the son of a bitch on a regular basis—wondered if her cousin would laugh, looked at the question mark in Cricket's face and turned away from him. She told her cousin how she'd gotten her number, and about the welfare department calling about their Aunt Dorien.

Lilianna was surprised because Social Services had called her with the same story. She found it strange that the agencies didn't cross reference their records. She said, "I only saw her once. I must have been about five, and I don't know why we were at her house. She and Mom were talking in the house, and I was playing with Dory in her sand box. All of a sudden she came out of the house and paddled both of us. To this day I don't know why. But I don't feel as though I should be the one to commit her. I've heard that people in the neighborhood say it would be the death of her."

Franniemarie wondered how her father died, and if anyone knew what he had been like. Lilianna wondered who her father was, and if anyone might know. Franniemarie tendered her doubts as to who she, Franniemarie, was, and that she kept finding additional layers of self through her writing; Lilianna said she didn't care who she, Lilianna, was. She just lived to enjoy what she did, and what she did was architectural photography. Before Franniemarie hung up, Lilianna invited her to come to her place in San Francisco and stay awhile.

"Come," she invited, "together we'll see what can be done for Aunt Dorien."

Franniemarie said she wished she could, but couldn't see how she could get away. She turned back to the table and watched Cricket's face turn from question mark to anger.

"What in hell was that all about?"

"Lilianna. I got ahold of Lilianna." Franniemarie felt an old terror rising through her.

"Jesus Christ, Frannie. Why can't you let well enough alone, damn family of yours is nothing but a basket of fruits—what the hell you doing getting involved with them anyway?"

"Dammit, Cricket, that bunch of fruits is my family. Why are you so set against my wanting to know them?"

"It's not just you wanting to know them. In the first place, Brooks and I are your family. You shouldn't need them. And second, a bunch of nuts can only spell trouble. I don't see where all this stewing about the past is going to get you anyplace. Give it up, Frannie. It's a damn waste of time."

Franniemarie swallowed her anger. In her heart she knew he only wanted what was best for them. "You're probably right, Cricket. Still, there are a lot of things that are the same about Aunt Dorien and me. We each lost a parent when we were young. Like her, I wanted to write."

"Yeah, an' did ya ever think that like her you'd be certifiably loony if it weren't for me?"

"Oh, Cricket," Franniemarie laughed ruefully. "Why do you think I've stayed with you all these years?"

Cricket took her words as a compliment, swallowed the last of his coffee, stood, stretched his back, gave her a hug, and was off.

Franniemarie wandered into the living room and sank into the large brown overstuffed chair that had been purchased by her great grandparents Anna and Spencer Freeman in the 1940s. And that's where Cricket found her when he came in for dinner. He peered through the doorway and watched her sitting all curled up and staring into space. "For Christsake, Frannie, where's dinner? The kitchen's a mess and nothin's cookin. What the hell you been doin' since I went out?" Franniemarie jumped up, rushed to the kitchen, opened the refrigerator, and in a flash she pulled out the fixings for red flannel hash. While the food was cooking, she quickly cleared and set the table. In less than fifteen minutes the kitchen was straightened and a respectable meal served. Cricket smiled with satisfaction, as if pleased he'd kept his farm running.

Franniemarie sat down, but could not eat. Inside she was shaking with a rage she could not comprehend. When Cricket gave her his "why aren't you eating" look, she swallowed several bites which turned around before they reached her stomach. She ran to the bathroom and vomited. When she returned, he patted her hand. "Sorry you don't feel well, honey. Why didn't you just tell me you were sick?"

I'm not sick! I'm angry! The thought squealed through her brain.

In the weeks that followed, the anger stayed with her. It stayed through the kneading of her breads, through the planting of the garden. Even Dog brought her no comfort, but then he was an outdoor dog. He had a job to do, guarding the place. Taking care of her was not a part of his job. And the anger kept her stomach in a knot, kept acid in her throat. Cricket became concerned. One day after lunch, he said, "Tell you what, you go take a nap. I'll clean up before I finish planting that damned side hill. One of these years, I'm going to fence it in and put it to pasture." In response to Frannie's, "yeah right! I've been telling you to do that for years" look, he quickly added, "with the price of corn what it's been, it won't be this year."

Franniemarie, snuggled under her grandmother's patchwork comforter, stared at the ceiling. In the white on white embossed paper she saw figures, clouds, waves, and in the raised patterns free associations began to take off. It was here that her poems often took form. Today, no poems played. Today, only questions ran through her, questions and rage.

Aunt Pru! I don't think she really likes me. She's short with everybody. But there's something else. She holds back. Like she has big secrets. Once she said indignantly, "Well, I don't tell everything I know!" So what is it she knows she isn't telling? She's never made any bones about the fact that she doesn't like my mother. How could she, she said, "I was a toddler, and a pampered one at that, when Mother brought Annamarie and Nannette to live with us. Everyone made such a fuss over them, with their pretty, naturally curly dark hair. No one made a fuss over me with my straight blonde hair that turned to fuzz while I slept. 'Poor sweet orphans' they said. Their mother wasn't even dead yet."

But then, her dislike doesn't seem to extend to either Annamarie or Dorien. She always said, "Dorien had the brains, Annamarie was the nicest—never a bad word about anyone. And what an actress, she was a scream in the film's noir she made in the fifties. Lord what a 'femme-fatal'. The strong type, not the simpering-type like some we know." Yeah like my mother. Well it's not her most attractive trait. Everyone always said Nannette was the beauty. Perhaps she didn't dislike her other nieces because, unlike Nannette, they never came back to live near her. Would it have been different if Grand had brought Dorien back to the farm when her daughter, Lilian, was in the sanitarium? It must have been strange for Pru to have been born an aunt—to have grown up with her nieces, and never known her oldest sister—my grandmother.

Damn Cricket! If he were dead, I'd go see both Liliana and Dorien. I wouldn't even tell my aunt I was related to her. I'd just talk to her about anything she wanted to talk about.

When she woke, the house was quiet and strange. The strangest thing was the lack of sound. *If Cricket were in the house, by now both the radio and the television would be blasting the air. Cricket's plowing the side hill—his damn side hill. Bet he's using the ancient, narrow-fronted John Deere.* With a start, she leapt out of bed and squished into a pair of loafers as she headed for the stairs.

Franniemarie drove the truck bumping and jumping along the rutted trail beside the fence line between the pasture and the grain field. In the distance, she could see the tractor's lights on the other side of the fence line where it followed the treacherously steep terrain Cricket kept promising to turn to pasture. The lights weren't moving. She was almost on top of the tractor before she could see Cricket pinned beneath it and Dog lying next to him. She rolled the window down and called, "*Cricket! Cricket! You OK?*" Cricket didn't answer. "*Dog!*" she called. Dog lifted his head. "*Dog, come!*" she ordered. The dog refused to move. Franniemarie sat in the running truck. *Okay. He's dead. I always told him he'd kill himself running that rig on the steep hill side. But would he listen? No! I should get out and check to see if he's alive. But if he's not dead now he will be by the time anyone finds him. Franniemarie, this is your big break. If you don't take it, you're a damned fool.*

CHAPTER 3

FRANNIEMARIE SPUN THE truck around, and spit gravel back to the house. In the house, she tossed some clothes into a box. *Okay, girl, don't take the truck. You never take the truck. Take the car. Go to town, buy some groceries, just like you always do, get a tank of gas and as much change as you can without looking suspicious. No, don't go to town, you just fueled up yesterday.*

In another box, she placed her family letters, the family picture album, Grand's Bible, her poetry, a notebook, and a leather attaché case filled with tax returns, legal documents, and bonds she'd inherited from her paternal grandmother when she was ten. She'd never tapped the fund and guessed it might be worth thirty-forty times over face value. Beneath her lingerie was a large rectangular tin filled with bills. Money saved over thirty years, the difference between the cost of groceries and the amount the store would actually cash. *The quilt! I can't leave the quilt. But I can't leave the bed stripped either.* Rummaging through the linen closet, she dug out an old chenille spread and an extra pillow. *I want to vanish. Vanish without a trace.* Meticulously, she made the bed, straightened the rug beside it.

Passing through the kitchen, she grabbed Lilianna's address and phone number, tucked them into the pouch, remembered Sunday's leftover roast beef, snatched it from the refrigerator, tossed it in a plastic bag, added apples, oranges, cheese, and a couple of small containers of yogurt, the last of a loaf of bread, then elbowed the door shut. Franniemarie put her belongings in the car, flipped on the headlights, revved the engine, and drove off without a backward glance.

Pedal to metal, Franniemarie raced the straight black top from Arapahoe toward I-80. She never registered the Elwood crossing, and the I-80 interchange came on her abruptly. Pumping brakes, she stopped the car a couple of yards past the turn. Glancing into the rearview mirror, she jammed into reverse, shot back three yards, and spun a left up the onto ramp.

Sometime later, she realized her face was wet with tears and she began to laugh; laughter rippled out of her body as freely as her tears, and she felt some great weight lifting. "So, I have to run away in order to cry!"

She punched on her radio and, like a gift from heaven, Jean Pierre Rampal's romantic flute filled the night with grace. In a euphoric trance, Franniemarie drove on, sheltered by the dark from the images of the lazy Platte River swollen with spring rain, the sight of rich black freshly plowed fields, the bright green of winter wheat and the variegated green of pasture that patterned the southern Nebraska landscape. The fancywork of utility poles, shelter belts, and the cotton-wooded river banks that stitched her home state together were never registered, and no after-image of Cricket lying beneath the weight of his tractor haunted her.

Beneath a star-studded sky, Franniemarie traveled a road made of Stravinsky's *Rite of Spring*, traveled a road straight into the landscape she owned when she was three.

She saw herself standing in the farmyard beneath a midday sun rubbing tears from her eyes in preparation for the smile she'd been taught the camera wanted. Bewildered, she watched her mother impatiently put the camera down, snatch her up, and rush her to the kitchen; felt the print of Mama's bare hand snapping against her bare butt, felt the room blur as Mama spun her back into the sunshine, heard Mama screaming in despair, "Damn you! Get your fists out of your eyes. I want the tears! You idiot! You bungling, stupid, brat, I want tears!" Over and over, the scene repeated itself until little Frannie began to vomit.

Grand, smelling of sun-warmed earth, scooped Frannie into her arms. Mama whined, "But Grammy, she's sooo cute when she cries! I just wanted to capture it. You know how cute she is when she cries!"

In a dark room Frannie heard her mother hissing. "Got me in trouble again, you little bitch! If it weren't for you, my life would be good. Was good before you. I told you not to stop crying. If you ever listened, I'd have my picture. But no! You wouldn't listen. Probably too damn stupid to listen. Ever seen dead puppies? Next time you get me into trouble, you think about dead puppies."

The Rite of Spring ended. Sobbing and sick, Franniemarie killed the engine and rolled to a stop at the side of the road. Huddled against the door, she rocked herself to sleep.

Two hours later, a high Nebraska wind slammed against the car—knocked her wide awake. She stared into the night, having shed its star-studded cloak, now grim. *Cricket's dead.* With a shiver Franniemarie tried on the thought. It settled comfortably. She turned the engine over. *And Mother's good as dead to me. No one can hurt me now.*

Fighting side winds, she drove on. The radio crackled and spit, the refuel light lit. *Where am I?* Her odometer read 984 miles. *Cricket always told me to reset it, reset it and figure out the gas mileage. Shit! Who wants to live a life computed in gas miles? If I run out before I reach a filling station, I'm screwed. I think I've got at least 30 miles before the tank runs empty."*

Franniemarie punched the reset button and fought the wind another 20 miles, the red light burning in a corner of her brain. *Don't panic! You run out, you can sleep by the side of the road till morning.* Yet another five minutes passed before the lights of Ogallala came into view. When she finally reached an open station, she cruised in on fumes.

Beneath the glare of filling station-artificial night light, Franniemarie held the cold gas nozzle, felt the fuel travel through it numbing her hands. The fumes made her sneeze. Returning to I-80, she did not forget to reset her odometer.

A Scott Joplin rag brought forth an image of Franniemarie's grandfather Francis Tourneau. She saw him crisp in a dark suit, celluloid collar studded to his neck with a set of garnet buttons. Through cigar smoke she saw the sweat that dimpled the piano player's silk shirt while he worked the *Old Piano Roll Blues*, then rolled it into a stogie-stoking *Wall Street Rag*. Francis Tourneau stood leaning against the side of an upright piano, drink in one hand, fingers of the other snapping rhythm.

The romantic flow of *Clair de Lune* brought Frannie back to driving a stretch of unknown road. *Cricket would say, "For God's sake, Frannie, you never even met the man." Ah, but Cricket isn't here and I know what I know. I know that man. What I don't know is why my mother would name me after him. Aunt Annamarie I can understand, but Mother told me he beat her when he was angry. I don't think she had any contact with him since sometime before my birth.*

That's not right. When she received word that Dorianna was dead, when she couldn't get ahold of her sister Dorien, she called her father. So she knew his phone number. But she didn't get him, got someone else. Her stepmother? Her half-sister? Francis Tourneau wouldn't speak to her, his daughter. Why?

I was seventeen when the call came. I felt relief for Dory. This cousin I'd never met. This cousin whom, I assumed, shared with me a life of household trauma. I can still see her in that stolen brand new red convertible, sailing full speed, aiming for the cliff, sailing over the cliff—sailing to freedom.

Sometime after Kimball, plumes of smoke lit by industrial lights filled the night with an exotic beauty evocative of some aged fairytale.

God sees that everything works out for the best. Poor dear Lilian, Grandmother Lilian. Was it best you took flight by death?

Four a.m.—Franniemarie took the first exit into Cheyenne, pulled up behind an open filling station, locked the doors, flipped back her seat, cocooned herself under the comforter till only her nose peeped out and snuggled into her pillow. Sleep came instantly.

Seven a.m.—she gassed up beneath a flat grey dawn. In the restroom she washed her face with a stiff brown paper towel and wished she'd packed a wash cloth. After filling her thermos with plain American coffee, after making payment for her gas to a gum snapping young woman who never saw her, after filling her go-cup, tightening the lid on the thermos and carefully placing the cup in the holder, after fishing an apple from the bag of food pulled from her refrigerator, she buckled up and hit the road.

Mid-morning—Laramie long behind her, Franniemarie drove into snow flurries. *Well, this can't last long.* She'd hardly dismissed the weather when wind hit the car and the world turned white. Slowing to a twenty-mile-an-hour crawl, she proceeded, barely able to see the edge of the road. In horror she passed an eighteen-wheeler jack-knifed on the median and slowed to ten miles an hour. The wind came in gusts, pummeling her car from different directions. *Do I quit? If I stop, then what?* She held her car to the road for the longest half hour she'd ever met. Then, as suddenly as it began, the storm was over. Light-headed and shaking, she accelerated.

I feel as if I've been beaten and bruised. Is this the way Grandmother Lilian felt when her husband beat her with a horse whip because the pie she baked for his lunch did not suit his fancy? Franniemarie saw her grandmother kneeling on dry autumn leaves freshly drifted into the carriage house, felt the whip across her back, and flinched.

On the far side of Rock Springs she passed a hitchhiker sitting under a viaduct, his back against a large green backpack, his thumb out. Something about him reminded Franniemarie of her son when he was about twenty. She pulled over.

Through her rearview mirror she watched the fellow unfold himself, gather his pack, and lumber toward her car. He wore a warped and worn gray felt cowboy hat, tennis shoes, and a neutral but pleasant, look on his face. Tossing his backpack behind the passenger seat and her bag of food on the floor, he climbed in beside her. "Where ya headed?" she asked.

"Salt Lake. And you?"

"I'm running away from home."

He responded with a hearty, life-affirming laugh that filled their space with good spirits.

"Apropos of running away, you wouldn't have something to cut meat with would you? I didn't think to bring anything, and I'm starving for some of that roast beef in the bag you just tossed on the floor."

He said he'd eaten breakfast, but he made them both sandwiches and didn't have any trouble tucking his down.

Men!

He said he lived with his folks in Salt Lake. Had come over to meet a buddy and hike in the Flaming Gorge National Recreation Area before the tourist season began. He said the area was fantastic, not something you could describe. He'd tried to write poems about it, but couldn't capture what he felt. She should at least drive through it.

Franniemarie mentioned she wrote a bit of poetry herself, and a lively conversation followed. He thought Roethke the finest. She thought Roethke sometimes sublime, but more often was left wondering if everything he put to paper found publication on notice of his fame alone. She was drawn to Sharon Olds and Luci Tapahonso. He'd never heard of them. Both agreed that each time they read Dylan Thomas or Pablo Neruda, they discovered new ways of seeing. He asked what she thought of Paul Zarzyski. She admitted she'd never heard of him.

In a flash, he unbuckled his seatbelt, twisted around, unzipped a side pocket on his back-pack and pulled out a book. "Time to change that."

Franniemarie took note of the first book's cover, a muted, surreal landscape of blues and greens taken from a minor key pallet. "That cover is a poem of invitation."

"Yeah! *Wolf Tracks on the Welcome Mat.* It's one of my favorites. He writes wonderful poems about Montana open spaces that give you a whole different understanding of life— people. What got me started reading him was listening to him at a Cowboy Poetry reading in Elko. When I was a kid I hung on to anything that had to do with horses and Cowboys. One summer Dad and I went up there just for the event."

The young man opened a paperback whose jacket featured a black-and-white rodeo cowboy coming out of the chute. Franniemarie caught sight of the title, printed in bold red: *All This Way for the Short Ride:* Listen to this poem—"Benny Reynolds' Bareback Riggin'" and with that he began to read: "A bacon slab a-boiled black in oil every day/Ain't as soggy..."

Now that's a poem Cricket could wrap his mind around. Franniemarie's mind shut down and the rhythm of the poem carried her through quite a distance. In the silence that punctuated the poem's finish Franniemarie asked if he was familiar with Robert Bly. Indeed he was. "Have you read his *My Sentence Was a Thousand Years of Joy.*

Her traveling companion nodded. She began to quote from Bly's "The Greek Ships." "I have heard that the mourning dove never says/What she means."

Jubilant he chimed in, "Those of us who make up poems/ Have agreed not to say what pain is."

Sharing poetry and laughter with this young stranger, Franniemarie shed her years, regaining a bit of the old buoyancy and confidence of her youth. And then Salt Lake City stole her passenger. His absence created in her a hollow that filled with a hunger that had nothing to do with physical need.

That's the kind of person I've always dreamed of having in my life. What on earth possessed me to marry Cricket?

Oh, Franniemarie, try trustworthy, honest, feet-on-the-ground safe. He knew who he was, where he was going. And he knew he wanted you. He was so damn solid. My rock, the rock that held us through life's tragedies—left me with this gnawing emptiness.

Now I am alone. Now it's up to me to find out who I am—what I'm made of, and to do something with what I find.

A fragment from the hitchhiker's reading of Paul Zarzyski's poem "Shoes" coursed through her mind. *"… Choose your most truthful / words, your most vital music …"*

When I've landed, I'm going to get that book. I'll pin those words to a writing table and try to live up to his charge.

After feeding her car gas and herself a hamburger in Wendover, Franniemarie continued into Nevada. By the time she reached Wells, she was ready for a hot shower and a motel.

The sun came up on beautiful clear skies. In the brief moment she took to place her bags in the trunk, a meadow lark sang promises of excitement and adventure.

Outside of Wells, a grizzled middle-aged man walked down the road with his thumb out. She slowed. He ambled to the car, tossed a duffle in the back, and closed the door.

"Where to?" By the time she reached speed, she knew she'd made a mistake. The car had filled with alcohol fumes.

"California."

'Elko 48 miles' flashed green and white as she drove past. "Elko. I can take you as far as Elko."

Hands shoved into his pockets he sat slouched next to her. Franniemarie felt him staring at her. Without turning her head, from the corner of her eye, she glanced at him. His eyes were a flat almost colorless blue—reptilian came to mind. Franniemarie drove faster. The silence, filled with stale fumes, felt heavy. In a low even voice, like some great cat purr, he spoke, "You're sure one brave lady." Again, Frannie glanced at him. His thumb, thick, nail broken, dirty, caressed a fine honed blade. And the blade reflected the sun's rays into her eye. "Yep, you're one hell of a brave lady. Pickin' up strangers." From the corner of her eye, she saw his lips curl in imitation of a smile.

Frannie swallowed, a reflex only, her mouth was dry. *Holy shit, this is it. Had it coming—leaving Cricket to die like that. What goes round comes round. Can't be any worse to die by knife than tractor. Unless—unless he rapes me first. And how would he do that? How can you rape someone and hold a knife to them at the same time? Wouldn't he be vulnerable—at least when he ejaculated. If I keep my head—maybe...*

"Yes, indeedie, one hell of a brave woman."

Franniemarie's heart pounded. Her body felt hot. She felt trapped. To her right, a great sweep of rangeland pulled her attention to rugged snow-capped mountains and a memory of Van Gogh's painting, *The Olive Trees*. It was one of those rare moments in her life when her mother took her on a trip. They had gone to Minneapolis, gone to meet some man, perhaps one of her mother's lovers. They left her at the Minneapolis Institute of Art. She remembered sitting on a bench in the museum entrapped by the painting, remembered feeling sucked into the picture. There she sat at the edge of a dusty road under an olive tree. The tree was no shelter from a sun so hot it filled the air with the smell of its heat. Sitting there she looked down the long road and into mountains, mountains harboring shade and water. If only she could get to the mountains. But the sun nailed her to the roadside with its heat.

"You know what's going to happen to you?"

This man isn't going to rape me. He's angry. Hurting. He wants to scare me good. Franniemarie felt the drunk tense his shoulders. "You hear me? I asked if you know what's going to happen to you."

Scare me good, then kill me. He thinks killing me will make him feel good.

"So, say something, bitch!"

Cricket always joked as to how I could talk a man's leg off. Joked? My ass! He made snide remarks every time I got on the phone. What would he know, I stopped talking to him within a year of our marriage and still he didn't get it. "I know you're angry. I know you think the more you hurt me the better it'll make you feel." *Well, Cricket, let's hope you're right 'cause all I got between me and the other side are words.* "Let me tell you something." Franniemarie kept her eyes on the road. "There isn't anything you can do that can hurt me any more than living already has. Take my life? Big deal. You just move me from one side to the other. Can't hurt anymore there than here." She kept her voice as heavy as his thumb on the knife, as flat as his viper eyes.

Franniemarie's traveling companion shifted in his seat, turned three quarters toward her, raised an amused eyebrow. "You are one brave lady."

Franniemarie pretended not to have glimpsed him from the corner of her eye. "Brave?" She snorted. "Hell, no. In order to be brave you have to have something to lose. Let me tell you, like you, I've already lost it all."

He continued to stroke his knife.

"My mother never wanted me. Bet your mother never wanted you. When I was a baby, my father died. Guess she hated him, too. Often said I reminded her of him, reminded her of the worst crap life could dish out. When I was little, sometimes she'd beat me just to see me cry, said I was cute when I cried. I ran from her to a man who didn't know the difference between a wife and a doormat. Had two sons." Two dead felt stronger than explaining three—and one still living. "Watching them grow was amazing. They were wonderful, made life worth living, worth the hell of getting to that place. My youngest was one of the brightest people I've ever met. When he started first grade, he couldn't read or write or figure, within three months he was working at a third grade level. He painted wonderful pictures, loved oatmeal cookies with nuts and raisins. They said he could start the new-year in third grade. He said, 'No, we have a dreadful teacher and the kids are counting on me being there.' He died before the New Year began—Encephalitis. He was seven. He was sick three days. He died Christmas morning. And you thought your sorry empty Christmases sucked! Five years later, his brother died of a cracked skull when he was tossed from a horse."

Franniemarie felt him shift in his seat, caught him looking out the side window, his thumb resting quiet on the blade of his knife. She let her voice take on a less mechanical tone. "I'd guess your life story's a lot like mine, a sum total of failed dreams and people who never believed in you until there's nothing left but that hollow hopeless loneliness."

From the corner of her eye she saw the man, eyes closed, a tear coursing his left cheek. *Gotcha!*

Before she entered Elko, she let him out, saying, "Peace be with you," then drove into a handsome residential section where the houses were well-set back and their parameters defined by tall well-manicured hedges. There she parked— double checked the door locks, flopped her seat flat, pulled the tulip quilt and a pillow from the back seat and instantly fell asleep.

Two hours later she woke numb, cold, and dazed. She managed to cross Nevada skipping from rest stop to rest stop and cat napping twenty—thirty minutes at each, forty miles to the stop outside of Dunphy, near ninety to the rest at Winnemucca, one hundred and twenty-five to the next. It was late afternoon by the time she reached Reno, by the time she began to warm.

As she drove west, the late afternoon sun seared her eyes, made them water. Franniemarie passed into California rummaging the glove box, searching for her sunglasses.

"Well, Cricket, I guess it wasn't my time. Glad it wasn't my time. I always wanted to see the state where I was born. Always wanted to find my past. Twice now, I'm given the chance. I wished you understood. I wished you'd cared. If you'd cared, we could have done this together." That's silly. Even if he'd supported my need to search, it's not like he could participate. Any search for self is going to be lonely.

I wonder what Lilianna will be like. How she'll react to my situation. I think she'll understand. She's the one who said if she'd married, she'd have killed him. Guess I'll find out soon enough.

Franniemarie white knuckled her path through traffic heavier than anything she had ever imagined. The high-speed California freeway sucked energy out of her. The houses, the housing developments, the sheer volume of people made her feel ill. *What did I expect? Orange groves? I wanted orange groves. I remember Mother talking about orange groves and mountains and San Francisco. Damn it! The people are supposed to be in L.A. and San Francisco—not living on the freeway.* It was dark by the time Franniemarie reached San Francisco. She refueled, then shivered in the phone booth, shook while she dialed Lilianna's number. Lilianna answered—her voice clear and pure as a bell. "It's me, Franniemarie. I'm at a phone booth. Lilianna, I killed Cricket."

CHAPTER 4

When Franniemarie—still shaking—pressed her finger to the doorbell, Lilianna opened the door and folded her into her arms. Then, at an arms-length, they scrutinized each other. Lilianna, tall, blonde, willowy. Franniemarie, fading brown hair, mid-height, mid-weight, mid-frame. They shared blue eyes, high cheek-bones, firm jaw-lines and competent working woman's hands. Lilianna's were slender and long, Franniemarie's sturdy and square. Neither wore jewelry nor nail polish. Both kept their nails short and serviceable.

"So, you what?" Lilianna asked.

"I didn't exactly kill him. I just left him to die."

"Oh, shit! You sure? Okay, you're sure. Why? No, don't try to answer that right now. Look, how about you unload your car, and I'll get us something to eat. You can put your stuff in this closet. You'll be sleeping on the couch. You drink wine? Good. A Pinot Noir okay? Good."

Lilianna passed the platter that included prosciutto and Greek olives to Franniemarie.

"Oh, my, I've never tasted anything so wonderful. What's the cheese?"

"Fresh Romano, the basil is from the plant that lives on the patio." Lilianna paused, "Okay, now why?"

"It was almost a reflex. I've wanted to know about my family, the history, all my life. It seems no one but Grand was interested or willing to share. The lady from welfare called. Then you called. I wanted so much to come out. Cricket just made fun of me—my family, that and so much more."

"You sure he's dead?"

"Well, I left him on the only hillside on the place, and when I left him he was pinned under an overturned tractor, it was running—he wasn't answering. If he wasn't dead then he would have been by the time anyone found him. Please, if anyone calls, please, don't tell them I'm here. Not that I think anyone will. They'd have to go through as much trouble as I did to find you, and I didn't leave any clues. Well, I did mention to Pru Ellen I wished I could come see you and Aunt Dorien. But I don't think she actually listens.

"I promised myself if I could sit next to Aunt Dorien at that coffee shop she goes to each day, I'd never tell her who I was. Have you seen her? I mean recently?"

"Geezus Franniemarie, I had her committed a couple of weeks ago. Don't look at me like that. You said you couldn't come out. Someone had to take control. It wasn't an easy decision. The neighbors were very protective of her. They would have taken care of her if she would have let them. They even raised several thousand dollars to help her out. But she was afraid of them. They said she harmed no one but herself, and putting her away would kill her." Lilianna drained her wine glass. "We all expected resistance. I parked on the street and watched when the police officer went to Dorien's door. Before the officer could say a word she nearly shouted, "I'm in the process of moving." The officer gently, but firmly, replied, "Mrs. Weaver, you know it's all over. Come with me." That was it. She walked to the car and went off without a murmur. I did go in before they locked up her house, but it was such a mess I couldn't focus on anything. You can't imagine it, holes in the roof, holes in the floor—clothes in plastic bags. After seeing how she was living, I only regret I didn't do something sooner."

"So where is she now?"

"A geriatric psychiatric center, I could take you there tomorrow, if you like. However, I must warn you, you can never know how she'll react."

"I understand. I want to meet her."

"I have a shoot in the morning, but the light I want will be gone by noon. We can go in the afternoon." Lilianna refilled their glasses with the tart, fruity wine. "Who you really need to meet are the Palladio's, Addie and Lew. They've lived next door to Dorien for years and years. I first met them while getting her committed. It turns out Lew absolutely doted on our aunt and they know a lot about her. They knew her before Dory died—moved in a few years after her husband was killed. They're sweet, fragile people." Lilianna looked at her watch. "It's early enough—I'll call and set up a time when we can see them. They don't take to strangers, so I'd best take you. As I said, they're fragile."

Lilianna hung up the phone, "That was easy. We can go over morning after tomorrow."

"When you went into her house, did you see any papers, notebooks, that sort of thing?"

"Actually, I was so overwhelmed I didn't think to look."

Franniemarie interjected, "Everyone said she wanted to be a writer. If she wrote anything, we might gain some understanding from that." She drained her glass again. "I have pictures of her when she's about eight years old and when she's a young woman, plus letters to Grand starting when she's a teenager and ending about the time her husband went into the military service."

"Got pictures of our grandparents?"

"Sure, Grand and Grandpa Freeman as well as their children. Well, Lilian and Prudence Ellen. Carl died of whooping cough when he was a baby. I brought my album with me. Want to see them?"

Lilianna nodded, uncorked another bottle of wine.

Franniemarie skipped the first half of the album, which was devoted to Cricket's family, and opened to their great grandparents' sepia-toned wedding picture.

Lilianna gasped. "She's beautiful. I guess I expected her to be worn and withered from the beginning."

Next came a picture of Grand standing behind Grandpa— Lilian stood with her hand on Grandpa's knee. She was dressed in a white cotton frock, white stockings, black Mary Janes. Her rich dark hair was caught up in a great lovely ribbon. Franniemarie turned the page. Puzzled, Lilianna asked, "Who is the blonde-haired toddler in Grand's arms?"

"That's Pru Ellen. She was born three months after her niece, Dorien, was born."

"So Grand is nearly twenty years older in this picture? How stately she looks, her black hair piled on the top of her head." Lilianna bit her upper lip. "It's still hard for me to wrap my mind around someone being an aunt before they were born.

But my mother hadn't even been conceived when Aunt Pru Ellen came into the world. I find it strange when I think of mother and daughter pregnant at the same time, stranger yet to think of having a child at forty-three.

Franniemarie pointed to the picture on the opposite page. Standing in front of a 1920s Ford, Grandpa Spencer stands beside Grand, his hand resting on her shoulder. Annamarie is in Grand's arms—Pru Ellen and Nannette stand at her side. "This was taken the day they set out to take your mother and mine back to their father. I think it was taken about three years after the one of Grand and Pru Ellen. Note, in that short time her hair has turned to white.

"But this is what you asked for." Franniemarie flipped to a page with a black and white image commemorating the marriage of Lilian Spring Freeman to Francis Dennis Tourneau. 30 August 1913.

They both sipped their wine.

Lilianna was pensive. "Do you realize they were both 21 when they were married? I thought that was old maid age in those days."

"Oh, yes. And Grand told me the story behind the dates."

Lilianna urged her on.

"The summer of 1906 Francis and a friend set off from Tucumcari, New Mexico. His mother had remarried that year, and she and her husband had moved out here. The two headed north and east on a pair of fine saddle horses, looking to see some of the country, looking for work along the way. When they reached Arapahoe someone told them Mr. Freeman needed help harvesting. Our great Grandfather, hired them. Francis nearly died of heat stroke the first day, so he sent him back to town. He knew the publisher of the paper was in need of a printer's devil and, as Francis knew his letters, he thought that would be better match for both of them."

"Lilian and Francis became sweethearts and finished high school together. They would have married then, but his mother wouldn't sign papers. At that time, a man could not marry without his parent's permission until he'd reached the age of twenty-one. Take note they married the day after he reached majority! The next day they left for Oakland to visit his mother. They never left."

"Francis' mother, she's the one who took Dorien when Grandmother Lilian went into the sanitarium. Right?"

"Right."

"My God, Frannie! It's three a.m. and I've got to be up by six."

The following afternoon, Franniemarie and Lilianna waited for their aunt in a spacious room built for visitation. Franniemarie clutched the large family album she hoped to share with her aunt. Dorien, tiny, self-contained, demure, walked in on the arm of a nurse and brought with her a heady scent of fresh ginger. "Mrs. Weaver, you have guests."

Lilianna stood and took her hand. "Are they treating you well?"

Softly Dorien replied, "Oh, my yes. I don't know why, but I'm having so much fun. And the food is terrific!"

"Aunt Dorien, I want you to meet my friend, Franniemarie. She's come all the way from Nebraska just to see you."

"Yes, many have come to see me." She extended her hand.

Gently, Franniemarie took her hand. It was cold, dry, brittle. She smiled, sniffed. "Your perfume is heavenly."

Dorien, ducked her head shyly. "It's ginger. Lilianna gave it to me."

"Franniemarie was born in San Francisco, but this is the first time she's been here since her mother moved to Lincoln during the war."

"I understand you've always lived in the area." Franniemarie released her aunt's hand.

"No. No, I was born in Paris."

"Paris? Where in Paris?"

"You know, in the hospital. My father was an officer in the big war."

"And your mother?"

"She died before I was born." Whoops, was written on her face. Quickly she went on. "We lived next door to the hospital. My mother was shot and they cut me out so I wouldn't die with her." Dorien leaned close to Franniemarie. "My dear, watch out for those Laotians. They're evil. Very evil. They're descendants from the clan of the Rhinoceros. Not like me. I come from the Seals."

"Really!"

Dorien nodded. Franniemarie leaned conspiratorially toward her, "I don't usually tell anyone this, but I am from the Porpoises. And as you well know, the Porpoises are good, too." Their eyes locked. In unison they nodded and smiled in some mutual recognition.

Lilianna addressed Aunt Dorien, "Franniemarie's family grew up here and she's brought her album. Would you like to look at it? You might be able to tell us about some of them."

Dorien smiled and suggested they move to a large table. There they flipped through pictures of Cricket's family, neutral territory where they could talk of the customs and fashions of the day. Cricket's parents' wedding picture recorded his mother's maroon wedding gown in black. Aunt Dorien brightened. "Black was common then. Yes, in those days a lot of women married in black. It was considered good luck." She showed no recognition when they came to her parents' wedding picture, nor the childhood pictures of herself or those of her sisters', but when she came to a picture of herself taken in her mid-twenties, she snorted, "I never looked like that," snapped the album shut, stood, and, in standing, dismissed her guests.

Franniemarie marveled at the ease with which Lilianna negotiated the hills and traffic in the city. *I'd have to get a car with an automatic transmission if I were to live here.* And she was charmed by the townhouses all lined wall to wall, tall and elegant, each with a distinct character.

Aloud she mused, "Makes you wonder how much of the mind is choice, how much genetic. Like my mom is as off the wall as her sister, but she keeps the conversation to people and events—real or imagined, mostly fabricated, always exaggerated. With her it's all about *her.* With Dorien, it's not even grounded. And yet, I get the feeling she, like my mother, has some notion of reality. Like when she saw she'd dug herself into a corner with her birth nonsense—she turned it around. When Mom talked with the men in her life she always watched them. If they looked like they didn't approve of what she was saying, she had the ability to turn the subject mid-sentence to a direction that met with their approval. Makes you wonder how a person ends up at that place. And when others in your family—well, do you ever wonder if you're straight?"

Lilianna giggled—then abruptly said, "No."

"What's your mother like? Here I'm named after her—well, her and our grandfather, and all I know about her is she was a talented actress and she was nice."

Lilianna gunned the car up a hill and made a sharp right. "Geez Frannie, to tell the truth, that's practically all I know about her. I hardly lived with her. I don't remember anything before first grade. I spent most of my childhood in boarding schools. She had friends. She baked them cakes for their birthdays. She was quite proud of her cakes. But she never talked about her friends. She never talked about the family. I know she left home when she was twelve. We didn't attend Cousin Dory's funeral. She never saw her father.

"You know, our grandfather Francis Tourneau lived in Oakland. Once I asked Annamarie about him. She said, 'When I was twelve, I was hospitalized with pneumonia. The Sunday after I came home, we were eating dinner, Father had a white envelope—he slid it across the table to me. It was the bill for the hospital. I left home the next day.' She went to live with the people she was working for. Needless to say, I didn't ask any more questions. I do know she acted in plays in grade school and high school as well as managing to graduate from high school in the same summer she was fifteen. That summer, she sailed to Argentina with some high mucky-muck family. In Argentina some producer saw her, took her under wing. She didn't return to the States for a couple of years. And then it was as an actress starring in those Tex-Mex Westerns, high on drama, short on fact."

Lilianna clicked her garage-door open and drove down into the garage under the house.

Franniemarie held her breath until her cousin had the car safely through the tiny opening. "My mother said Francis brought home a divorcee and three children. Just went away for three weeks and returned with them. She was twelve. Mother said it nearly killed Dorien. That Dorien had been his favorite and they spent most of their time together. They had a telescope on the roof of the house and they would spend time studying the stars. My mother said they all hated their stepmother. And that the stepmother's daughter was Dorien's age. Pru Ellen says our grandfather was probably sleeping with her.

Lilianna snorted, "He probably slept with all of them."

"What makes you think so?"

"D'no. But think of it. All three of them had husbands, lovers, and not one of them stayed in any committed relationship. I don't know about Dorien, but you say your mother played to men, manipulated them. I only heard the rumors about my mother, but the rumors relate a similar story."

"Wow. I'd like to meet her, too."

"Don't hold your breath. She's in retirement—lives a reclusive life in Bakersfield. She isn't well. We talk occasionally, but briefly. I haven't seen her in years, and that's fine with me. After all, she won't talk about the past or friends, just their children, theater, and politics. So what's left after the lovely cake is finished?"

"Dishes?"

Lilianna's phone rang. Laughing, she answered it, walked into the kitchen and began rummaging through the refrigerator. By the time the call was finished, the table was set with linen and laden with an exotic array of deli tidbits. "Shit, Frannie. Have a shoot in the morning. I can't afford to turn it down, so you're on your own with the Palladio's.

It's not hard to get there. I'll draw you a map. However, I do worry if they'll let you in without me. I'd call, but then they'd want to change the date and who knows when we could get it together again. They don't warm easily to strangers." Lilianna poured wine, held her glass up with a toast. "To family, such as it is. And to the search for what it is, and who—possibly *why*—we are."

Franniemarie bit into a cold, spicy, giant prawn. "Pru once told me Grand said Dorien always was a strange one. That Francis was more than handsome and brilliant, and that he could be the devil himself. Grand said he had a terrible temper—said he ran hot and cold. Grand told me, once he whipped Dorien so hard she started foaming at the mouth. She said life would have been different for all of us if her daughter hadn't died. Aunt Pru lays Dorien's mental state on her father, but the death of her husband during the war and then the death of her daughter couldn't have helped." Tearing off a bit of bread, she continued. "I remember the day we got the call. Dorianna stole a red convertible and ran it over a cliff. I remember I thought, 'Good for you Dory. You made it. Now you are truly free.' And I wished I'd had that kind of courage."

"That's not how I remember it." Lilianna said. "I remember Dorianna with dark unkempt hair. I remember thinking of her as a biker chick. My memory is she slammed her bike into a truck in the middle of the night. We did not go to the funeral."

"I have some letters our Mothers wrote way back when they were in grade school. They're still in their original envelope. Wanna read them?"

"Sure.".

The small packet was addressed in adult hand to Mrs. Freeman, 1337 Kulien Ave., Centralia, Washington. The letters were small notes written in childish hand.

Sept. 26, 1924

Dear Mama:

How are you? All of us kids got promoted. Now I am in the low 4th. I got so I like oatmeal mush now. On Wednesdays we had geography Thursday we had language. Now I use ink at school it is lots harder work than in the 3rd. to Mama from Prudence Ellen Freeman.

Lilianna frowned. "Okay, I'm confused. This is Aunt Pru Ellen. She's writing from Grandpa Francis' house. What was Grandma Anna's youngest daughter doing at his house? Why were the girls all with him? But Pru Ellen! Especially why Pru Ellen?"

Franniemarie looked at the postmark, 1924, and the return address is Centralia, Washington. "I don't know. It's confusing. If I remember right, at some point Francis invited them out to live with him. After all Aunt Pru has said about him and his temper—that he could never keep a housekeeper because of it—it doesn't compute. Grand's mother, a brother and sister were living in Centralia and Grandpa's mother was still living, and she was there. I remember once Grand said she'd taken care of both her mother and her mother-in-law for two years before they died. She was so proud of herself because neither one of them developed bed sores. I think Grandpa got a job with a logging company. Grand was always outspoken, Grandpa never said much, but they held the same opinions. I wouldn't be surprised if Grand and Grandpa Francis got into it, and they left for Centralia. Perhaps Centralia didn't have a suitable school for Pru. That's the only circumstance I can think of would be more important than having her with them.

Oct. 18, 1924

Dear Grandma,

How are you? We go to pioneer memorial my teacher's name is miss Thomas are church is on 37th and telegraph Daddy bought a new truck I got two Es on my report We had a fine rain yesterday an last night I went to the bakery. I saw how they made bread we saw from the beginning to the end the men did not handle the bread he gave us a little hot."

Lots of love, Nannette

Dear Grama,

I hope you are well, I have a bad cold. I like to go to school. My teachers name is Miss Marjorie. I dried the dishes for Dorien this morning. I am a big girl now and do lots of work for Aunt Betty. I don't cry much anymore. Aunt Betty gave me some new paper dolls. Little Bo-Peep and Red Riding Hood. Give my love to Grandpa. I will send him a card for his birthday

Lots of love, Annamarie

Lilianna held her mother's note in her hand. With soft awe she said, "She would have been six years old."

"You can keep it?"

"Really?"

Franniemarie nodded. "And I'll get copies of the pictures made for you if you'd like."

"I would. Truly, I would. Thank you," Lilianna looked at her watch. My God, it's the middle of the night again. I'll make you a map right now. It's not hard to get there from here. I just hope they'll let you in."

"Welcome to Mexico"

Jose Remariez, swarthy
knight in shining
from your bed you rose
to aid this aging damsel
whose briefcase has traveled on
vanished in some taxi beneath
the city's Christmas glamour
You turn the Reforma into a speedway
we engage in pidgin Spanish and sign
defining my situation, your choice to trade
slumber for a wild ride on the town

racing to recover our identities
locked in that briefcase
I have three girls
Ustade quatro Nino—pero adulto
Back at the airport I watch you weave
conversation before cab stand after
cab stand, miming the look of eldest
in her man's fedora, youngest a beauty
husband with a mustache curl
Each time you meet with negative nods
my heart stops and we move on until
at last you find a friend of our driver
together you race off leaving me in your wake
you rouse the fellow from happy slumber
having enjoyed showing us the city
in all its seasonal glory he had
gone to bed without even cleaning his rig
in a flash they returned
our lives reconstructed,
our introduction
complete

On rereading her words Franniemarie wondered, *Where in God's name that came from. So foreign—so complete.* In awe she curled up and promptly fell asleep.

CHAPTER 5

Franniemarie banged the brass knocker against its plate. *Please, oh please, don't let them be difficult.* She banged the knocker again, waited, replayed Liliana's caution, "They're reclusive, timid, private. You'll have your work cut out getting any information, let alone cooperation breaking into Aunt Dorien's house." At last, the door was unbolted and opened a crack. Addie's frail voice quavered, "Who is it?"

"Dorien's niece."

"Where's Lilianna?"

"She's on a shoot."

"A what?"

"A shoot. You know, when a photographer is working an assignment."

"I thought Lilianna was bringing you."

"She was, but she got a call, so she had to work today. I wanted so much to meet you. She said I should come anyway. She said to tell you how sorry she is she can't be here. I'm her cousin Franniemarie." Franniemarie shifted her oversized picture album to her left arm and pushed her right hand into the room as far as the chain would allow. "She sends her regards. You must be Addie." She felt Addie's tiny hand in hers and gently shook it. "So pleased to meet you. Lilianna speaks highly of you and your husband Lew."

"You goin' to let her in, or just stand there till the heater comes on?" Lew's voice did not carry the punch of his words. Addie slipped the chain and Franniemarie eased herself into the foyer.

Keeping her slippers flat on the floor, Addie shuffled into the living room, Franniemarie trailing behind. Lew rose and plumped up pillows on a chair. "Here Addie, let's not overdo it. You know how it stirs up the rheumatism. You could have waited for me to get the door. You've no patience, no good sense."

Lew settled Addie into an overstuffed rocker, then took a seat across the room from her. Looking up, he seemed almost surprised to see Franniemarie still standing in the middle of the room hugging the family album to her chest. "Sit down. For heaven's sake, sit down." He nodded toward the couch.

Franniemarie sat on the couch with the album in her lap. Lew fetched them coffee and they all sat sipping in awkward silence. "I never met my aunt—that is till yesterday." Franniemarie considered telling them about the seals her aunt Dorien was convinced she'd descended from and decided against it. "But I have these old pictures from her childhood. Even a couple of her and Gill, and some of Dorianna when she was little."

Addie leaned forward. Her beady eyes glinted with curiosity. Lew sat down beside her.

"My mother would never talk about her family. And she tried to keep me as far away from my great grandmother as was possible. Grandma was a treasure trove of stories. I suppose that's why I've collected all these pictures and what family anecdotes I could. Even when I was little, I was all ears. Here's a picture of my grandparents with Dorien. Looks to be about seven years old. She's told the people at the center that she was raised by thirty families. But she wasn't."

"Everyone here knows that. The Tourneau's were all crazy." Addie looked into Franniemarie's eyes, caught herself. "Not Lilianna, of course, she seems all right to me. And maybe not her mother. I never knew your mother, so I can't speak for her. Nannette and Annamarie left the Bay Area so long ago, no one remembers much about them."

"Except for their beauty. God knows they were all beautiful." Lew fairly choked on his admiration.

Addie snorted. "Never was a damn lick of sense a man could hang onto around any of them girls."

Lew continued, "I remember Dorien singing. Some mornings she'd come out on the porch at sunrise and sing. Lord that woman could sing."

"Like I said, men lose their heads."

"And dance, she sure could dance." Lew stood and looked out their dining room window. "From here you can look right over the fence and into her porch. Sometimes she'd sing and dance the length of that porch just as free as some wild creature. Didn't she love to dance, Addie?"

"Glory yes." Addie's eyes lit with some pleasant vision. "Remember the dance club we all belonged to back in the forties?"

"Aunt Dorien belonged to a dance club?"

"Oh, my, yes. Warmed to the shimmy." Addie leaned forward in her chair.

"I was under the impression she was reclusive, didn't socialize."

"Well, that was sometimes true and sometimes not. She could be very social when she wanted. Come dance night, she always wanted. And she had her share of suitors. I don't think she liked the idea of men in a personal way, though—just loved to dance. Maybe to dance and to dream."

Lew poured more coffee. "Remember that funeral parlor chap? What was his name?"

Addie snorted. "Rodney Sankovitch. Only a man could forget a name like that. Rich as Croesus, would have given her anything."

"Would have given her anything?" Lew raised an eyebrow.

"Okay. So maybe he did take care of the balance and taxes on the house after Dorianna died." Lew stated defensively.

"Pish!" Addie snorted. "That realtor, one of the Conrads—well you know the rumors. He's more likely the one."

Franniemarie sucked in her breath. "I always wondered why the bank didn't foreclose. Was she, you know, intimate with these men?"

"She never let a man even come to her house—always had him pick her up here."

"Once, Sankovitch invited her to spend a weekend at his Lake Tahoe retreat."

"Big mistake. After that, she never said another word to him."

"He came here begging us to intercede for him. I tried to talk to her. All she said was she never liked short fat men. And that was the end of that."

"How strange," Franniemarie murmured.

"Everything about that woman was strange," retorted Addie.

"Now Addie, she could be charming and she could be so much fun."

"Indeed she was!" Addie snorted.

Franniemarie quickly turned to a picture of Dorien and Gill standing beside their Piper Cub. "I think this one was taken about 1938. I've been told he taught her to fly." Franniemarie looked at the small, soft-featured woman. She could envision her dancing easier than navigating the plane.

Lew looked at the picture. "Before our time, I think she moved here in about '46—year before us. He'd been dead a long time."

"Never knew her to drive a car. Walked every place she went, unless of course Lew took her." Addie peered closer at the picture. "Don't doubt that she could fly a plane, though. That woman was a strange mix."

"Smart, that woman was smart. On a good day, you could talk to her about anything. Well, anything but family, always claimed she didn't have any family."

"They were all smart. Like that doctor uncle of hers. He could cure most anything. But hadn't a lick of sense when it came to women and couldn't leave them alone either. And money! He made loads of money. 'Course it ran right through his fingers. His poor wife could hardly keep the family together for lack of money and trying to keep the family tony enough to please him."

Doctor Uncle? Must be talking about Francis' brother.

"'Course, she was crazy. Just like her father, her uncles. Everyone around here knew they were nuts."

"In these pictures she looks so normal. Look at this one." Franniemarie turned the page to a picture of Dorien standing in front of a fountain in a calf-length princess style coat. Head whimsically tilted to the side, she looked coyly into the camera. "The way she holds her purse, sort of clutching it to her chest, the way it matches her shoes, prim, she looks sort of prim."

Addie laughed. "Prim, yes she could be prim. One moment prim, the next cussing you out like a riverboat madman. 'Course, her father was the same."

"Problem was," Lew interjected, "you could never know what would touch her off."

"My Great Grandmother Anna said when Dorien was young she wanted to be a writer. I've always thought that if she did write and if I could find her writings, somehow through them, I could better understand my family."

"Oh, she wrote all right, filled steno-book after steno-book with her scribblings. One time, Lew saved a bunch of them from vandals."

"It was in the afternoon. Addie and I saw Dorien leave in the morning for her usual walk to town. She never came back till after six in the evening, so we knew she wasn't home."

"She used to go down to the library to wash up. They shut her heat and electricity off back in '59, you know. She used to read in the library and have coffee and a doughnut at the coffee shop in Marietta. It's three miles down and three miles back. And back is straight up."

"I used to offer her a ride up in the evenings after I closed the pharmacy."

"He was the Marietta pharmacist for twenty years."

"Sometimes we'd have a good conversation, friendly as you please, other times she'd curse and swear at me like I was the devil in person."

"The vandals, what happened with the vandals?" Franniemarie kept her words soft, gently nudging the conversation back to a direction she was interested in.

"Oh, just a bunch of high school kids. The house was boarded up just like it is now, excepting for the doors, so a body wouldn't know someone lived there. They had gone in and started a fire in the fireplace. You know that was the only heat she ever had. Once, I came in and she was feeding it a branch that stuck out into her living room. Could have burned the place down, and I told her so."

"Lew used to chop wood and put it on her porch when she was gone. She wouldn't take anything if she was home. If she was home and you brought anything, she'd just cuss you out and maybe start throwing the stuff back at you."

"Once, after they'd shut off her utilities, I saw that she'd been defecating in the garden. I did tell her she couldn't be doing that without getting into trouble with the authorities, and I showed her how to dig holes and bury it properly. She seemed glad I did that and it wasn't a problem after we talked."

"And the vandals?"

"The vandals? Oh yes, the vandals. I chased them out. Pulled a bunch of papers and notebooks from the fire, and I put it out."

"Do you think the papers are still in the house?"

"They're in there, alright. Right along with Dory's toys and everything else that was there when she died."

"I'd sure like to get ahold of those notebooks."

"Shoulda been here a few weeks ago. They hadn't boarded up the doors then. Now they have no trespassing signs all over the place. Now it's posted. The sign says violators will be prosecuted." Lew looked up at the clock. "Time to get my bride fed. Will you join us for lunch?"

Franniemarie hesitated.

Lew reassured her. "It's no problem. I've got some potato soup made up already. I'll just put out some whole wheat bread. Our bakery makes the best whole wheat bread, and there's some fresh fruit. Can't make Addie dessert anymore, her diet won't allow it."

"Do stay." Addie leaned back in her chair.

Lew set a simple but fine table replete with sterling. Franniemarie ran her fingers over the fluted pattern along the stem of her soup spoon. "This is so beautiful. What a pleasure to eat with sterling."

"The silver's Addie's. She always loved silver, but she couldn't make up her mind what pattern she liked best. So I bought her three chests of it."

"I still don't know which I like best. It's my pleasure to be surprised by whatever pattern he brings to the table."

"Have some more bread." Lew passed the basket." That's real butter. We never did believe in margarine. Sure a shame that Dorien's house is getting bulldozed."

Franniemarie choked. "When?"

"Scheduled for next week."

"Lew saved it twice. The first time was several years ago, not long after they'd condemned it. He pulled up all the stakes with notices on them and posted signs on each of the doors. He wrote "*This House is Occupied*." That got people to looking into her problems. And a lot of people tried to help her. But, of course, she wasn't able to understand that. Too far gone, she was. The last time was three years ago. That time, he got a bunch together to stand up for her, and the city backed off. 'Course, now there's nothing for it her not living there anymore and all."

After Franniemarie and Lew washed the dishes, he said he needed to run a couple of errands, and suggested she keep Addie company while he was gone. Before he left, he helped Addie into her comfy chair and tucked her in.

Addie directed Franniemarie to the silverware chests, and the two of them admired the patterns. Then she asked Franniemarie to fetch a family history she'd written, down from the bookshelf. Franniemarie became captivated, then lost in a family history that was outside of her life. Addie's writing was colorful, clear and crisp. After some time she looked up and said, "You certainly have a way with words. This reads more like a story than a family history."

"I'm the one my parents should have sent to college. I was smarter than all of them put together. My brothers were all dumber than posts. I'd have gone to college, if it weren't for my uncle. My damn uncle! He's the one who talked my parents out of it.

"So I got a job teaching normal school. I met Lew dancing, and we married. Damned old fool he was, and just as crazy for Dorien as the rest. Never did meet a man with a lick of good sense."

Addie quit talking when Lew came through the door. He showed Franniemarie a picture of Lake Como nestled beneath the mountains of Italy, the homeland he hadn't seen since he was a child. He invited her out to see the yard. They walked a path of brick and rock that transformed the space into a work of art. "Addie is the horticulturist in the family. I don't know what half the plants out here are, but if she could get out then she would. But she's crazy," Lew stopped, pointed to the path. "Take this walk. I told her it would be better to do it right, to do it in concrete. But she wouldn't hear of it. She insisted that I lay it in brick, bed the brick in sand not concrete. Now I have to work like a dog to keep the weeds out of the sand. If she'd let me do it right the first time, I wouldn't have to be working so hard all the time. 'Course she always took care of it before.

"I just don't know what's going to happen to her after I'm dead. I will die before her, you know. She's just like Dorien, crazy, you know? That kind always lives on. They are the survivors. So I'll die first." Lew shook his head. "Don't know what will happen to her after that. No one to take care of her."

The path meandered until it opened into a patio. "We used to keep a huge four poster bed out here. Right over there." Lew pointed to a lush arbor. "We'd sleep there at night under the stars." His eyes glazed as if looking back in time, and he smiled. "Oh, my, I cannot tell you how good that memory is."

Franniemarie looked over the fence into Dorien's place. "I'd like to walk in her yard. Do you think it would be all right?"

Lew looked dubious.

"I'd just like to take some pictures."

Lew softened. "You go on. I'll tell Addie what you're doing."

Ancient trees towered over Aunt Dorien's once white bungalow. Looking up, the sun filtered through leaves and spun Franniemarie dizzy. *It's like a church. No wonder she didn't want to leave.* Franniemarie lay on her back on the littered ground beneath the trees. *She must have written poetry.* The patterns were as fine as any surrealist painting she'd ever seen. She lay there and took pictures. *Dorien had to have written poetry.*

The doors were posted "*NO TRESPASS: Violators will be Prosecuted*", and in fine print, "Trespassing is a misdemeanor and all violators will be prosecuted." A misdemeanor. A misdemeanor? *What the hell are they going to do if they do catch me? Lock me up? Not likely. Bet the Oakland jail is full. Besides, who's going to know? Unless?* She looked toward the Palladio's well-manicured parcel. *Unless the Palladio's call.* The doors were secured with simple sheets of plywood. *If I just had a crowbar, even a hammer I could get in easy enough. But how am I going to get them to cooperate?*

Breathless Franniemarie burst into the living room. "Lew, have you read those notices."

"No"

"Well, it says that trespassing is a misdemeanor. I really want to go in."

"I don't know anything about this misdemeanor stuff. I don't want to get into any trouble. I've lived in this country since I was fourteen years old. I've never been in any trouble. Served in the army, became a pharmacist. Never been in any trouble."

"Lew? You do know the difference between a mortal and a venial sin, don't you?"

Lew snorted. "Everyone knows that."

Franniemarie exhaled a sigh of relief. "Well, Lew, a misdemeanor is the legal equivalent of a venial sin."

"You don't say? A venial sin? "

"Would you lend me a hammer?"

With the energy of a mischievous youngster, Lew fetched her not only a sturdy claw hammer but an armfull of canvas shopping bags and, unbelievably best of all, the keys to Aunt Dorien's back door.

"You go in, get those papers. I'll put the wheelbarrow this side of the fence and you can just toss anything over. I'll put it in the wheelbarrow."

A wren was nesting in the rotting fascia above the door. Blood pounding, Franniemarie quickly pried the door open, taking care not to disturb it.

Franniemarie adjusted to the dim light inside. Sunlight filtered through missing shingles, much as it had filtered through the leaves outside. Near the side of the fireplace was a rusting typewriter on an equally rusting typewriter table. A large square oak table of lasting quality was pushed against the living room wall, and on it were stacked boxes of rotting clothes. Moldy stuffed toys and a rusting red tricycle littered what must have been Dory's bedroom. There was no food in the cupboards, no dishes. *Did someone take them?* Dorien's bed was framed in 2x4's like a four-poster and covered with a clear plastic that Lew had put up to keep the rain out. Under her bed were more clothes zippered into neat plastic bags. They did not appear to have been worn.

In high gear, Franniemarie snapped pictures and hoped she had enough. Then she started stuffing every piece of paper she found into her bags, starting with what was on the mantel. She found steno-pads stuffed in dressers, on shelves, under beds, in the corners of closets, and books smelling of mildew, yet irresistible. She filled the wheelbarrow full—then nailed the door shut.

Together, Franniemarie and Lew wheeled the treasure to the other side of the house, and carefully transferred the books and the writings from the canvas bags to the trunk of her car.

Addie was visibly relieved when they returned. "I worried and worried. It seemed to take forever. I was thinking that maybe Franniemarie fell through the floor. I wished I could get the window open so I could tell Lew to go in after her. I'm so glad you're safe. Did you get what you wanted?"

Did I get what I wanted? Yes. God, I got what I wanted. Now I'm half afraid of what I've retrieved. What if she can't write? After all, she was never published. I do want her to write well—probably, I want that as much as I want to understand this family.

Franniemarie had all she could do to remember the three turns she needed to get to the Bay Bridge. Her mind kept leaping ahead—visualizing Lilianna's delight with her catch. She fairly shook in anticipation of opening her aunt's notebooks, peeking into her aunt's mind.

CHAPTER 6

FRANNIEMARIE LET HERSELF into Lilianna's empty town-house. Its midday darkness surprised her. Not till she opened the curtains did she realize the fog had rolled in. *How strange. At Aunt Dorien's it was sunny. I must have driven into this fog. Strange, I never noticed.* She pushed away an uneasy feeling that pressed for recognition, dug up some plastic grocery bags from Lilianna's kitchen, transferred her clothes from the box to the bags, and then took the box and a brown paper bag to the car. Leaving the musty books in her trunk, she placed loose papers in the bag and the steno-pads in the box.

Aunt Dorien's handwriting was crabbed and small, covering the cardboard covers as well as the margins. Unfortunately, some of the books had charred edges; others were spoiled by water stains. Franniemarie diligently stayed the task till she'd sorted the two dozen notebooks by date. Besides the complete notebooks, she had a pile of disordered pages unbound by the action of rust on wire. She stacked them neatly and began a search through each one, looking for first dates, when her attention was captured by the following lines:

> *In the park, the flowering acacia bleeds scarlet thru every break in foliage, a scarlet banner raised especially for me. Every time the acacia blooms, I'll remember today and see its color flung against the gray sky and smell damp air and green grass and city, and that peculiar mixture of happiness and melancholy I've felt all my life on a dull gray day with the fresh smell of rain in the air—rain, or the promise of rain, and the slightest touch of fragrant wind whispering over lawn, and macadamia.*
>
> *I'll remember that acacia flame flung high against the sky as long as I live. And I'll remember I was happy on that day. Happy in an astonished way because a dream came true. A piece of Heaven fell in my lap.*
>
> *Gill, dead, has given me more than Gill, living, denied me—and he said he was going to get me. Ha! I have the last laugh on him. And that takes away the bitterness in me.*
>
> *Mr. Stell of the Veterans Administration says I will receive $40 and Dory $20 a month through high school, and $40 through college. Oh, my! I just came to pieces as soon as I said goodbye. It was the way talking to Clay used to be. Ten years off my shoulders and I felt relaxed to the very core of me—so much for worry and*

planning. And of course there's Gill's insurance, another $105 a month. Now I can go to college and so can Dorianna.

Because he's dead, we'll have the things he couldn't and wouldn't have given us had he lived. Gill died for this as well as for his country, even if he was more a soldier of Fortune than a Patriot. Now the book is closed, he's dead and the evil he did while living no longer matters. Not to be able to love him doesn't matter—the thing that did matter was to have hated him and wanted to hurt him for having hurt me; now he is where I can no longer hurt him. To feel grateful is a relief. There was a time when I sincerely tried to be a good wife to him—that I failed was no fault of mine. I couldn't be what he wanted in a woman. So I can feel peace without qualms of conscience. I don't quite believe it yet. I haven't felt so joyous since I met Clay. It's wonderful!

It's hard to write tonight. I feel empty of words and spilling over with relief. Today I was supposed to sign the papers for the college fund. I'd have gone today, but I knew I'd never make it with tears in my eyes and half-hysterical laughter bubbling from my throat. Silly woman, why don't you cry like other folks do? Oh, Glorious Tomorrow!

By the time Lilianna let herself in, Franniemarie, surrounded by Aunt Dorien's papers, was crying. Sobbing she called out joyously, "Lilianna, she could write, she really could write. Listen to this." Reading aloud, she followed Lilianna into the kitchen, the bedroom, the bathroom and back to the kitchen. Is this beautiful or what?"

"Interesting."

"Just interesting?"

"I don't know about you, Frannie, but I'm half-starved." Lilianna pulled a pizza from the oven.

I don't think she even listened to what I read!

Lilianna mused, "Wonder who in hell Clay was?"

Franniemarie hadn't noticed Lilianna putting the pizza in the oven, but having watched her cousin take it out, she was suddenly famished. She could hardly keep herself from wolfing down the first slice.

"I take it your visit with the Palladios went well?"

"God, yes! Lew even gave me a hammer to pry off the plywood covering the door and a key to open it. You won't believe the stuff I pulled from the house."

"How are the Palladios?"

"Seemed fine. They're an interesting couple."

"They are very fragile."

"I suspect they're a lot stronger than you think. They've had to be to survive together."

"And what do you mean by that?"

"She thinks he's a weak overbearing jackass; he thinks she's weak in the head and he's always been her hero."

"Frannie! What a thing to say."

"You asked."

Lilianna poured cups of strong coffee and tossed a couple of shots of Maker's Mark into each. She handed one to Franniemarie and raised hers. "A taste of San Francisco to ya!"

Together, they sat on the rich Persian rug that graced Liliana's living room. Franniemarie continued sorting the loose pages. Liliana started sorting piles of letters, large notebooks and odd pieces.

"Good Lord, Frannie, there are heaps of utility bills going all the way back to '57—and none of them opened. I'll put all that sort of thing into one pile."

Franniemarie opened a stained notebook. "Here's something about Clay. It was written in May of 1946."

"If Clay had minded his own business, my marriage to Gill would never have outlasted its third year. He was already looking for a prettier, more musically accomplished wife and simply wanted to make sure he could be rid of me without giving me any money. When he saw Clay take an interest in me, well that brought him up short."

We're missing something 'cause the letter bottom is scorched, but it continues mid-sentence top of the next page.

"… he stopped the car outside the house on San Antonio Street. It was warm and quiet and the car was very comfortable. He had begun the short trip talking nervously, trying to amuse me, and I remember being completely astonished that he should feel that way about me. Then, when we stopped, I wanted to stay in that little space with him and in the moment when he sat still beside me, I cuddled down in the seat and put my head back. He turned his head and I realized suddenly I had no right to behave as if I had a proprietary interest in him and sat up quickly. I wished with all my heart then to be free and to brush the sky clear of sunlight and let it be night, and no place either of us had to go. Just to wish for one unspoken hour to be alone with him in the darkness. That is comical.

I'm the girl who finds kissing disgusting. Nor do I dislike it less at my age than I did in my early teens."

"Lilianna, I think we just met Clay."

"Sounds like she was playing with him before her husband left for the war."

"Hard to tell, she's talking about something that happened in the past—but how long in the past? Uncle Gill was killed in '43. So at least five years."

"We have unopened bills from furniture, grocery, and clothing stores as well as one from a funeral parlor. And I have a bunch of newspaper clips."

"Does the letter from the funeral parlor have a return name on the envelope?"

"No. Just Sunset Mortuary."

"Lew said she had a suitor who was a funeral director. Perhaps they're one and the same. Do open it."

"Sankovitch. Rodney Sankovitch."

"That's him. Addie said he was really rich."

"Look Frannie!" Lilianna held up a news paper clip featuring Dorianna, aged two and a half, accepting her father's medals."

"This is interesting.

"Tho where Mrs. Cassidy comes off criticizing Mrs. Coy for charging $80.00 per mo. a room, I don't quite see. Mrs. Cassidy frankly says she patronized the Black Meat Market and justifies it by saying, "Well, we wanted steak." That sounds like Gill—so does Mrs. Pollan's, "Well, we figured out that some child liked Sue's scooter better and took it, and left hers. Now that's pure nonsense, that scooter was found days after Sue lost hers. Dory found it so I know. She and Sue lost scooters near the same time. Dory found this scooter and she knows finders are keepers if there is no claimant. To Dory, being intelligent enough to reason a little, these people found a way to steal: no different than Gill's 'reasons'. The lesson isn't lost on Dory and I've had my first really serious trouble with her for taking things since that happened."

Liliana snorted, "Chip off the old block, already. That letter got a date?"

"Yeah, August 29, 1946."

"Dory would have been about 4."

"Here's a snippet. It's dated the 26th of July, same year.

"Dory liked my worm but when I went to put him on paper, I began to realize that I had a very nice worm without any well-defined story structure, just unrelated adventures of a worm."

Wouldn't it be fun if we found the story?"

Lilianna did not reply.

Franniemarie read another fragment featuring Clay.

"I remember, once, Clay was smoking a pipe and accidentally blew smoke my way. Without thinking I blew it back to him and he ducked. Then he laughed, and I blew at it the easy way you blow at soap bubbles, reflecting that a faintly bluish color and a woodsy smell that reminded me of late autumn and yellow and brown leaves on the trees outside a room with a fire burning, a light southwest wind blowing softly outside. Of blue sunny skies, yet a touch of frost in the air and the bluish smoke of leaf fires."

"Isn't she wonderful with words?"

Lilianna yawned, "I hear infatuation has a way of doing that to you."

"Oh, and here's an undated fragment. The tops are charred on this one.

"… my proper poker face calm or smiling—my voice stayed calm and the right words came out even tho blackness closed over my vision and all my body was like it had gone to sleep and my brain was scalding hot: but, when my vision cleared, no one seemed to notice anything amiss. Yet, looking down, I saw my own little fists clinched tight till the knuckles were white with tension, the skin drawn almost beyond its ability to stretch. Only Clay ever noticed my hands. At times of stress my hands say much. It was emotional stress that the tension of my fists bespoke—he noticed and knew the reason for that tension and kindly eased it so that my fingers unfolded and relaxed."

"Looks like Auntie was well on her way to gone before Dory took her dive." Lilianna said dryly.

Franniemarie sucked in her breath. "Listen to this…"

"… I'd condemn her except that I am sometimes a stranger to my daughter. The other way around, my daughter is a stranger to me. I only hope I find her before it's too late. She's so elusive now, like a warm breath on a frost-cold window-pane. She's young and her character is not yet formed. I trust I can reach her and make sure she's given a chance to grow safely in the way that will be of advantage. I can't have her destroy herself and others thru misuse of inherited capacities. I want her to use them for her good and others, yet I don't want to tie her to my decisions. She must stand on her own two feet."

"She may be misguided, but doesn't she sound like she's trying to be a good mother?"

"Wasn't my mother's focus, but there is this: her kid's dead, we're alive. That oughtta tell us something." Lilianna had made stacks of Dorien's papers, the bills, miscellaneous typed papers, large notebooks, newspaper clippings, and the last was a pile of sketches and drawings of rooms and notes on interior decorating. "Look at this, Frannie." Lilianna picked up the pile of papers, spread them out on the round glass top of her dining room table, made some more Irish coffee. Together, they sorted through the notes and sketches. "I think this was her calling."

"Geez, Lilianna, no one ever mentioned anything but the writing."

"She probably never shared this with anyone. These shouldn't be left loose—they deserve better. I've got an extra acid-free picture album. You mind if I mount these in it? "

"Go ahead. It's a neat idea."

Lilianna was soon lost in building the book, leaving Franniemarie to peruse her unbound pages.

"Found more Dory stuff. Again, no date.

"…has admitted she may have spit at someone accidentally and she's sorry, and she says she forgot she was to get the money after school instead of at lunch, and she's promised not to do either of those things again."

"Kid on the road to perdition."

"Lilianna, that's a judgement easier to make after the fact. At least Aunt Dorien was trying. She says,"

"… I'd rather train her to do her own thinking with some solid foundation to do it. That's what bothers me. Wondering if I'm getting that foundation in right. It isn't quite like laying cement. Last night we listened to Red Ryder and during the commercial we talked about the moral as we often do. It's really the only way I can tell what she gets of what I've tried to teach her, and she said she wasn't good or bad, she said (with-satisfaction) that she was the "in-between—part good and part bad."

"Frannie, I'm thinking of having a party for you."

"You don't need to do it on my account." Franniemarie continued reading.

"Queer, when she was dressing this morning, before morality came up at all, she said something about it not being very much fun, did I think, for a girl to be engaged to a man who wanted to murder her."

"Wouldn't you like to meet my friends?"

"It's not that. It's just—what I came here for was to get to know you, and of course learn what I can about Aunt Dorien." Franniemarie resumed reading:

"She knows her father did steal things, and her little throat went tight over the words for a moment. It was on the bus coming home. But I've always said, and I insisted, quietly but firmly then, that her father was both a thief and a hero. He wasn't just one or just the other. He was a bad man and a great man—both. And that he was not entitled to respect as a good man merely because he was a hero, nor could anyone take from him his right to be remembered as a hero because he had done some bad things. And Dory managed very well, as she always does if I tell her squarely the whole story without subterfuge and making anything different than it is."

"My friends are very important to me."

"I'm sure they are." Franniemarie hardly missed a beat.

"Nor do I talk to her teacher about her without telling her what was said in our conversation. That would be dishonest. She seems more secure when she can trust me."

"I haven't given a party in a long time."

"Mrs. Cox is right. Dory's nightmares and sleepwalking are related to fights with other children and rare school difficulties. I don't see how you can take a sleeping child's temperature, though. She does feel as if she had a fever; but even covered only with a sheet, she will perspire until her clothing has to be changed and her pillow turned. She has had dreams and cried without tears and talked in a way that is unlike her self-possessed awake personality."

"You sure you wouldn't like a party?"

"I didn't say that. I never mentioned a party preference. Aunt Dorien seems really concerned about Dory's nightmares, she says:"

"… however, lately, she has neither sleep-walked nor had nightmares. For a while she dreaded sleep for fear of nightmares."

"It's been so long since I've thrown a party—seems I owe everyone I know."

"It is easier for us to be friends the last few days than it has been, and she seems to have toward me the good-will she had when she was a baby. That wish to please me that was so characteristic of her early behavior disappeared completely the last few years and only now is reappearing. Wish I could go to that organ program, but I just haven't the money to pay Shirley to stay with …"

"That must have been written before she knew the government was going to give her money."

"Must have."

"It's queer that Dory can never remember what happens in her nightmares. She's so terrified of them, but can't remember what happened. Tonight she was afraid she'd be killed in her sleep. She's a bit of a stoic. Her voice may shake; but she doesn't break down easily."

"Geesus, Frannie, here's a note written on the bottom of a living room sketch. She says,

"Sometimes I don't take such good care of Dory—like now when my mind is full of plans. Yet once the plans get going, I'll probably take very good care of her simply because everything finds a place in the routine of my schedule.' Bet it never happened. Bet she thought a lot about mothering, talked and wrote a lot about mothering. Bet it ended there. For sure, that's the way it was in our stories."

Tears came to Franniemarie. "It's no wonder she killed herself."

"Lord, Frannie, just look at the time. Don't know about you, but I'm going to bed."

"Wait a minute… I think I've found something telling! Listen to this charred undated fragment."

"… Clay, if anyone tells you. You know better than anyone else that a thick screen hangs between me and other people. You alone penetrated that screen, loved me without restraint and proved it. Forever we shall be wed in our hearts. Oh, I know you married another and I forgive you that. I'd forgive you anything in honor of the secret we hold as dear as our love. Each night, I thank you for what you did that night in Egypt. Each night I …"

"Egypt? Where the hell does Egypt fit in here?"

"Lilianna, I haven't a clue. But the answer is probably buried someplace in all this—this stuff."

"Each night I thank you for the gift of freedom. For freedom from that evil that promised to destroy my life. You have been the only person who loved me, so you have been the only one whom I loved in return. The bond between us is deeper than any other I have known. For that I will protect your life, as you protected mine. I will never tell what we planned; what you did. In this world of maudlin sentiment, a murderer is excused on the ground that he has a charming manner. And I have nothing against charm."

"My God, Lilianna, the newspapers said Gill was missing over North Africa. We had bases in Egypt. Could Dorien have had her husband killed?"

"Shit, Frannie, she could have done anything. But I'm too tired to try to make sense of this stuff." With that, Lilianna left Franniemarie for bed.

Franniemarie, too wired to sleep, carefully repacked Dorien's materials. She poured herself a shot of whiskey, sat at the table, her own pen and pad in hand, and let a poem come through her.

> *Cousins*
> *You remember her—motorcycle maniac,*
> *dark-haired 50's chick—leather-jacket*
> *hair flying.*
> *You remember her—slicing midnight into*
> *before and after*
> *For you, her death was one clean shudder*
> *against the memory of the day her mother*
> *blistered your butt for no reason—for*
> *no reason at all.*
> *I remember her—fair-haired tragedy*
> *toddling in the shadow of her legendary*
> *father's distinguished flying cross. I*
> *remember her—red convertible,*
> *top down—aiming for the edge—kicking*
> *wind and sailing free. For me her death*
> *ascended our hell warped inheritance*
> *gave me faith I might wrest my wheel*

from destiny.
My mother remembers her sister sitting
at their father's feet—memorizing
incantations, tracing paths that stars make
making real their father's sky.
My mother could not know the incantations
her sister taught—'your father was a hero
your father was a thief'
my mother erased the garbled communications
that circumscribed her death that same autumn
morning their father refused to answer
her isolated call. In her world
her sister married best, a military hero
soon missing over North Africa
that he'd received le croix de guerre
for bravery in action—her sister was the family
genius—the one her father loved the best and her father
is a saint she hasn't seen in over thirty years.
The Oakland Presspaints the picture black and white
GIRL DIES IN HIGH SPEED CRASH ignores police
shots—at 90 miles an hour rams a tractor trailer with a
stolen 1956 Lincoln and never touched the brake. From
her fractured flesh she cried out, "shoot me—take me out
of this misery"—three hours later—7 A.M.
she copped a trip
to the other side.

Franniemarie had not been aware she'd been wound tight
until the poem focused her tension and she'd spilled it
across the paper. Only then could she contemplate sleep.
Tomorrow I shall see my city. Tonight I sleep.

CHAPTER 7

LILIANNA WAS GONE before Franniemarie was up. She left a note on the table. "Hey, girl—have a party in motion for tonight. See you then, Love, Your Cuz." Franniemarie shook her head. *That woman sure works fast.* Under grey skies and morning mist, Franniemarie walked a glorious seven blocks to Chinatown. She reveled in foreign smells—asphalt mingled with the scent of the ocean, and something else, something astringent, perhaps eucalyptus. And she was charmed by the sight of row on row of town houses that shared common walls as casually as Nebraska farms and ranches shared common fences. *More than half a country, I'm a world away from Nebraska. And, Lord, I do like it."*

Chinatown's crimson arches called. Franniemarie accepted the invitation. *I'll have a real Chinese breakfast—as new to me as these sights and smells.* Walking down the street, she passed merchants opening doors, hanging out signs, sweeping sidewalks in front of their establishments. Two clean cut airmen in uniform came round the corner. Heart pounding, she swiftly crossed the street where she found a small café with a rather uninteresting facade and numerous tacky signs in English and Chinese, she supposed, plastered on the windows. Quickly, she slipped through the door.

Inside, the smells were both strange and enticing. Booths lined the walls either side of an aisle leading to the kitchen. Near the kitchen a group of Asian people sat, eating with chopsticks and speaking a language foreign to her ear. "Probably employees, possibly owners," she thought. When she seated herself in the booth across from them, one of the women stood, fetched a menu and brought it to her.

Franniemarie waved it away, pointed to their food. "I want that."

The waitress frowned as if she wasn't sure what this patron had said.

"I want what you're eating."

The waitress raised an eyebrow, "You sure?"

"I'm sure"

Eyes wide, the waitress shrugged, "Okay."

In minutes, the waitress returned with a pot of tea, a large bowl of soup, a plate of small steamed buns, and a pickled egg. Franniemarie admired the fine dragon on her porcelain spoon before she dipped it into a viscous soup and released some marvelous fragrance she could not identify. In the soup, she found flakes of fish and kelp and bits of sea urchins. It was delicious. The bun was both soft and firm between her teeth and she was pleasantly startled when she bit into a shrimp. The egg, dead brown and slightly slippery, did not invite.

Franniemarie looked to the table of native diners. They were all intently watching her. She smiled broadly, picked up the egg and took a healthy bite, chewed and tasted. It tasted like a pickled egg with spices she'd never used. *What did I expect?* She looked at her fellow diners again and smiled an approval that they returned. Still savoring the new spices, she looked at the egg in her hand. Felt a puzzle forming. That isn't yoke, Oh, my God it's a chick—a chick embryo. Her stomach started to churn. *For heaven's sake Franniemarie, they thrive on this food. You liked it fine before you looked at it.* With studied ease she leaned back, closed her eyes, popped the rest of the egg into her mouth, and made her face into a portrait of sublime enjoyment.

Before Franniemarie left Chinatown, she'd purchased three silk scarves and a giant wok. The sight of the wok reminded her of Lilianna's expressed interest in entertaining. *Why, with this Lilianna could make something special, some delight guaranteed to be a hit. Heaven knows it's big enough to hold food for a crowd. I just know Lilianna will love it.* She never entertained a thought of weight, or the miles ahead that she'd be packing this treasure. By the time she'd traveled a few blocks, she was both grateful and charmed by the cable car she took to the harbor.

Midmorning found Franniemarie maundering Fisherman's Wharf in the sunshine. *I've never seen so many creatures from the sea. To think you can eat all of them! I could never have imagined it, neither in dreams nor nightmares. And the smell, I shall never forget this smell, this mingling of sun-warmed sea and sea creatures. The closest Nebraska could come to this smell would be a mingling of fresh mown hay with silage.*

Clutching the wok awkwardly to her chest, Franniemarie walked to Ghirardelli Square. There she wandered for hours, fascinated by kitchen wares and exotic merchandise gathered from Earths' far-flung corners. From India she purchased small, round clay ornaments covered with tiny geometric mirrors imbedded in colors of orange, fuchsia, blue, and mustard. From Japan a set of chopsticks inlayed with mother of pearl, from Africa a carved wooden comb.

In the square, she discovered a pub. There she sat at a small window facing the ocean. The sky was filled with kites, kites in an array of colors and sizes to defy imagination. She ordered Irish coffee, settled back, and watched the kites crisscross the sky in a colorful, graceful, ballet.

From the bar behind her, two fellows held a lively conversation about some mission. "It's an absolute must see. Franciscan friars built it using slave labor. Way back—1790s, I think. Story goes the Indians painted some kind of mural, using color they made. But that's all been covered up by an altar. Still, even the altar is impressive. It's massive. It was built in Spain and sent here in pieces."

"I was in an ancient church south of Mexico City once. An older Mexican gleefully told me that the natives, when forced to build that church, worked into the building symbols of their own religion. They did it so when they prayed they still prayed to their gods."

"The Spanish called it Nuestra Senora de los Dolores— Our Lady of Sorrows. It's not far."

When three small kites attacked the largest, loveliest kite, her heart fairly stopped. She feinted and soared with the great kite holding her own against the enemy until a little kite, striped like a neon zebra, entered the fray, darted in, and severed her line. Free, the great kite soared on a current until it was lost over the bay.

Franniemarie hadn't walked three blocks, when she spied a cab. Mission Dolores called, and without a moment's hesitation she hailed it. Full of pride, the cabby told her the mission was built of adobe and redwood beams tied together with rawhide thongs. Its walls were six feet deep. When they arrived, she asked the driver to wait.

Nothing she'd heard that day prepared her for the awe she felt passing through the mission's massive hand-carved doors. In the hushed cool interior of the mission, she nearly became lost in the mustard-yellow, gray, white, and red primitive designs above her—the heavy, ornately carved altar before her. Inside, the mission felt full of people past and people present. *Behind every altar there's some hidden story. It's the hidden story that obfuscates the present.*

An image of her son Brooks and his bride, Christina, raptly staring into each other's eyes as they vowed their troth, filled her with a poignant mix of joy and sorrow. Immediately she shut it out, left the mission, and ordered the cab to Chinatown.

Franniemarie wandered into a Szechwan café. There she randomly pointed to an item on the menu. By the time she finished her meal, she'd tasted eighteen dishes—not counting the pot of tea and the thin, pancake-like rounds of bread kept hot in a covered pottery dish. Eighteen servings, starting with salty dishes which morphed into sweet, and the sweet ones into hot, and the hot increasing until the last bite felt like it would blow off the top of her head. Franniemarie shivered with delight.

The trolley clanging behind her, she walked into evening's twilight as it gave way to street-lit dark. In the distance a soft glow of light beckoned from Liliana's living room window. Anticipating Lilianna's reaction to her gift, Franniemarie could already see herself passing the wok to her cousin—could see the corners of her cousin's eyes crinkle with delight. She fairly ran up the steps. Then, disoriented, stopped short. Beyond the oval beveled glass door she saw a room filled with people—shadows milling beyond the lace curtain. The party, oh, my God, I forgot the party! How could I do such a thing? Inside, overwhelmed by a babble of voices over-riding some Latin-sounding rhythm, she leaned against the door.

An obviously distraught Lilianna slipped and twisted between her guests till she reached Franniemarie. She hissed between clenched teeth, "Geesus, Franniemarie, where the hell you been?"

"Downtown. I told you I was going downtown."

Franniemarie followed her cousin to her bedroom. Lilianna closed the door behind them. "Christsake, Downtown doesn't take fifteen hours. I didn't even know where to start—police or hospitals. At the very least, you could have called."

"I'm sorry."

"Sorry doesn't cut it. Here I invited all my friends—put together this party—all for you, and you don't even show."

"But Lilianna, I didn't know about the party. You never …"

"Oh, yes I did! How in hell was I to know you'd be gone so long? "

"Lilli …"

"Put that junk on the other side of the bed, go wash the city off, and I'll introduce you." Lilianna turned on her heel, closing the door behind her.

Lilianna, in a shimmery gown that skimmed her lithe body and fell to the floor, stood by a dining room table laden with wines and seafood delights. Unnoticed, Franniemarie worked her way toward her lovely cousin—wove her way through snippets of conversation. "Renee Fleming … Ariana …"

" … Dvorak … last, or next to last symphony? *God, I wish I weren't in blue jeans.* "Little mermaid …"

"Ah, yes, Hans Christian Andersen …"

" . . *New World Symphony … 9th Symphony…*"

"THE great Bohemian sprit!"

Lilianna picked up a stemmed plastic wine glass, "Merlot or Chablis?"

"I'll take the white stuff." Franniemarie looked through the dining area, through an open door to a patio where figures twined, dancing beneath the lights of paper lanterns.

Lilianna raised her glass to the guests in the room, "To my long lost cousin, swept to our fair city from the prairies of Nebraska."

Franniemarie heard someone exclaim, "Nebraska? Where in hell's Nebraska?" This was not a San Francisco moment of her dreams. She smiled, raised her glass in a salute to Lilianna and guests, drained it, then poured another—worked her way to the patio, found an inconspicuous spot at a table. Leaning back in a deep wicker chair she sipped her wine, listened to a rhumba rhythm, and watched the couples dancing. *Cricket was never a flashy dancer, but he was steady. When did we stop dancing?*

The music ended. Someone was fussing with the CD player. A couple crossed to her table. "Great party, this?" Franniemarie nodded. "Mind if we join you?" Franniemarie tipped a chair in invitation. "So how do you know Lilianna?"

"I'm her cousin."

"Oh, you're our excuse for a party."

"Guess so." Franniemarie found herself smiling.

"I'm Rachael, and this is my partner Davida." Rachael, wrapped in layered diaphanous materials was pleasingly plump, sort of a matronly aging hippie. Her partner, sporting a crew cut, was wearing skin tight leather and enough metal in her ears to set off a metal detector. And that's when Franniemarie realized they both had breasts. They were both women. Davida held up her empty glass, "I need a refill, how about you?" Franniemarie nodded, tried not to stare, and handed over her glass. Rachael leaned toward her. "What do you do in Nebraska?"

Again, Franniemarie swallowed. "We run a farm."

"Really? Like with cows and chickens and stuff?"

"Something like that."

"So," Rachael hesitated, "You're straight?"

"I think so."

Rachael sighed, "You know when I came to San Francisco I didn't know what I was. It's a long story, but I was a student at the Minneapolis Institute of Arts—we're talking '60s. To make it short, this guy tells me he's sterile and I get myself pregnant. He was some asshole. Anyway I was friends with this guy who was about to graduate and had a job offer out here. He's gay, but he says, 'Why not come with me, and we'll get married.' Sounded like a plan to me. We did, and here I am."

"So you're a mother?"

"Try grandmother."

"Oh, wow. Then, did you divorce him?"

"Heavens no! He's a graphic designer, and I'm a fiber artist. We raised Juni together, but now we live with our lovers. There's no way I could afford health insurance on what I make. We're good friends."

Franniemarie nodded sympathetically.

Setting their drinks on the table, Davida said, "We've known Lilianna nearly twenty years and never knew she had a cousin until today."

"Could be because Lilianna and I didn't meet until I got here this week."

"No way!" Davida exclaimed.

"It's a long story. But we're just getting to know each other."

"Lilianna's a kick."

"Sooo talented."

"Too bad she picks such jerks for partners."

"Lilianna's gay?"

"Honey, everyone at this party is gay."

"Oh my God!" Franniemarie looked around confused. "I mean …"

Rachael and Davida let her stew.

"It's just … I never met anyone who was gay before."

"Don't you mean—you never met anyone you knew was gay before?"

"Yeah! That. Lilianna didn't mention it."

"Guess now she has."

"Yeah! I mean—I guess she has."

Rachael leaned forward, and using her best disinterested-in-the-outcome-pseudo-counselor voice asked, "So how do you feel about that?"

All three burst into laughter.

"But seriously," Franniemarie replied, "I've never even thought about it much, except I never could understand what the big deal was about marriage. You know, how it destroys family values and all that. Seems to me a family is a chosen unit, hopefully built to last—certainly built to nurture."

"Yeah! And we aren't contributing to overpopulation, so all you heteros really ought to be cheering us on."

"I'll raise a glass to that." Franniemarie lifted her wine. "Guess these days it's a plastic one."

"Shit, look who's with Clarice!" Rachael nodded toward a couple slow dancing near the dining room door.

"Brazen."

"Totally." In response to Franniemarie's face turned to question mark, Rachael explained, "Clarice is the tall one. Bubbles is Lilianna's ex."

"Lilianna's ex?"

"Latest ex."

"How many has she had?"

"Bubbles is number four."

"This one was nasty, though."

"Nasty? How? Why?"

"Lilianna has a history of entering into relationships with women who need saving. Once collected, she tends to micro-manage their lives, trying to get them on track and up to speed. Then she expects them to take over and leave her free to do her thing. What she doesn't understand is this, not one of them can hold it together."

"It's not long before they drive her up a wall."

"They only function well while she's managing them."

"I don't know if they're needy, stupid or lazy, but when she turns back to her pursuits they feel aggrieved."

"Abandoned."

"Whatever. In the past, they've always left her and she's been fine with that."

"By the time they left, she'd already given them up for a lost cause."

"Lilianna never looked back."

"What was different with this—" Franniemarie glanced toward the couple, "Bubbles?"

"Well, Bubbles is a sculptor—actually, a very fine sculptor, probably an idiot savant."

"Rachael! That's the long story. The short of it, Bubbles didn't want to leave. Bubbles would have stayed on and on and on."

"Lilianna had it up to here," Rachael interrupted. "If Bubbles pulls on socks, they don't match—she can't even remember to put gas in the tank, and it never occurs to her to look at the gauge. Lilianna literally had to dress her, and she never knew what she was going to come home to. One time, Bubbles used her new fondue pot to melt wax—totaled it. That kind of thing. The last straw came when Bubbles acid-washed a bronze in her porcelain bathtub. It cost a small fortune to replace it."

Franniemarie watched Bubbles moving freely in a lovely white-crinkled, cotton peasant dress. "Looks like she found another to dress her."

"Oh, yes. Bubbles is also charming."

"What Lilianna needs is someone who can match her strength."

Archly, Rachael asked "Someone like you?"

"Get outta here."

*****

Before Lilianna closed the door on the last of her guests, Franniemarie had the patio cleared, darkened the lanterns and was nearly finished putting away the food.

"Let's not do this." Lilianna yawned.

"The food has to be put away."

"I need to be up by six."

"That's okay. You go on to bed, and I'll just finish up. Go on now… I'm not a bit tired."

Franniemarie hadn't finished clearing the table when Lilianna came storming into the kitchen with the bags that had been tossed beside her bed. "Jesus Christ! Franniemarie, I damn near killed myself tripping over your junk. The least you could do is get it outta my room." Before Franniemarie could reply, her cousin had turned heel and tromped out.

A line from Sharon Old's poem *I Go Back To May 1937* skittered across her mind: "I say / Do what you want to do, and I will tell about it." *I should be writing poems. That's the only way I can sort my life—I toss the events in piles, file them, then take them out and try to make sense of it all. Only, perhaps that's not what I should be doing with them. Perhaps I should view the emotions, the words, the events, as bones piled in my file, bones to be dug up when I need to chew on them, and just maybe I can morph them into something else like the Szechwan dishes, salt into sweet into hot till it becomes something else. Something beautiful, I hope. Something as beautiful as the smell of fresh baked bread. Bread. That's what I'll do for Lilianna. I'll bake her a couple of loaves of bread. And while they're rising, I'll read some more of Dorien's letters.*

Hours later, the scent of baking bread brought Lilianna storming into the kitchen.

"What the hell's going on here? It's damn near morning, the house smells like fire!"

"Lilianna! That's not the smell of fire. That's the heavenly smell of bread baking."

"Bread baking! You're baking bread in the middle of the night? That's it! Franniemarie, you're gonna have-ta get out of here!"

"Get out? Geez Lilianna, we haven't even read all the letters."

"No shit! Ya got a zillion of them."

"We haven't found out who she is."

"Oh, yeah? She's a psycho old lady in psycho center."

"Don't you want to know why?"

"Hell, no. What I want's you out."

"Lilianna, you're crazy!"

Lilianna sputtered. "Crazy? Me, crazy? I sure as hell will be if you don't get out."

"What the hell's that mean?"

"Christsake Frannie, you come out here, never sleep, never stop talking, and the talk is all about YOU."

"Me? I thought it was about our aunt?"

"Same difference."

"Anyone crazy here it's you, Lilianna, you. You're the one invited me out. You're the one keeps asking me questions—invited a buncha dikes over for the night."

"Damn you, Franniemarie, those women are my friends."

Franniemarie began stuffing her clothes back into plastic bags. "Friends, my ass. Plain as the nose on your face, they're just acquaintances glad to suck your beer."

"It was wine, not beer, and what would you know about friends? Only three people in your life, and you're related to all of them."

"I thought you wanted to know me?"

"Ditto."

Franniemarie retrieved her personal grooming supplies from the bathroom and placed them next to the bag of letters already neatly stacked on top of the steno-pads. Last, she added the wok. Hooking her left arm through the handles of both her purse and the plastic bags filled with her belongings, she picked up the box and worked the door open with her right hand.

"Where the hell you going this time of night? It's because I'm gay, isn't it?"

"Yeah, and that's why I was baking you bread." Franniemarie lurched though the door. "You said, leave. I'm leaving."

"It's damn near 3 a.m. You can't leave now."

"Oh, yeah? Just watch me."

Lilianna grabbed the door, "Frannie, what about the bread in the oven?"

"Take it out when it's done."

Lilianna called after her, "How long till it's done?"

"When you thump it and it sounds hollow."

Lilianna yelled, "How do you thump hot bread?" But Franniemarie had slammed the door and was gone.

CHAPTER 8

Blinded by anger, Franniemarie drove through an industrious rain, a rain hard at work cleaning the streets and watering the plants of San Francisco. *What does she know? She doesn't even know me. I don't give a damn with whom she sleeps. I thought we were more alike. I thought we both wanted to know how and why we are the way we are. That's what's important. That's what hurts.* Mindless she paid a toll, crossed a bridge, found herself on a freeway without a clue as to the direction she was headed. *Sex. Big deal! I used to want sex. Every time I saw a man I was attracted or repelled. Physically I was never neutral, but I wanted them all to want me.* A truck passed, casting a huge spray. Franniemarie turned her wipers too high. A police car came up behind her, lights flashing, siren screaming. Automatically, she checked the speedometer. Her heart pounded in her ears. She gripped the steering wheel, felt her body go into the familiar sweat she experienced each time she came in contact with a policeman. Ahead, she could see him pull the truck over, yet she could not relax until the scene was swallowed by dark. Then she shook her head and laughed. *Why do I always do that? Why do I associate uniforms with men? I don't think the image of a woman in uniform would cause me to sweat—to feel faint. And I don't know the officer wasn't a woman.*

Interstate marker I-5 NORTH registered in the recesses of her mind, and she shivered in response to some association of north with cold. Her fingers played staccato searching for classical music. *How can anyone be so absent-minded? I can't believe I forgot Lilianna's party. Before I left, I glanced at her note, but then the memory disappeared. It was gone. Totally gone. I've always been this way. If anyone asked Aunt Pru where I was she'd say, "Oh, you know Franniemarie, she probably just forgot to come home." Worse, everyone would just nod in agreement. Most of the time it doesn't matter. Cricket gets mad, but his mad is short lived.* The second movement of the first *Brandenburg Concerto* responded to her searching fingers, and visions of violins dancing played a backdrop for her thoughts.

What have I learned? Lilianna isn't like me. I do know a lot more about Aunt Dorien, and I have some of her letters and her journals, so I may learn more, but I don't know any more about Lilianna, or her mother than I did before I came. Hell, Lilianna doesn't know much more about her mother than I do. Maybe that's why she's gay, looking for her mother's love in all those women. But then why would she choose weak women? And, if that were the case, wouldn't I be gay? Lord knows my mother never loved me.

Some of the things Cricket did to me—the things I liked the best—could have been done by a woman. When did we stop making love? When did it turn into his release? When did I stop wanting to be touched in those special ways? And why did I stop wanting?

And what about Aunt Dorien? Could she have had her husband killed? Perhaps she was delusional. How did she come by the idea that her daughter would be better prepared for this world if she knew the worst of her father, weighing the bad and the good equally? She was only five, maybe less, for Christsake. Like me, she never saw her father after she was a year old. Lew says Dorien isolated her for days on end and sometimes whipped her unmercifully. Mother never isolated me, we just lived apart. But that is isolation. Perhaps in Aunt Dorien's mind she was protecting them. I can't believe Mother ever protected me from anything, anyone. Cricket's right, I'm just one member in a family of loonies. I don't think they were born that way. In my box of letters—letters written from the time the authors could print and ending while they were yet young women—the letters read like normal. Does the mind look around, then imitate what it perceives is normal? Does it work hard at imitation until it can't make normal work?

Franniemarie's headlights caught a skunk ambling toward her on the right-hand-side of the road. *Oh Shit!* She glanced at her mirrors, not a car in sight, she swung into the left lane, and thrilled that her ancient Chevy responded handsomely, just as it always had. She patted the wheel of her old friend. For years, Cricket had been urging her to trade it in. A hundred thousand miles ago he was saying, "Franniebaby, I know you're fond of that old heap, but let's face it, ya got near two hundred thou' on that puppy and no way it's gonna run forever. Besides, I worry about you driving with that many miles on it." Franniemarie looked at new cars, but she just couldn't find another that felt so completely right.

The rain was long behind her and the road was now so dry it seemed never to have been wet. Franniemarie stared into a black night, and the night worked on her mind in the same way her prairie screen had, sucking her into a vortex made up of introspection, memory, and vision. Before her, in black and white, Dorien and little Dorianna sat on the steps in front of the duplex on High Street. In a snap that image was replaced with one of Franniemarie and Brooks on Grand's porch swing. As fast as the image came, it vanished and the black and white photo of her Aunt and cousin returned, then dissolved into color. Aunt Dorien looked charming in a tailored teal silk blouse with three-button cuffs, and a long pointed collar tucked neatly into a gored navy blue serge skirt draped over her gracefully crossed legs tucked modestly to the side. *She must have been about thirty in that picture. She looked crisp. She looked as if she had it all together.* The scent of ginger first warmed Franniemarie, then caught in her throat. She could feel her aunt's presence. Her hands froze to the steering wheel.

"I must tell you," Aunt Dorien's voice was clear, gay, and familiar, "Dolly really liked the excitement of having me hurt. She thought it was 'interesting'."

Who in hell is Dolly? Is this real? Franniemarie fought the urge to look at her aunt. *If I look, she'll disappear.*

"Once she told me a story about a girl whose husband died, and later the fellow she loved married another, just like Clayton married Camilia."

If the love of her life's emotions were so intense he would kill her husband for her, why did he marry another?

"Dolly said this girl told her it was for the best because he loved the girl he married. Then one day she gave Dolly her earrings and told her to keep them 'to remember me by' and she seemed alright, but she went out and killed herself. Dolly knew about the earrings Gill once gave me that I'd given to Janice. I had the strange feeling she was trying to work me up to a dramatic ending in which she could feel she figured as the star performer. If she thinks I'd do such a thing simply to provide her with a little amusement, she's a fool!" Aunt Dorien's voice resonated vibrant and young. "People like Dolly have no standards, no understanding of logic, therefore they have no capacity to judge the veracity of what they're told. They are a potential danger to a democracy. They could sit on a jury, but haven't used their brains enough to sustain a reasonable doubt."

Franniemarie didn't dare turn her head for fear her aunt would disappear, disappear as unceremoniously as she'd recently dismissed Franniemarie and Lilianna in the rest home.

"That's the way it was with the women of the JCA. Just as sure as smoke curls upwards, some people are born to lie maliciously. Others are born to believe the lies. Once Dolly said, 'Oh, people like to gossip. Don't you know gossip is sweet?' Then she pursed her lips and made two smacking noises. Gossip is not dangerous because of the gossip itself, no matter how revolting, it's dangerous because of the mental incompetence of the listeners. And gossip has always been my undoing."

Franniemarie winced with recognition. *How many times have I heard Mother say, 'The gossips in this town will be the death of me?'*

"We're supposed to make friends of our enemies, but who wants friends like that? On the whole, I don't know why being unable to be close friends with everyone depresses me. I wouldn't have time."

Mother never had close friends. Annamarie surrounds herself with groupies, Lilianna with shallow relationships. She accuses me of having only three friends and being related to all of them. She's right. I haven't had friends since I married Cricket. I haven't even tried to keep in contact with my old friends. What is it about this family that doesn't allow us to commit?

"Edward and Victoria told me, 'Pink had enough on Gill to send him to the penitentiary'. I was crying. They always had me crying. I wondered, if they could send him to the penitentiary, what could they do to me? They were always saying bad things about Gill. That's why, when I invited Clay to dinner, I arranged it so he'd be a witness if I ever needed one. Clay was the one person whose testimony in support of me would be believed without question."

Were Clayton and Gillian buddies?

"Gill was no angel, but whatever else he was, he was a hero, too, and Dory will never need to hang her head."

But what on earth did he do? What was your part in it? Franniemarie dared not ask.

"Since I was seven I've said to myself, don't even breathe a word of it to any living mortal."

Say what? Seven. What secrets does a seven year old need to hide? Franniemarie could feel her aunt's eye's on her. *She's watching to see how I respond to her words. She's looking for reassurance.* Franniemarie nodded encouragement and hoped it was enough to keep her aunt talking. *If I speak, she'll be gone.*

Dorien continued, "Of course, Dory knows she's going to live with the Conrads if I go to Heaven in a hurry."

Franniemarie nodded.

"I'm sure you understand I would never have become Mr. Conrad's housekeeper. It was the principle of the thing.

Them saying it was immoral made me furious. Besides, all the Conrads seem to be sort of glad-hand muscle builders. I'm just not that type. I may be uneducated, but I tend to be intellectual."

Guess that's the Tourneau motto. Not one of us a college graduate, but the mantra lives on.

"It's no wonder Clay was the one who endeared himself to me. Once, I went to work without makeup and he said he admired naturalness in a woman. And him a mechanic! Dad always said, "Have no truck with a man who has to use his hands to make a living.""

Dorien giggled, "He wanted to know what I thought. In those days he seemed interested in me, as no one else ever had been. He looked at me as if he wanted to possess me. He was concerned because he thought his tummy wasn't flat enough to please me. He was troubled because he thought maybe I wanted his fingernails longer and he didn't want to look effeminate, and I think he actually grew that moustache because he thought it would please me. He was the most delightful person I've ever known. And I know he joined the service because of me. That, and Gill urged him to join because they needed mechanics.

"Those months have spun a sunlit pattern over all my days since. They've spilled a little magic into even the worst things I've known since. No one and nothing can ever entirely destroy that golden memory."

Franniemarie reached out and gently squeezed her aunt's arm without looking at her. Dorien did not flinch.

"And the psychiatrist is right. Sensitive people should marry only sensitive people. Makes sense to me. Mixed marriages provide a large percentage of failures. But I'll never marry Clay. It would be crazy for me to marry into that family. Lucky for Clay, Camilia is not shy."

Franniemarie was startled by her aunt's new turn. *What? You've already said he's married to Camilia. Of course you'll never marry him, you goose.*

"I am beginning to understand our long ago quarrels. I realize I never really loved him. His brother Arthur and Gill both said I didn't know what Clay was like, and Gill said I'd never marry Clay if I waited until I found out what he was like. And Gill was right. Conventionality and goodness are too dear to my sensitive, humorless soul.

"I think the Conrads fixed it so I couldn't go to college last fall."

Franniemarie felt her aunt shift. She kept her eyes on the road.

"However, I suppose it's true, I'm a snob. I don't think highly of people who misuse the English language. I suspect the reason beauties marry more often than intellectuals do is that a beauty wants admiration, not competition; however, an intellectual wants companionship, a meeting of minds."

Oh, bother. Franniemarie stifled a yawn.

"The cruelest way to sabotage another person is to be so kind you swallow up his personality and all his free time. That was what I resented most about Gill and Victoria. They could not let me go, not even for a few hours. If I wanted to go anywhere without Gill, Victoria wanted to drive me over and back. They just killed me with kindness. I just couldn't get away from them. That's simply brass dressed up in virtue. Christian doctrine may be all very well, but too many people make a vice of Christian virtues. A little Christianity goes a long way."

So who is at fault here? She thinks they're bad for trying to be kind to her? Got news, sweetie, that doesn't work for me.

"I want a view of San Leandro Bay, but for $6,000 not $10,000. I know, that's asking a lot of one's realtor. Some think I want too much color and I ought to have wooden scallops in my kitchen. I detest wooden scallops. I like stippling and painted canvas. I like paint with depth. Aqua wallpaper with cream-colored woodwork. Phooey!"

Good Lord, this could be Mother talking. If they're alike, she'll go on and on and on and never get to the stuff I want to know.

"Perhaps I would be wiser to take a small loan on the Walnut Street house and use some of the money learning to write. Of course, that's a bigger gamble than real estate. And with real estate, I always feel like I am playing pinball machines with thousands of dollars instead of nickels."

Dorien paused, and Franniemarie thought it was probably the time to squeeze her aunt's arm again, but by now she had to pee so bad it was all she could do to listen, drive, and watch for a rest stop.

"I'd rather have been a spinster than have married a rude man." Dorien stretched, stifled a yawn, continued in a husky, almost conspiratorial voice. "In the wakeful middle of last night, I caught myself having the most wonderful conversation with my pretend Clay. It was all about my plans, how I'd use the money, furnish the house, go to school—just as if he'd be interested. If I don't watch out, I'll find myself living a double life in which I imagine myself married to another woman's husband." Dorien giggled. "Reminds me of the night before Dory was born, thoughts of Clay seemed irresistible. I kept saying to myself, don't think of him. Don't think of him. Don't think of him! But it was heavenly thinking of him!

It was heavenly last night, too. I've done it for years. Then, when I meet him, I'm tongue-tied. I feel shy because there's so much I've told him that he has no way of knowing, and I'm afraid I'll begin in the middle the way I take up an imaginary conversation with him. Sometimes I'm not sure anymore what things we've really said and what things I just made believe we said. I think I can still separate the reality from the dream with him, but sometimes I wonder—and I get frightened. I'm so familiar with the make-believe person that I'm surprised when the real one doesn't respond as if he knew me at all."

"What bothers me about this Clay thing, it swims to the surface of my consciousness when I'm in the middle of making my plans, or when I'm talking to somebody or even resting my mind. It isn't a dream exactly—it's more like a spirit."

Franniemarie saw a deer by the side of the freeway and touched the brakes. The deer bounded back into the darkness.

Without pause, Dorien continued, "Gill called himself Arthur Marsh to conceal his married status. His mother let folks think she was divorced, although she was still married to Sam Marsh. She called herself Mrs. Weaver all the years she was married to Mr. Marsh.

"The Mt. Whitney incident was worse than either the thieving or the out-of-season killing of the fawn. I don't think MacIvers came into it until after Mt. Whitney, but he might have. Yet I can prove nothing. Once I thought Maynard Morris knew something about it and I played him along, but he came back with all the wrong answers. Be that as it may, Mac was for hire.

For the criyii! Who in hell are these people?

"I tried to avoid Anita at first because I didn't like her. Then she gave me the one lead I had been looking for, the one that only the person who was guilty would be likely to know. I had tried to meet each person Gill had known well. All bug-eyed and angel innocent, I tried to draw them out. However, I only drew blanks until I cultivated her. Gill let it seem he just ran into Mac from time to time and didn't really know him. I did pump Anita dry, and I got all the right answers, but I still have no proof. I'm helpless without actual proof."

What in hell did she tell you?

"They were afraid I'd guess too much, so they tried to break up our acquaintance. But they feel secure now. Maybe they'll slip."

REST AREA 2 MILES Franniemarie squeezed her thighs together tight.

"Gill frightened me by threatening to hire a professional gunman to kill Clay if I left, and succeeded in getting a divorce. He threatened to have fake photographs, supposedly of Clay and me behaving immorally, introduced as evidence in court if I tried to divorce him. He said, that way, he could get the court to take my baby from me and wreck both Clay's reputation and mine. Anita knew all about this. She even knew how to fake photographs."

Franniemarie pulled off to the area. Under the lights she could not resist glancing at her aunt before she split for the john. Dorien, staring straight ahead, offered her the profile of a healthy woman in her thirties. Her aunt's profile stayed with her as she reveled in the pleasure of the warm stream of her relief. Washing her hands, she hoped her aunt would still be there.

CHAPTER 9

W HEN FRANNIEMARIE SPUN onto the street, Lilianna slammed the door after her. Leaning against it, she inhaled the smell of yeast and wheat baking. *Thump it! Oh, shit!* She opened the oven door and a blast of hot air hit her face. She jerked back. The loaves stood tall and white in their pans. Quickly, she closed the door. *At least I know what color the loaves are supposed to be. That's easy. I'll never know who my father was. Or is it, is? I'm never having children, so why should I give a rat's ass? I never cared before, why rag on it now? Damn that Franniemarie, she comes in spinning like a dervish, stirring up more questions than a gossip columnist. Do gossip columnists ask questions?*

Christ, it's after three! Might as well stay up. Damn I'm getting too old for this! What am I saying? Fortyish isn't old. Look at Frannie. She's in her fifties. Older than I and she can go, and go, and go. Damn Franniemarie. Thoughts, rampant as rabbits in a warren, coursed through Lilianna's tired brain. Irritated, she poured herself a cup of cold coffee, then nuked it. As she sipped, she began methodically trapping a snippet of thought, and cat-like she worried it—worried it to no satisfaction.

We each called the other crazy. How many times have I called my mother crazy? How many times did she return the compliment? Crazy seems an automatic epitaph in our family. Why? Because we have more than one certifiably insane member in the family? Because we're afraid we might belong to their club? Or, are we trying to get comfortable with our close relationship to insanity, to the possibility we, I, might not be operating with a full deck?

"*You cannot imagine what tragedy is until you've lost a loved one.*" Annamarie's low melodramatic voice echoed across time, and Lilianna shivered. *Mother never loved anyone. She doesn't have close friends. Well, neither do I, but I don't claim to love. I don't call them dahling and sweet-ha't She hugs them, listens to them, feeds them cake, gives nothing of herself. They never know her. I don't know her. I've never felt comfortable asking her questions. Well, how could I? We were hardly ever together.*

Would it have been different if she had married my father? Would he have wanted me, wanted me to live at home? Is he alive? Perhaps I'm a war baby and he's dead. But then she'd have told me who he was. She wouldn't pass up a chance to become a bonafide martyr. Maybe he was married. What if she doesn't know who my father is? Rape?

A memory, shadowed beneath those thoughts—a memory from a time when she had been expelled for misbehavior from a private school. She was at her mother's home waiting until Annamarie could get her into another school. She played with sticks she'd broken. Pretending they were cars, she crashed them into each other as she drove them along patterns the sun made on the ground beneath the bush where she was hiding from her mother, hiding because she did not want to change into party clothes and now she couldn't leave because mother's guests had arrived. Two lovely ladies in wonderful wide-brimmed hats were seated at the patio table not five feet from her, heads together, mourning some aborted film. *Something about a director and Annamarie on a sail boat. He'd died in the ocean. They were appalled with his wife's behavior. They said she showed a definite lack of sorrow over the whole affair, that Annamarie seemed more broken up about it than his wife. And then there was that deadly hush when Annamarie returned with drinks. And later, that strange look they exchanged when they realized I'd been beneath the bush all the while they were talking.*

Lilianna carefully opened the oven door. *Who was that director?* The loaves were a light golden brown. She gave one a tentative tap, then snapped her finger on another making a hole in it. Quickly she closed the door. *I don't think this is what my cousin meant when she said thump them.*

Dressed, she struggled to slip in her earrings, tossed her head, felt the turquoise baubles against her cheeks and smiled with satisfaction at her reflection in the mirror. Back in the kitchen, once more she checked the bread. The loaves were darker. She removed them to the cutting board. Again, she snapped a loaf. To her surprise it made a rather dead sound. It did sort of sound like a thump. *I think I thumped it. I really thumped it.* Proud of herself, she drew a knife through the hot loaf and shredded off a very crooked, steaming, slice, then slathered it with butter.

Oh, my God, this is wonderful! Frannie really did want to make me a gift. Lilianna began to cry. *And now I'll never be able to thank her. That's the way this family is. One wrong move and it's over. Why was I such a bitch? Because she didn't show up at the party when I wanted her to? Because she is so focused, she'd blow anyone away. Because she opened up in me some long buried curiosity? She wasn't ill-intentioned, she was just being Frannie, and now she's gone.*

Lilianna washed her face and hands in soft warm water. *After the shoot, I think I'll visit the library. See what I can find out about that accident.*

CHAPTER 10

WALKING TO THE car, Franniemarie was not surprised her aunt was absent; however, she was disappointed. Under predawn skies she brought her Mazda up to speed. She'd been awake twenty-four hours and wasn't ready to sleep. *I wish she'd stayed—wish she'd stayed and I could ask questions—find out who she is—what she is. But then, she's rather like Mother. That being the case, my wishes are useless. She and Mother never answer questions. They just natter on and on, taking whatever track they will.* The sky lightened, revealing the shapes of vineyards checker-boarding the landscape. The sun came up turning the vineyards into exaggerated, elongated, exotic patterns.

"I've never been this far north before." At the sound of her aunt's voice, Franniemarie sucked in her breath and nearly hit the brakes. Leaning into a deep curve to the right, she surreptitiously looked at her aunt. Dorien, jaunty in a red rayon dress with short sleeves gathered at the shoulders and a red and white straw cloche which framed her face, was taking in the scenery as casually as if she'd never left.

"Oh, my! Perhaps I haven't changed after all. I did have a caller last night. I'm certain he came in through the bedroom window. I must have stirred. He went into my closet. For a long time, I lay wondering what he would do next. After a while, I got weary waiting for noises; and I'm ashamed to admit, I went sound to sleep."

"I'm not frightened, but curious. I wonder who my caller was. It makes me wonder about the time I found two cigarette stubs and some ashes on the hearth in the morning. I do try both doors twice, once before undressing, once after. I wonder if he will come again. I'll probably sleep through it if it happens, darn. I would like to know who came. It's exciting! Adventurous!"

Was it exciting to plot revenge on your husband? Exciting to know he was going to be dead?

"'They'll remember it against you when they're grown.' I don't remember where I heard that expression, but it's true. I remember Grandpa giving Pru Ellen nickels to buy ice cream cones and wanting to give me one too, and grandma saying no, 'Her father can give it to her if he wants her to have it.'"

Franniemarie blurted, "Surely you have it wrong, Grand wouldn't …"

"This is my story, not yours." She snapped. "You tell your story on your time. This time is mine."

That doesn't sound right. The Grand I knew wasn't mean. However, from all I've heard, your father could be. Perhaps he and Grand got into it over money—possibly money and treats. Perhaps he's the one who set that up. Certainly the man in his letters to Grand was capable of that. Did Grandpa give Aunt Annamarie and my Mother nickels?

"Dad rarely threatened to commit suicide, but he constantly said, 'I wish I were dead.' I suppose I should have asked for help from the juvenile authorities. Except what we really needed was to be adopted into homes able to take good care of us. We were a terrible burden for Dad, and I, most of all,"

That's what Mother used to do when she was angry with me. She used to say, "You've made me so unhappy I'm going to kill myself." Then I'd beg her not to and I'd promise to be good even when I didn't know what I'd done to make her life so miserable. It quit that late fall day the year I was fourteen. That was the day I laughed at her and said, "Be my guest. No great loss to any of us." That day she dramatically swung her red wool cape over her shoulders and strode out the apartment house. My friend Joan passed her on the walk and asked, "What's with your ole lady?" I shrugged, "Oh, she's going to the lake to commit suicide." We both laughed. I did not tell her she'd spent some time before leaving on the ledge outside the living room window.

There have been times I wanted out. If I'd had energy, I'da been gone. But I never threatened my children.

" … Dad was always saying, if we did without while we were children, we'd have a nice home where we could entertain our friends and have nice clothes and furniture and go to college later on. So we did without and look what it got us!"

Sounds like mother. Grand would have said, "The apple fell close to the tree." Timbered rolling hills replaced the gentle vineyard-laden terrain. Franniemarie's stomach began to complain.

"The one bit of unbelievable good luck for me is that the child is not like her father at all. Sometimes my blood runs cold when I think about what kind of grandchildren I might have."

Franniemarie shivered. The words seemed to clatter against something metal, some shield that faded into the welcome sight of a Red Bluff Flying J sign.

Inside, she picked up a couple of corn dogs, a couple of cups of coffee and two dark chocolate bars. Aunt Dorien did not seem to notice her struggle to get into the car with her booty. But she gaily accepted her portion. "Oh, I do hope you remembered the sugar and cream."

Yes. Yes. Just like Mother, you smother your coffee with cream and sugar. Franniemarie rummaged in the glove compartment and came up with a fistful of crumpled packets.

"Just like going to a circus! I've always been drawn to the clown, lovely in his red tights, so colorful and gay, I'm afraid I'll never get over circuses. Tightrope walkers and trapeze artists, animals and tumbling acts. Oh, to be able to watch all three rings at once!"

Dorien continued, talking around bites of her hot dog and sips of coffee. "Gill could never sit still long enough to enjoy a circus. We were incompatible. We held nothing in common. I was the girl who graduated at 16 in spite of working full-time after school. He was the fellow who attended high school four and a half years without ever becoming a senior. He could box and jump hurdles, shoot almost as good as I, and drive a car. He thought trucking, hunting, and fishing were the alpha and omega of life. His idea of a swell vacation was camping, sleeping on the ground, cooking over a campfire, going unshaven and unwashed, and killing everything in sight whether or not it was edible or out of season or even on a game preserve. His idea of a party was a few sandwiches, plenty of liquor, and songs in mixed harmony. His idea of a pleasant evening was drinking, playing the pinball machines, and speeding as fast as the car would go. To him, friends were good drinking companions, a desirable woman was a little tramp—and he called that kind of woman 'choice'."

Franniemarie winced. *Her assessment of Gill sounds a lot like mine of Cricket. Oh, the issues are different—but the rant is basically the same. Hardly cause enough to have Gill killed.* Her mind shut down before her reflection could turn a corner into personal introspection.

"He wasn't interested in art, story, excepting maybe Tarzan, or composition. He hated opera, art galleries, museums, excepting trucks, mining equipment, or guns. But even that sort of thing couldn't hold his attention for long."

"If any conversation outside of hunting, trucking, fishing, drinking or choice gu-urls came up, he promptly changed the subject, and if you brought it up again he began a tirade, the gist of which was that nobody wanted to be bored by such dull talk. He kept telling me to try to be interesting to other people and improve my personality."

I'll concede. Reason enough to think murder.

"The first time I saw Gill I thought, *that man has the face of the man I want to marry.* His face greatly resembled my grandfather's, right down to the moustache, but there the resemblance ceased. Gill was nothing like the kind of man I wanted for a husband, and I was jittery before I'd known him three weeks, jittery before then, when he told me he was married."

He told you he was married and you proceeded into a relationship? Talk about a loose screw! At least Cricket was eligible.

"I think I'll almost never use my telephone anymore. And when I do call, I'll watch the clock and never talk over five minutes. And never have any visitor to my house without other visitors present. And never visit anyone else unless she has other callers, that way I'll be protected by having a minimum of two people hear anything I say."

Franniemarie burst out laughing.

"And just what do you find so funny?"

"It's just—here you are talking to me and we're alone."

"This doesn't count."

"It doesn't?"

"Of, course it doesn't. You're just a figment of my imagination."

"I am?"

Dorien reached out, gently patted her arm, and with reassuring certainty replied, "Yes, you are."

Pay no mind, she's outta hers. Franniemarie set the car to cruise and relaxed into the escalating curves of the road.

"If I married now, I'd want a man who'd be good to my girl and not someone like Emma. All of us girls would have been happy for Dad to have married someone who loved us as well. She definitely disliked us from the beginning. Nannette and Annamarie had a fit about it even before the marriage because they knew she didn't like us. And that was no malarkey. Dad went with other women—and they didn't object to any of the others."

Really? Mother's story was that her father left home for three weeks and when he returned, it was with a wife and three children. All was news to his three girls. But then, she never mentioned his dating anyone. Mostly she talked about how much he doted on you.

"There must be some form of penance somewhere to relieve my guilt for any happiness I take, especially a thing of beauty. And I did penance to compensate for my ugliness and lack of charm, my inclination to be lazy and sleep or sunbathe. I made a fetish of collecting occupations I hated, especially housework, of depriving myself of good things and pretty clothes.

She sure isn't depriving herself of pretty clothes now. Perhaps she's just talking about her understanding of herself as a child. And housework? Mother always said they had housekeepers. I have pictures of the housekeepers. Or could it be that in the death of her dreadful husband she found the freedom to enjoy herself?

"To be criticized for my thinness, or for not getting along with people, only made me redouble my efforts to compensate by pleasing in other ways. My occasional revolts were put down as bad temper and lack of control, and I was severely punished and isolated from them. Sometimes after a temperamental burst, no one in the house would speak to me for several days. If I asked for the butter, they passed it mutely, nor would the children play with me. When I tried to play with them, they talked to each other as if I weren't there. I'm glad that's past. My life is good now. I'm not a chameleon for nothing."

However, the question remains—did you kill your husband?

"The ocean at Santa Cruz is lovely. Once, we went to a restaurant overlooking the beach there. That was after his mother had threatened to make Alameda so hot for me that the women would tar and feather me and ride me out of town if I didn't stay away from Clay, and Gill had promised

I'd never marry Clay even if he gave me a divorce. He told me he'd do 'anything at all' to keep me from divorcing him. That day his mother was with us and they discussed it at the table in the corner of that fish restaurant at Santa Cruz. Gill said, 'Why don't you get off the dime?' And I thought, 'And have Clay accused of being my lover?' Oh, no. That kind of accusation sticks like tar even when it has no foundation. I wasn't giving him a chance to say of Clay and me what he said about his first wife and more than one man."

Okay, already. I'd kill him.

"Dad's sister Fern accused me of seducing her husband and then turned on the silent treatment. I tried to tell her that I screamed against that dirty old man. I wasn't even ten years old."

"No, I don't love my people. We three girls were father's guinea pigs in an emotional and social experiment in which he took no responsibility for the outcome. He didn't even make any effort at common decency."

"In the early months of our marriage, Gill said, 'Marriage, like life, is a survival of the fittest. It is immaterial what the weakest feels or wants because the strongest will prevail.' In the end, he came to know what I meant when I replied, 'Who is to say who is fittest to survive, who is to say what strength is—power, endurance?' The last laugh is on me. He's dead. I live."

Franniemarie could no longer contain herself. "Did you kill him?"

Dorien continued as if she hadn't spoken. "I remember the morning after the telegram came, saying he was missing in action. I sat in his mother's living room while she talked about his will, and I kept admiring my legs and thinking they were a better way of compensating for ugliness than ceaseless humility and hard work. I think that was the beginning of my emotional escape from the misery of my lifetime of penances. Admiring my own legs in the net stockings and silly shop-girl pumps that Gill always liked so much."

"I would have killed him."

Dorien ignored the comment. "Somehow the horrors of concentration camps leave me cold. All those tales of horror, they're not surprising. My own people did to me all they dared and still they appeared to outsiders to be good citizens."

How do I get her to respond?

"What happened to Gill and me was not the sort of thing that could happen to a couple if they had a healthy approach to life. Even in legal marriage, I paid by having taken a man I did not love. He wasn't good to me. He, plain and simple, wasn't good. I doubt I could marry a good man who loved me and whom I loved."

"So you had him killed!"

In the silence that followed, Dorien began to shake with rage. "How dare you accuse me? It was Annamarie who killed her lover. Oh, don't look at me like that. You're supposed to be driving. It was so easy. She got him drunk, smashed in his head, and pushed him over the side of his yacht. Since she didn't know how to sail, by the time they found her she looked a wreck.

Franniemarie felt lightheaded. "Why? Why would she do that?"

"He was a pig she had to sleep with to become a star. He wouldn't marry her because he liked having both her and his wife and a few others—and he liked it that way because his wife was lovely and Annamarie was choice. She did it because, she was pregnant."

"Lilianna?"

"Indeed, Lilianna."

"Did my Mother know?"

"Of, course she knew. Who do you think taught Annamarie how to survive?"

A chill coursed through Franniemarie.

"Annamarie was smarter than your mother. She worked it out with his wife. Together they split his estate in exchange for Anna's courage."

"And you. What did she teach you?"

Dorien hissed, "Don't you dare compare me with them. You can read about them in the newspapers. Of course Gill was in the papers too. He was missing over North Africa. He was a hero. Don't ever forget it."

"And Clay?"

Dorien's voice became a whisper, "Clay loved me. Don't misunderstand. He has never touched me except to shake hands or to give me change except once, but only then, to prevent me from being run over by an automobile. But I've known moments with Clay when I knew I mustn't be long alone with him."

Oh, boy have I heard this one before. What's with this generation? I've watched my mother all but mate a man and yet she always says the same thing. 'It may be most hard but I've always kept myself pure.' Pure, my ass.

"Certainly he didn't break up my marriage. That was on the rocks already before the end of our first year. He was just one more complication. When I told him that Gill and I were going to have a baby, that gentle, agreeable, easy-going Clay suddenly went Lord and Master on me, asking me searching and frank questions about my moral behavior previously and my intentions from then on. I thought he was being impertinent, considering what he had in mind. After all, if there was a child, he could wait and see if it resembled him. He didn't have to take my word for it. But he didn't intend to wait.

Excuse me. If you never mated with him, why would he need to wait to see if this child looked like him? Something of this rings like the 'My mother was murdered before I was born' episode in the geriatric psychiatric center.

"And, when his mother talked to me on the phone, she talked about adopting the child as soon as it was born. At first, his father said it would have to be kept a secret. After all, why insist on advertising an extra-marital relationship just in case a child should be born of it? Clay Conrad insisted he wanted to adopt the child. He said, 'Why make it hard for the child?' The mess I was in was shamefully complicated. We had to make a plan."

Lily-white and pure, my ass!

"Gill left for Texas to attend aviation school, I was up to my ears in his mother's dirty tricks, and before I knew it we were in the war and Clay followed him. Followed him and kept his word to me."

"But he was listed as missing in action. That would leave Clay out."

"Oh, no it wouldn't." Dorien's voice became harsh, strident. "There are ways. Anita could tell you all about the ways. You can set it up so that when the plane reaches a certain altitude the gas won't flow, or you can make it so the oil seizes up. Either way, it's curtains. And you know Clay was a pal of his. Gill trusted him. Clay was part of his ground crew."

"Okay, say he did it. Then how is it you didn't marry when he came home?"

"I don't know," Dorien whispered. "I thought at the time that Clay and I were engaged, but his folks say that was all in my imagination. His sister Anita says I must have misunderstood something he said because she knows he never felt that way about me. And she says she knows more about Clay than anyone else in the world, because he always confided everything in her." Dorien began to cry.

Franniemarie reached out and stroked her hair. *What a dumb question. She's been trying to figure that out all these years, figure it out and come to terms with it.* Dorien rummaged in her purse for a hanky, dried her eyes, and then stared out the window in silence.

Franniemarie rounded a curve and drove into view of Mt. Shasta. It took their breath away. Looking for a place to stop, she slowed down—then turned off on a road that soon became dirt. Wordless, they got out and leaned against the car. Franniemarie unwrapped one of the chocolate bars and together they enjoyed the warmth of chocolate shared in the beauty of a tree-lined road that framed a spectacular snow-capped mountain. A flickering breeze caressed their arms, lifted the loose tendrils about their faces. In that moment, they became one beneath a clear blue sky.

When they slipped back into the car, Dorien said softly, "Thank you." Franniemarie smiled, popped open the sunroof, and set the cruise control.

"It's this splitting of life into tiny fragments, always addressing the fragments and never considering its relation to the whole, that makes it so hard to figure out."

"I have no surplus energy. I need the relaxation of a switched off consciousness.

I worked so much even as a child that I learned to disconnect my mind and hold it vacant and empty of thought."

The gas gauge was hovering dangerously near empty. Visions of filling stations eclipsed the beauty of the forest that Franniemarie drove through.

"... might sound strange, but it takes eternity to think and I didn't always have enough energy to think. That's why I don't always hear and see things any more than if I were asleep. Some folks call it preoccupied, but it isn't really. It's just turning the switch off and inducing a kind of mental unconsciousness."

The familiar gas, food, telephone sign popped into view bringing with it a sigh of relief from Franniemarie.

"It's very simple to do. Sometimes I sit down or lie down, but quite often I just go on automatically with my housework. That used to irritate Gill. I'd be silent for hours and he'd start asking me what I was thinking. I'd say 'nothing,' and he'd keep at me. It's kind of funny though to get a whole ironing done and not remember doing it and not have had a single thought the whole time."

Franniemarie slowed for the off ramp. Filling her gas tank, she wrinkled her nose against the fumes' sharp smell. *Damn, I miss the good old days when you never pumped your own. Cricket would say it's better than no gas at all.* When she climbed back into the car, her aunt was still talking.

"I don't mean fall asleep ironing. That's different again. It isn't self-induced, it's more like …"

Franniemarie drove on to the drone of her aunt's voice. She did not notice her aunt's absence until sometime after she crossed into Oregon. By then she was too exhausted to care.

CHAPTER 11

CRICKET'S COUSIN CHARLIE waited for him at Uncle Dick's Café. Uncle Dick was related to everyone in Arapahoe, well most everyone. If you weren't blood, he'd adopt you. Cricket said he'd meet him at ten. Now it was eleven and Charlie was puzzled. He called, but then left when there was no answer. Come evening, he called again, but there was still no answer. He thought perhaps his cousin had gone off with his wife. Still, it wasn't like him not to have called.

Seven a.m. and still no one answered at Cricket's. Charlie called Pru Ellen. No answer there. He called Brooks, and to his relief Brooks did answer. However, Brooks hadn't a clue where his father was. They agreed to meet at his folks' place at nine.

Beneath cloudless blue skies, Brooks drove down the familiar cottonwood-lined lane of his home place. It was a beautiful cold, crisp morning. He noted his mother's car wasn't in the drive next to the house where she usually parked it, but his dad's Chevy S10 was. Inside, the house was quiet. So quiet that not even the smells of breakfast lingered. Immediately, he called out, "Mom! Dad!" He peeked into the living room, and then ran up the stairs. No one was home. By the time Charlie arrived, he'd discovered the ancient John Deere missing.

"Charlie, no one's home. Mom's car is gone. Dog's gone. The truck's here, but the old John Deere isn't. It's my guess, Dog's with him. Let's check the fields. You take the road to the north, and I'll take the lane east. I'll check out that field where he planned to put corn."

Brooks' heart raced as he drove past the home-site shelter-belt and on toward the east field. Threequarters of the way there he could make out the tractor. And the tractor was on its side. *Christ no. Please, dear God, please.* Brooks could not formulate any thought past *please.*

Before he reached the tractor, he could see a portion of his father's body under it. Dog was hunkered alongside him. Dog whined when he knelt beside his ashen cold father, while he searched for a pulse. Finding none, he dialed 911, shed his jacket, and covered him. He returned to his truck and blew his horn in a staccato SOS, SOS, SOS, for Charlie. Not knowing what else to do, he took off his shirt, opened his father's jacket, clawed a space next to him in the dirt, then molded his upper body to the shape of his father's in hope that he might be alive, in hope that he, Brooks, might be of help.

CHAPTER 12

WHERE AM I? Franniemarie woke bewildered and confused. She smelled mold and something else—something almost sweet. And there was dampness in the air. The room was pitch black—dark as she remembered her cell in the asylum some thirty years earlier. Gently, she rolled onto her back and slid her hands, palms out, over the mattress. To her relief, she found herself in a full-sized bed. The room did not smell of disinfectant; it smelled of mildew and cheap room freshener. And the bed was not nearly as firm as the one her mind had returned to.

Cheap hotel? No, motel. No one sleeps in hotels anymore. Gingerly she explored the tables on either side of the bed, hoping to find a lamp. She swung her feet to the floor, reached out and found a wall. Gingerly, she followed the wall. It angled right and she came into an open doorway. Exploring the edges, she found the back of a door, reached to the opposite side and came upon a light switch. The bulb was bare and did not soften the rust stains in the sink, the corroded metal of the shower. However, the worn towels were clean, packets of bathing amenities greeted her, and best of all the water was hot.

The spray from the shower nozzle was narrow and sharp. *Why am I here? Wherever here is.* She answered herself. *I'm Franniemarie Martin Hanks. I'm here because Franniemarie Martin is musical and the Hanks just clunks. I'm here because I've run away from home. I've killed my husband. So, why do I feel no remorse? I'm perfectly comfortable with it because, killing husbands and lovers is a Tourneau tradition.*

To the rhythm of predawn traffic, Franniemarie pulled on the same clothes she wore the night she left Lilianna's. Beneath a neon sign, *Seaview Hide-a-Way,* she checked to make sure her belongings were still packed in her car. *With a name like that, the ocean must be near. I wonder which way I was going when I turned in. Guess I'll find out where I am soon enough.*

Funny how I thought meeting Lilianna and Aunt Dorien would change my life, change what I know. Having done that, I don't know anything and I still haven't seen the Grand Canyon or the redwood forests—been close to them, but I've been in too much of a hurry looking for me to make time to find them. Cricket used to say, "Franniebaby, what's the big rush?" Here I am driving in the dark through country I've never seen. And what did I drive through to get to this place? Some winding road I think. I left home to meet some family. Did that. What do I want now? Now I need to find a place to stop. Look around me. Look at me. Pay attention. Maybe write a bit. Rest and write. But first I need to refuel and eat and find out where I am.

Driving North on 101, she entered Yachats. On her left, just before crossing a bridge into the village, a *Shamrock Cabinettes* vacancy sign caught her eye. Cruising the town, she found neither filling station nor restaurant open and returned to the Shamrock Cabinettes. There, she asked for the least expensive cabin she could rent for a month. The clerk offered her what she called the hippie cottage for a price that wasn't greater than that of an inexpensive apartment. Taking care to write Franniemarie Martin, Lincoln, Nebraska, and carelessly omit her license plate number, she smiled when the tired clerk did not notice.

Buoyant, she crossed a small side porch taking note of the little table, two chairs, large wood box, and most especially a view of the ocean. Inside she found it clean, sunny and charming, the rooms painted white and accented in primary colors. The furnishings were birch, the lines unembellished. The living room opened to a dining area, and the kitchen nestled in a nook just beyond. A bath, bedroom, and small study made up the rest of the unit. Best of all, across from the freestanding fireplace, the windows opened to another view of the ocean. Worst of all was a huge television set that dominated the side wall. Franniemarie shuddered with revulsion. Before she would agree to marry, Cricket had to promise there would be no TV in the living room, the idiot box would never invade nor dominate their lives. Before bringing in so much as one box, she unplugged the offending presence, wrestled it into a closet, and all but locked the door.

Scrambling down a bank of rocks, north of the cottage, Franniemarie reached the beach. It looked to be, she thought, a small shallow bay. It was low tide and the sand stretched before her in wide ripples. On the beach a couple walked a dog, three children engineered sand castles, another fellow repeatedly tossed a Frisbee for his chocolate lab, and across the bay from the resort the Yachats village rose like a picture in some book of fairytales. On reaching the bridge she came upon a wide shallow river of water flowing into the bay. Rivulets of a darker, almost charcoal, stain of sand seemed to overlay the more prevalent tan sand of the beach. Franniemarie pulled herself up on a rock and sat taking in the colors of the sand; how it changed with the light, how the sand changed shades depending on the depth of water left on it, how water and sunlight made the sand shimmer. The salt smell of the ocean made her shiver with delight. *Maybe this isn't a bay, maybe this is what they call an inlet.* She climbed the bank, crossed the bridge and found herself in a coffee shop. Over an American coffee and an apricot Danish, hot from the oven, she contemplated her needs and began making a list. Coffee / Milk / Total / Nuts / Fruit / Vegetables / Whole wheat bread / Peanut butter / Olive oil / Cheese. *That ought to do it for food. I'm so damn tired of cooking. Besides, I need to lose weight. Mother never cooked, but she always had those things in the fridge. Well not the nuts but the olive oil, the cheese. No mother had Sweetheart—roll it into a grey marble, flick it out the door, Sweetheart bread and Wheaties, breakfast of champions, sogg in your bowl then upchuck in the toilet—Wheaties, and Franco American Spaghetti and Campbell's Soup.* Franniemarie felt nauseated with the rememberance. *Growing up, I felt so deprived that with due diligence I taught myself to cook. What a waste. Fresh is better.* She was mostly right.

Classical music, I left it all behind, the whole damn collection. I have to have the music, a CD player, a radio. Franniemarie remembered the Corel-ware dishes at the cabin and the flatware, graceless, thin stainless, she shuddered. *I don't need much but I do need fine china and sterling. If I'd ever truly*

*thought about leaving, I'da paid attention. I'da taken the time
to pack those things.*

Before she entered the grocery store, an Estate Sale Notice
posted on a bulletin board caught her eye. *Waldport. I wonder
where Waldport is from here.* At the checkout counter the clerk
told her eight miles north, and not to worry there'd be signs
leading her to the estate sale.

It took Franniemarie longer to walk home and put away
her groceries than it did to drive to Waldport and find the
estate sale. There, she found a sturdy basket filled with pottery.
The pieces were glazed in earth tones, each complimenting the
other like sands on the beach. In a bowl were two mugs, each
different in glazing yet beautifully proportioned. Franniemarie
caressed the ripples some potter's fingers had left in their
making. Beneath the bowl a stack of slightly concave square
pottery pieces, each approximately the size of a salad plate,
filled her with awe. *How absolutely cunning! These would be
perfect to use for plates, perfect with the lacquer chopsticks I
found in San Francisco.* She looked for a price and could find
none. Carefully replacing the pieces in the basket, she asked,
"How much?"

An obviously bored young woman shrugged, "Five
dollars?"

"That's for the basket and its contents?" Franniemarie
dared not hope.

The woman shrugged, "Yeah, sure."

She was so taken with her find that she nearly missed a
couple of very plain, round soup spoons made of coin-silver.
Holy Moly, all I need now is a good radio.

"Know where I might get a radio?"

The young woman called into the house, "Hey, Dad. There's a lady here wants to know where she can get a radio?"

At the hardware store, a gracious gentleman helped her select a good AM-FM radio with a tape deck and a CD player. However, when she asked where she could find a selection of classical music, he laughed so hard his eyes became moist.

"I take it that's a 'no'."

"Oh, lady, you got that right. No one listens to that stuff."

"Excuse me. I do."

The man sobered. "You might find that sort of thing in Portland."

"Portland? How far is it from here?"

"Maybe a hundred and fifty miles."

Not going to happen today.

Franniemarie hadn't driven two blocks when a quaint little house with a sign MIM'S WHIMS caught her eye. Braking, she stopped directly in front of the place. When she opened the door, the strains of *Mahler's Ninth* nearly knocked her out. *Ha! So much for 'no one listens to classical music'.* Behind a glass case, a beautiful, perfectly quaffed and manicured lady removed an airy diamond and peridot dinner ring from the case and slipped it on the proffered finger of a patron. "It fits," the patron murmured with pleasure. The music filled the room while the purchase of the ring was weighed, and in the weighing it was not found wanting.

Franniemarie breathed a sigh of relief, as if she were the ring wanting a home. While browsing, she felt like an audience to the little shop, the shop playing host to a seeming endless stream of people coming and going, some to peruse the charming mix of small antiques and jewelry, others to say hello. Mim greeted most by name, and everyone with warmth.

A small Nippon plate decorated in a blue bird motif, a silver and agate pill box, and a silver plate wire basket captured her material heart. Mim greeted her as if she were the first person to come through the door, as if she were a dear friend. In no time at all she was calling someone who had been in the previous week wondering if Mim would buy her late mother's collection of music. Mim laughed, "I didn't think music would sell here, and as you can see I haven't a lot of space. However, I think it was mostly classical." Mim left a message.

The phone rang while Mim wrote up Franniemarie's purchases. "Don't leave yet. She still has them and she's on her way down." While they waited, Mim shared her opinions on the best restaurants in the area, as well as snippets of local lore, sights to see, and the beaches she and her husband liked to walk. Breathless, a young woman came in toting a fair-sized box of CDs. In short order, Franniemarie had the classical music separated from the rest and offered the woman twenty dollars, which she seemed happy to accept.

Exhilarated and hungry, Franniemarie headed toward the docks and to a restaurant Mim had recommended. In the block just before the docks she passed a row of small, brick, Victorian vintage houses. Several doubled as businesses. SMOKIN' JOAN'S, a tobacco and rock shop caught her fancy. *Not now. After lunch.*

The eatery was a rather shabby mostly soup, sandwich, and seafood shop that also sold bait. However, the clam chowder and the biscuits were both fresh and as hot as the coffee. The chowder was a pleasant first, the regular coffee a familiar treat. In the booth behind her a group of young men were smoking, gossiping, and talking tough.

"You hear Joby got busted?"

"Yeah, but his old man's already got him out."

"How'd he do that? I mean, he was dealin' big time. He tole me he had enough green stashed away to last him a lifetime."

"Shit, if it were me, I'd disappear about now. Disappear permanently."

"Yeah, right."

"No. Really. There's ways, man. Ya just go to another state and get a driver's license … in your new name. It's so simp, man. Whatcha gotta do is take your title and sign off on the back and write in who ya sold it ta. See, what you're doing is selling it to your new self. Course you have to use an address in that state for your new self. Lotta people just use a friend's address. Then what you do is type up a paper saying you sold it to this person who is now you, and sign it. You can get forms for this shit from state motor vehicle offices. They even send ya an envelope.

Then ya send it in with a bunch of money. When ya get that shit back, you now have a car in your new name. Then you get a social security number in a new name. You can just make up that crap like when you's born and who your parents are. They don't check jack. Pretty soon ya have a social security card in your new person. All ya have to do now's get someone to drive ya to the driver's licensing place and show them your shit and take their tests. Voila! New identity, Dude."

Franniemarie thought, *Indeed, there's something exciting about disappearing.*

"My old man knows this dude who made it big selling cocaine. He quit before he ever got caught. Now he has this car wash and he's livin; real laid back."

Maybe I can do that. But I think I'll have to do better than the Shamrock Cabinettes for an address. I doubt that would pass without raising eyebrows.

SMOKIN' JOAN'S was closed.

In the late afternoon, she explored the rocky beach west of her cabin. In a sandy nook she found a pretty red rock mottled with white lines. She slipped it into her pocket.

Franniemarie more felt than watched the sunrise from her porch, grateful for the old wool cape that held permanent residence in the trunk of her car, insurance against the vagaries of Nebraska weather. Sucking in the ocean air with her morning's fresh coffee, she felt a calm that energized her.

A maintenance worker, near young enough to be her son came by delivering wood. He asked her how the wood was holding up, and if she was warm enough, and if she was enjoying her stay. She showed him her rock. He said, "Red jasper and agate. You'll find the greatest quantities of fine rocks on the gravel bars the ocean opens up. The best times to look for them is when the tide is low and most especially after a big storm." She asked about low tides and how one might know when they occur. He smiled and softly replied," You'll find one next to your phone book, compliments of the Shamrock Cabinettes. There's a place to the south where you can find loads of beautiful agates. Best time to find them is when the sun slants low and they're wet. That's when the light comes through them. That's when they beg you to take them home." They talked of dreams and rocks and poetry. She told him she was a poet. He told her, "I write poetry, too. My name is Yves. "Y V E S, pronounced Eve. My parents are French. Yves Montagne." Franniemarie was drawn to him in a way that frightened her. She chose not to offer her name. A breeze came up and she retreated to the warmth of her fire.

She spent the bulk of the day reading Dorien's chaotic scribblings, trying to make sense of them, trying to understand her aunt, trying to make connections that could help her understand herself. The effort made her sick to her stomach. Tossing a sheaf of papers on the table, she pulled on a windbreaker and headed down to the beach.

This day, she and the wind were lone visitors. Hunkered in the lea of the rocks Franniemarie built sandcastles and mused. *So Aunt Dorien thought she was untangling threads by some convoluted denial of the events that she remembers. She thinks that the women who accused her of being her father's mistress, if they truly believed their accusations, would have reported it to the police in order that she could be protected, as if that would have made a difference in the 1920s. Her father, after all, was a respected man. Children and wives were no more than chattel. She thinks that since they made the accusations, her father should have sued them for slander, and she then goes on to state that he shouldn't have slept with her after the age of seven—that he should have ordered a medical exam to prove she had not been molested.* Again, Franniemarie felt sick to her stomach. *At least I have never been molested.* She took some noble pride in the notion that she was special. She had never been molested.

That night, she wrote a short poem: Caustic winds dry seashells brittle / Endlessly, waves polish this beach / Ripple claw-marks down its spine / A grain of sand caught under your skin / I'm still festering our last trip. She titled it *The Effects of Time, Wind, and Water.*

By the following morning, a deep depression had settled in. Listlessly, she studied the tide table. Today it was lowest at

11:45 a.m. In the absence of another desire, she climbed into the car and headed North on 101. Driving through Waldport, the thought of stopping at "Smokin Joan's" crossed her mind but was dismissed. *Too early. Not likely to be open.*

Entering Seal Rock, she pulled into a parking lot in front of giant rocks rising majestically out of the ocean. For the longest time she sat, watching the ocean batter them, contemplating their beauty, reveling in their power.

When she returned to the road, those behemoth rocks filled her mind, obliterating time and place. Mid-afternoon she found herself wandering a beach. And on the beach she found a perfectly-shaped pink shell, a shell reminiscent of the Shell Oil Logo, an infant pink shell no bigger than her thumbnail. It touched Franniemarie, and in some strange way made her long for Cricket. *I wish he were here. I'd say, "Close your eyes, hold out your hand," and he would, and I'd drop it in his hand. He'd open his eyes, look at it, look down at me, his eyelids softened, the skin at the corners all crinkled, and his smile would fill me up.* Driving out of the parking lot, she noticed the sign *Lost Creek. Oh, my, Lost Creek—lost me.*

Late afternoon, the OPEN sign welcomed her into SMOKIN' JOAN'S. The weathered door creaked when she opened it; however, only the smell of cigarette smoke greeted her. To her right, a room that looked to once have been a library was filled floor to ceiling with rocks, polished rocks, cut rocks, carved rocks, and fossils. To the left, the smoke shop portion of the establishment was filled with cases of pipes and lighters and all sorts of smoking accouterments, mostly unidentifiable by Franniemarie, and shelves filled with boxes of cigars and tins of tobacco. In the rock room, a glass case was full of small carved stones and open cigar boxes. In the bottom of each cigar box, sand—black in some, white in others—had been raked in patterns, and on top of each pattern rested a few effectively-placed polished rocks and in some were placed a shell, or a small piece of driftwood, or a bit of fossil. The carvings were mostly faces, reptilian creatures, and flowers. "Sorry to keep you waiting." Franniemarie had not heard the proprietor enter and was startled.

"My God! Franniemarie? Franniemarie Martin?" The voice was familiar but Franniemarie did not at first recognize the body.

"Yes?" In a rush it came to her, this hefty woman was Joan Hilton, her best friend in high school. *For Christsake, we went off to college together. What a difference thirty years makes!* "I can't believe it's really you! What is the probability of our meeting like this after all these years?"

Joan smiled knowingly and shrugged, "Happens all the time out here."

"Really! The last time I saw you was about a week before you ran off with that Flamenco Dancer, Felix. I heard you'd gone to Spain."

"Seems like yesterday. And you? I always expected to see you on the tube. The famous Franniemarie Martin, novelist… Best-selling novelist."

In the interaction, Franniemarie lost her gloom. In fact, she began to rev like a well-tuned engine. "I was never that good."

"Yeah, right. You were assistant editor of the school paper. I remember you had a column and wrote stories."

"That was college, not the real world."

"So what did you do? Become a teacher?"

"No, I never finished. I married."

"So now you're married. I can't even imagine you married."

"I'm widowed."

A young woman breezed in. "The usual?" Joan asked.

"No, this has to be real special."

"What did you do now?"

"You don't want to know."

"Smashed his bike?"

"Not that bad. But I did dent it. How did you know?"

"Only three things your man loves ... The bike, you, and cigars."

"Ya got that right."

"Try this. It's not Cuban, but it comes from the same seed. It's just grown in the Dominican Republic."

The woman sniffed the cigar and smiled.

"I must warn you, this one is pricey." Joan floated a cigarette ring into the air.

After the woman left, Joan stubbed out her cigarette and turned out the CLOSED sign. "Of course, you'll stay to supper. You have to see what I've done to the house. And we've a lifetime to catch up on."

"Of course." Franniemarie laughed. Joan was still that powerful decisive person she once knew, and now her body and her personality matched. She followed Joan through the smoke shop, through a set of massive, carved pocket doors and into what had been a dining room, now transformed into a living room. An oak paneled stairwell led to the upper story, a downstairs powder room was tucked beneath it. In the far back, a generous kitchen was flanked by a glassed-in porch furnished with wicker furniture.

"Originally the upstairs contained four small bedrooms," Joan rambled on while she tossed together a shrimp salad, "I knocked out one wall to make a big bedroom and converted the other bedroom to a walk-in closet and a bathroom that has doors to both bedrooms."

"The place is lovely. Can I help?" *What happened when you ran off? And how did you end up out here?*

"You could set the table. The dishes are in the hutch on the porch."

A varied collection of china was housed in the hutch. Franniemarie held up a hand-painted bowl, *Chinese*, she thought. Holding it to the light she could see through it and, even more translucent, was a pattern that looked as if it were made by pressing rice seeds into the unfired porcelain. Blue dragons lived in the bottom of the bowl, and geometric blue and crimson patterns further enhanced with gold graced the rim of its bowl. Next to the bowls was a set of salad-sized matching plates. These she placed on the table along with the sterling, two simple crystal water glasses, and two wine glasses with crisp cut stems.

"Ah, I see you've picked my favorites." Joan brought to the table the salad, a loaf of ciabatta, a bottle of wine, and a pitcher of cold water.

"And Felix?"

"First we went to New York for the International Dance competition. We won the samba, took second in the tango. Then he took me home to Spain to meet his family. I was so taken with them. Then he dumped me for another woman. Well, not quite. I found him in bed with another woman, and I left. There I was in Spain, didn't speak the language, didn't know a soul. I ended up in Italy. I'm told I would only talk to Italian men. I'm told I kept saying we understood each other perfectly, that I was found nude in a fountain when they locked me up. I really don't remember any of it. I just remember the mental institution, making little clay figures, and the shock treatment. I'm not sure how I got back. I think my mother got me back. You know? The really dumb thing is I still love that man …" Joan paused, "More wine?"

"No. No," Franniemarie covered her glass.

Joan insisted. "We only go this way once, girl. God, you were something else in those days. I'll never forget, you were the first liberated woman I ever knew. Hell, you were liberated before woman's lib."

"Remember the night that cop stopped you, driving ninety in a thirty-mile zone?" Joan laughed. "He asked if you knew how fast you were going. And you said, you said, 'Yes, sir. I just washed my hair and if I do ninety it will be dry in five miles. And I really want it dry before I get to the party.' God, the look on his face! He just shook his head and drove off."

What always puzzled me was this, that was the only time I can remember that I was not afraid of the police. I guess I was so emotionally high I lost all fear.

"You ever wonder what happened to that philosophy professor you had an affair with."

"Nope."

"One sure way of acing a class."

"I never took a class from him."

"Joke, Frannie. Same ole Frannie, never did get it."

So Cricket kept telling me. "What brought you here?"

"I taught dance after I got home. Mother died a couple of years later. I got tired of Nebraska and came out here. Truth is, I was going with this guy who grew up in Corvallis. He wanted to come back, got a job in Portland, and I followed him. We spent a lot of weekends out here, and I got hooked on the ocean, the rocks, and all that."

Franniemarie's mind stalled when Joan mentioned the death of her mother. "Your mother's dead?"

Joan nodded. "Stroke."

"She was so good to me. I can't believe she's gone. I don't want to believe she isn't in this world."

"Yeah, she sure fed us good. Remember those potatoes she used to make. They were sort of like giant French fries."

"She didn't just feed me—she got me out of so many scrapes. Remember the time we stole her car? It was raining and we got stuck in the mud in front of some old lady's house, and she came out ragin' on us. Your friend Edie yelled, 'Stick it where the sun don't shine,' and the old bag called the cops."

"I remember sitting in jail with you and Edie playing cards and waiting for our folks to come and bail us out."

"Your folks came for you, but when they called my mother she told them she wasn't about to waste her time. Your mother got them to release me into her custody. I was the only one in real trouble—I was the one driving. To this day I don't know how she did that. She also went with me to the hearing."

"Geez, Frannie. I don't remember that part."

"Probably 'cause that part wasn't you."

"And when they expelled me from school, she's the one who got me back in."

Joan continued her earlier thought. "When our relationship took a dive I put my inheritance into this place."

Franniemarie wondered, "*Could it be Joan was jealous of the attention her mother gave me. Perhaps it strained our relationship back then, caused me to pull back. Could be why we didn't stay in touch.*

"Now I carve rocks and …"

"You carve the rocks?"

"Yeah. And I make-up the boxes."

"How do you carve rocks?"

"I have a shop out back in the garage. I use a variety of tools. Come by on a Monday or Tuesday and I'll show you around. It's the off season, so I close the shop on those days. Just remember to come round back. I only answer the front door during hours."

Two bottles of wine later, Franniemarie drove home under a star-studded night listening to Gregorian chants. Altogether wired and over-tired, she opened the bedroom window to air-out the cigarette smoke that filled her clothes and her hair. All night she tossed, visions of old lovers floating uncomfortably through her sleep.

Too soon she woke to the blast of her new neighbor's TV. Irritated, she slammed the window shut. She tried to go back to sleep, but the rugged rocks haunted her. After half an hour, she gave it up and headed for Seal Rock.

CHAPTER 13

For hours Lilianna scanned 1944—45 issues of the *Los Angeles Times* and the *Hollywood Citizen News*, looking for any mention of her mother. The gossip columns carried plenty. "Miss Tourneau has been seen with Mr. Sedgwick ... bets are on when the announcement of ..." and pronouncements "... no, Miss Tourneau is not engaged to Sterling Sedgwick." And three months later, "Miss Tourneau has suffered a nervous breakdown brought on by overwork. She will be sailing for Sweden next week." *That's one story I never heard. According to Mother, she's the only one in the family who is brick solid, never known a day of depression.* Another column stated, "Miss Tourneau's mother was from Sweden, and she's always wanted to travel." *Grandmother Lilian from Sweden? What a crock! Did my mother make that up, or was this just studio PR?*

The *LA Times* seemed to have stayed out of the fray. *Mother did say she and the Chandlers were friends. In fact, weren't they the family she worked for when she went to South America? Yes, she was nanny to their children. She said she learned to sail while on that trip. Perhaps relationships do count.* However, they did report. "After lengthy negotiations between MegaMount Picture Co. and the Asling Studio of Sweden, Miss Tourneau has been engaged in the making of a murder mystery under the direction of Johannes Sveen." *Wonder what happened to that nervous breakdown? Guess it didn't make it across the ocean.*

Then she found it–JOHANNES SVEEN SWEPT OVERBOARD

"Sveen, best known for his epic screen play *The White Lily* which he wrote and directed while he was yet in Sweden …" Lilianna drank in stories of Johannes Sveen's death, his family, Miss Tourneau, his boat. One article spent more time covering the boat than the accident. "This fabulous 36-foot craft designed especially for Sveen by Herreshoff himself …" Another article primarily focused on the movie he was currently directing, Annamarie Tourneau playing the lead, of course. "… *End of Time*, a surreal futuristic film … the world has been destroyed by bombs and biological weapons … people dying en masse … a Messiah-like creature comes to recreate the world in his image … All goes well, those remaining are preoccupied with survival and have focused their collective energies on agricultural, social, political, and artistic endeavors …"

Lilianna scrolled on. "… The tragedy of Johannes Sveen's death … seasoned sailor claimed by the sea in a boating accident. Sveen and Miss Tourneau were alone that afternoon on the *Lyckodam*, a boat as trustworthy as she is beautiful … When picked up by the *Sea Scamp*, a trawler piloted by Captain Joseph Cornelius, Miss Tourneau was hysterical. According to the captain, Miss Tourneau kept repeating, 'It's all my fault—all my fault.' She told him, 'When the winds came up the *Lyckodam* listed, salt water washed over the deck and washed him, Johannes Sveen, into the sea.' She stumbled on, 'I lost the wheel and he was swept away. I threw out the ring buoy, but he went under. He never came up."

By mid-afternoon Lilianna's eyes burned from squinting at reeling microfiche. The librarian tried to be helpful. "What is it you're looking to find? We can narrow the search. Two years is a lot of fiche to look through."

"No thank you." Lilianna preferred to chart her own course.

Johannes Sveen's publicist released a statement to the *LA Times*: "Johannes Sveen's wife is prostrate with grief. Her husband begged her to come sailing. She had been tempted as she and Miss Tourneau are quite close; however, she didn't feel up to it. The trio had been on the water the week before when no wind blew and she'd found it quite boring; further she was frustrated by the lack of control one has when one is dependent on the vagaries of the winds … Johannes Sveen's body has not been found."

For her mother, MegaMount released but one, what seemed to Lilianna, terse statement. "Annamarie Tourneau is distraught and under doctor's care."

I can't believe Mother couldn't hold the wheel. She's always been so proud of her athletic prowess. And she often said she learned to sail on that trip to South America the summer of 1930. She turned sixteen on board ship. Talking about that trip was the closest thing to bragging I ever heard from her.

Argentina! That's where she got her first chance in the movies. That was the trip that led her to the Argentine director who got her started in those sleazy Tex-Mex Westerns everyone doted on.

Mid-musing, the image of Johannes Sveen scrolled into her screen, Lilianna fairly gasped. The grainy image of Sveen could as well have been of herself! *I need to get a good copy of this picture.* Now she was ready to accept the librarian's help.

In the late evening, Lilianna ate her supper slowly. The librarian had unearthed an archived picture of Johannes Sveen taken by the studio a week before the accident and copied it for her. She studied it as if by concentrating on his face she could learn something of his fate—their relationship. *I can see the reason for an attraction between these two. I always wondered who I looked like. Now I know. His tall forehead, the squared off eyebrows, the angular shape of his face are all mine. Both he and Mother had full lips, so that doesn't count. But I don't have a dimple in my chin to match his. He and I are fair. I wonder if his eyes were the same as mine. I wonder if I look like his sons. I don't remember ever seeing them. Now that's strange. My mother and Solvieg are still close friends, that is, they see quite a bit of each other. And there was something strange about Solvieg's behavior after her husband's death.*

While cleaning the kitchen, Lilianna took a notion to call her mother, then thought better of it, but finally gave in to the urge to dial her.

First, they chatted. Then she asked her mother point blank, "Who is my father?"

"What makes you ask?"

"I've always wondered, but I never felt like I could ask. I've gotten up the courage and I'm asking now."

"Dahling! You know I don't believe in dwelling on the past. As to your father—if you can't say anything good about someone, you shouldn't say anything at all."

Christ, Mom, just cut the crap. "What can you tell me about Johannes Sveen?" The question floated on dead air.

"You know I'm not well. I can't believe you'd be so rude as to bring up such a tragic time in the life of our film industry. I did not raise you that way."

"That's right. As I recall, you did not raise me at all."

"This conversation is ended."

Shaking, Lilianna returned the receiver to its cradle. *My, God. I think she really did kill him.*

CHAPTER 14

THE MORNING WAS cold and windy, the sky grey. North of the rocks Franniemarie found a steep path that wound down to the beach. Not far south the rugged rocks rose almost straight out of the sand. The tide was low and she was able to walk right up to them. And there was a cave, the opening a couple of feet above her head. Franniemarie walked inside. She began a low guttural howl that reverberated against the rocks and inside her person, and the howl transformed into sounds of some Asian mantra. On and on the sound coursed through her until rock—until body and rock—disappeared, and all that was left was air reverberating in her ears. When the sound wore itself out she felt stunned, then she discovered some center of calm lying deep inside she'd not known existed.

From the cave she saw an agate bar about a half mile down the beach. When she reached the bar, it was laden with agates and jaspers. *What a marvel, that I can find such treasures. I, who never won a thing in my life, feel like I just won the lottery.* She was so totally absorbed in the act of searching out the beautiful rocks she hardly noticed the tide change. A woman in an Aqua slicker yelled, "Hey, sneaker!" Franniemarie looked up in time to see the truant orphan wave roll toward her. Together they dashed ahead of it. "I take it you're new to the beach?"

The woman said she was a writer. In fact, she used be a journalist. Just now she was looking for a used car. Something about the exchange left Franniemarie feeling that they had not connected. *Lilianna is probably right, I don't have friends. Well, there's Joan. How is it we never kept in touch? Friendship is a game of catch. One tosses the ball, the other catches it. That goes on till someone tires, gets bored, or the ball gets lost. All these years I had a friend. But I didn't know it. How is it that only now, so late, I see what was right under my nose?*

That night she found herself writing a poem titled "Missing YouYou." Stoned on your kisses / I am a magma reservoir / passions pressured full / these thirty years I've lived / with you. / Last night I kept waking, / your soft fingers on my pulse, / your earlobe caught between / my teeth in the same way / my iron once pressed your scent / from freshly laundered shirts / I seek coffee's early morning / on your lips.

The following morning, wrapped in her wool cape, Franniemarie sipped her coffee and rewrote her poem. She did not dwell on its meaning, nor the issues that prompted it. Instead she concentrated on its shape on the page. Not far from the porch, to her great pleasure, her TV-blaring neighbors were packing to leave.

"What's this?" A shrill voice rent the early morning's quiet in two.

Mumbled masculine words obscured any meaning.

"We don't have room."

"We have plenty of room." His enunciation carried.

"You never have room for the stuff I want. You always have room for your junk, but not mine."

"That's crap, Millicent, and you know it." His voice rose.

"That's not crap! It happens all the time. I say we need to take this, and you say we haven't room."

"One time, tell me one time, that's ever happened."

"It happens lots."

"Okay, tell me one time. Come on, one time."

"The lamps."

"That was over four years ago." And on and on they wrangled.

"Damn you, Harold …"

Franniemarie fled the porch. *Kind of puts missing Cricket in perspective.* She collected her rock treasures and took off for SMOKIN JOAN'S. *It's Monday. Cross my fingers and hope she's home.*

Joan welcomed her in a way that melted the years between their youth and this moment, pulled her in and taught her about working rocks, how to operate the tumblers, the various grits used, and the lengths of time needed for each in the tumbler. With great enthusiasm she encouraged Franniemarie to fill a small container with the stones she'd brought. "You have a good eye," Joan told her.

Franniemarie shook her head. "I don't know how you do it all."

Joan sighed. "Problem is, I don't. The trim on the house needs painting. I hate the book work, so it piles up until I can't find the stuff I need, and the list goes on."

"I can paint. Really! I'm good at it. Why don't you let me paint the trim?"

Joan hesitated. "It really needs to be scraped first."

"I know. I know. Like I said, I do know how to paint. Let me do that in exchange for teaching me about polishing rocks. Really, I'd like to do it."

Joan agreed, then insisted on fixing supper for the two of them.

"Oh, Joan, I just love the ocean. So much so, I'm seriously thinking of buying a place here."

"You won't regret it."

"I think I should get my driver's license and my car plates changed out to Oregon. If I need to get a loan, I think that would look better. Would you mind if I used this address—just for that, of course?"

Joan shrugged. "No problem."

Over pasta they talked of books they'd read and artists they admired. "There's this fantastic sculptor, or is it sculptress? Dixie Jewett, she lives in McMinnville." Joan said. "She's positively amazing. Her sculptures are beyond description. And she does all her own work—from finding and hauling in the scrap metal, to the welding, and I mean all the welding—to transporting the finished pieces to their destinations. A friend and I are going up to see her tomorrow. Hey, you wanna come with?"

Driving home, Franniemarie mused. *Maybe that's what friendship's really about, the ability to pick up where you left off no matter how many years have passed.*

Franniemarie chose the back seat for the trip to Dixie Jewett's studio. That was her way of avoiding the inevitable small talk she'd always found so deadening. There in the backseat, traveling behind the chit-chat of two comfortable friends, she relaxed into watching first the Oregon coast, next the wooded hills mixed with small farmland clearings, and finally rolling farmlands and small communities. When she saw a giant mastodon, she knew they'd arrived. It must have been fourteen feet tall, constructed of tons of metal. From the aluminum ice it stood on, to the knot at the top of its head, bronze tusks included, it looked real, alive. Traversing the drive they passed horses, people, sheep and buffalo, each an illusion made of scrap metal, each imbued with a life of its own—a life Franniemarie felt privileged to be introduced to.

Dixie, unlike her massive creations, was a bit of a woman, and a shy one at that. The contrast took Franniemarie's breath away. And though they had little to say to each other, she felt an immediate bond with her—felt that were they alone, they would be comfortable with each other—would not bother with polite nothings.

On the way home, Joan took her friends to lunch at a casino. Franniemarie had never been in a casino and found it puzzling. *This is where people go and throw away hard earned money in the hopes that in doing so they might take home a lot more. How can they do that? Why would they do that? What prompts them to think that way?*

That evening, she wrote: In dark of morning light I lie / Pinioned beneath stampeding / Images screaming across my past / Skewer me to time and distance / Kaleidoscopic turnings massage / Memories into potent unguents / Acceptance, leeches, sucking / Tears—purifying nights.

Franniemarie woke eager to begin work on Joan's place. While brushing her teeth, she imagined herself already on the ladder, felt the wooden handle of the scraper in her hand and the wind in her hair. *Better take a cap and gloves. Maybe I'd better pick up an old sweatshirt before I begin.*

In a thrift shop, in addition to a bundle of work grubs, Franniemarie picked up a bathrobe, a wool sweater and a couple of wine glasses. On her way to the counter, she spied a short rabbit fur jacket about the color of her mouse brown hair. She slipped it on and found it pleasing. *It's supple and in good shape now, so even if rabbit doesn't wear well, its warmth, softness and style will please me so long as it does. Besides it's only thirty-five dollars.*

Wearing her new old clothes, shins braced against the top rung of the ladder, Franniemarie scraped away the flaking paint of the Victorian cornice. As she scraped, the ornate decoration faded into the wallpaper that dressed the walls of the living room in the flat where she lived when she was five.

Now five, Franniemarie lolled on the floor, coloring, while her mother and Mrs. Riggs, Mrs. Mabel Riggs, landlady, sat on the couch, drinking coffee, getting to know each other. Franniemarie finished her picture, and jumped up, eager to show them her work. Mrs. Riggs didn't look at the picture. Instead she stared intently at Franniemarie and bluntly asked, "How'd she get that scar?"

"Scar?"

"Yeah, under her chin—into her neck. Such a shame, she coulda been a pretty child."

"Oh, that." Nannette paused to choose her words. "She was really little. Had a big abscess growing there. Took her to the hospital. She was in the hospital for a week, maybe a bit more. Finally, they lanced it and cleaned it up."

With a gasp, Franniemarie dropped her scraper, pressed her hand to the scar on her neck—fell off the ladder in a swoon that took her into a long-buried, late infant space.

Nannette reclined on a couch, deep into a book.

"We go out?"

"Not now."

"I go out."

"No."

"I go out!"

"Go play with Kanga."

Frannie take Kanga. Go hoppity hoppity hop round the room. That's the way Kangas and Roos go. Hop Hop Hop. And they Hop Hop Hop above her head. Hop Hop on the table top. Crash! Splinter! Mother comes screaming, "Damn you! Look at what you've done! Rotten brat!" Mother swoops down. Franniemarie is on the floor hurting, really hurting. Mother is gone. Franniemarie's cheek is sticky. Her hair is becoming sticky. Mother will be angry again. And then there is nothing.

"Frannie! Frannie! You okay?" Joan knelt next to her on the ground.

"I'm fine, I think. I fell."

"No shit."

Franniemarie rolled into a sitting position. Then stood—hand yet pressed against the scar on her neck. "I just need to lie down."

Joan put her to bed in her guest room.

In the black of night she woke. Yesterday's incident on the ladder seemed more a story belonging to someone else—someone far removed from her person. *Would my mother have done that? Why not? She always said she could never love me. I was the reminder of her husband—her handsome, charismatic husband who died, she said, dancing in the arms of another woman. I remember standing on the toilet seat looking into the bathroom mirror above the sink, stretching to see the scar. Until*

Mrs. Riggs, I did not know I had a scar. I remember feeling uneasy—haunted.

Franniemarie's bladder begged attention. After peeing, she remembered asking her mother about the scar. *I must have been eleven, twelve, not yet beyond wanting her love. She was irritated—nothing new, her being irritated. She said, "How should I know? It happened a long time ago. Perhaps you cut yourself. Yes, that's what it was—you cut yourself on a broken bottle. I had to have it stitched up. Did you know your father raped your aunt? Yes! He did! But that was before his brother married her. His brother loved her so much he married her anyway." Until that moment I don't remember her ever talking about my father's family. Were there any other's besides the brother and his family? Those twists, bizarre and unexpected, always threw me off subject and left me with questions I'd never thought of before.*

Joan rapped on the door. "Frannie? You okay?"

Sheepish, Franniemarie came out.

Concerned, Joan asked, "Can I get you anything?"

"How about a glass of warm milk? My stomach feels nervous."

Beneath the kitchen light, Joan listened to her tale and gave comfort with gentle caresses, warm milk and gingersnaps. "Your mother always was crazy." she reassured. "I'll never forget the day I came over and she was heading out of the apartment in a huff. She was so dramatic in that red cape. Guess she should have been an actress. I asked, 'What's with your old lady?' You casually answered, 'She said she was going to commit suicide.'"

"I remember that day. I remember it because that was the last time she pulled that number. We were what? Fourteen?

Fifteen? I'd been sorting clothes for the laundry and when she came into the room with that preoccupied look that meant she was absent. I said, 'Boo!' She jumped and started screaming at me, telling me what a rotten kid I was and how miserable I made her life. And how I made her so unhappy that she was going to kill herself. I especially remember that day because that was the day I stopped begging her not to do it. That was the day I said, 'Then do it.'"

"But that's not what's important about yesterday. For years, I've had these—what I call absent times. I don't know what triggers them, but suddenly I'm gone from the present, but not really gone. I'm just not doing what I planned to do. I don't know how to explain it. Try this: Once, I invited an ex-lover and his fiancée over for dinner. She was a friend of mine I'd introduced to him and it was important to me that she be comfortable. That afternoon I went to an art museum and I never even returned home. They showed up and I wasn't there. I felt awful, but I couldn't explain it to them. I couldn't explain it to myself. That's just one example of what happens. I think something triggers a memory, and when I start to retrieve the memory then I end up in some no-man's-land. Eventually, I come back, and when I do, I remember everything I've done and what it was I was supposed to be doing. But here's the big thing, every time I get close to some important memory, some memory that might help me understand myself, a huge curtain comes slamming down. I've revisited that curtain for hours on end. It's too tall to fly over, slams too deep into the earth to dig under, and so wide it would take several lifetimes to walk beyond its ends. The wall is embossed with figures— allegorical figures looking like those populating old Greek urns. But, of course, I don't know the allegories. Yesterday is important. Yesterday I fell off the ladder when the curtain started coming down. I fell off the ladder as I slipped under the curtain before it hit the ground."

As Franniemarie talked, she shivered against a cold that was not caused by lack of heat in the kitchen. Joan wrapped her in a quilt. Franniemarie emitted a sharp laugh, almost a snort. "At least now I know the worst. My mother left me for dead. That's the Tourneau way, you know. You don't really kill them. You just let nature take its course. Leave them for dead."

"But Frannie, she must have taken you to the hospital."

"I don't think so. Look at the scar, it's all jagged, no stitch marks. You knew her. Would the woman you knew have taken me to a hospital?"

Joan stared into space as if traveling back to the years of their youth, the years before they'd gone off to college. "I guess not. Guess that's the reason my mother kept feeding you."

For two weeks the weather held. Evenings, Franniemarie read her aunt's journals; early mornings, she walked the beach, and then from eight to six she scraped and painted trim as if her life depended on it. Joan shook her head, "You're gonna kill yourself working like that. What's your rush?" Franniemarie found the question maddening. *Sounds just like Cricket. This is the way I've always worked. Guess my way of tackling a job drives everyone nuts, but at least I always finish what I start. And thanks to my 'ways,' I've finished that job.*

Early morning, heading home from the cave, Franniemarie passed a *For Sale* sign half way between Waldport and Yachats. *Nah, it's too far from Seal Rock. I want to be near my caves. Those sacred caves. I want to be able to walk to them each day when the tide is low. There I'll scream myself into health. I know the right place is waiting for me. I just need more time. More time! Damn, I only have a week left in the hippy pad.*

Franniemarie pulled up in front of the Shamrock's offices and practically ran inside. No one was at the desk. She pressed the bell and waited. The clerk came out carrying a carafe of fresh coffee. "Morning. Here, have a cup. There's cream and sugar on the table." Franniemarie accepted. "Is there a chance I could extend my stay another month?" She asked.

The clerk pulled out the registrar. Shook her head, "Looks like we can do two weeks. After that the tourist season begins." Franniemarie accepted the two weeks. "I see here you're a writer."

"Poet." Franniemarie blushed.

"We have a published writer, living right here. Her book is about a religious sex cult that was in existence about the turn of the century, right in this area. It's *Holy Rollers; Murder and Madness in Oregon's Love Cult.* If you like local history, you might enjoy it. There's a bookstore other side of Yachats. I'm sure he carries it."

Franniemarie smiled, "That would really be a treat."

"I'm sure she'd enjoy getting together with you, autograph her book, talk shop. Not that many writers here, you know. Her number's in the phone book. You be sure to give her a call."

That night, as if to validate her way of working, a great storm rolled in. *Now aren't you glad I got that job done in jig time?* Franniemarie told herself. *Nuts to those who don't understand.*

Six a.m. her phone rang. "Today's the day, my friend! Meet me at Ona Beach. I'll show you some real agate hunting." Within an hour, she and Joan were trotting to a sandbar. To

Franniemarie's amazement, about a hundred people were already there. The crowd parted to give each space enough to span their reach, and no more. Facing the ocean, between waves, each snatched up beauties as the sea offered them. After a couple of hours plucking rocks, Joan left to open shop. Franniemarie stayed on filling her canvas bag till its heft surprised her, till the tide became dangerously high.

Walking back to the car, she became aware of the wind and the chill in the air. Again, she met the woman in the aqua slicker. This time she'd come to walk the beach with a friend from Portland. She still hadn't found a car. They talked a bit about the weather, the rocks, the tide, yet still Franniemarie felt no connection.

She drove south where a wonderful horse sculpted in blue neon pulled her attention to a very sophisticated building whose shape undulated beyond the sculpture. It was called the TRIAD ART GALLERY. Franniemarie glanced in her rearview mirror, and without braking, pulled in. The Gallery was closed. *On to SMOKIN JOAN'S.*

Inside, eager to share her find with her friend, she found the place filled with shoppers. Holding up her bag, she grinned and gaily called out, "Fabulous day! Thanks." Back on the road, as she headed to her cabin, the day became grey, and she felt deflated.

Listlessly, she poured herself a glass of wine and opened another of her aunt's notebooks. Reading through the slush of grocery lists, what I want lists, and paranoid evaluations of the true nature of Dorien's acquaintances. Half-bored, she read on.

" … I don't want her friendship. I've always had a queer feeling she was watching me like a cat watches a mouse for something she could use against me. Toward the last, I had that same strange feeling about Anita Z. Janice had to have said something. They greet me with fake smiles and sugar plums, but they're not friends. They are really spies."

Lord, how she natters! Franniemarie sipped her wine. Pushing back a darkness that she felt herself settling into, she returned to the notebook.

"Even Gay didn't sound friendly. I think she knows what's been said. I was sick all yesterday and I couldn't go to bed until morning. Sick with shame and humiliation just remembering. No, I can't be friends with Gay either."

Ah Christ, Dorien, I've journaled off and on all my life, but unlike you, my purpose is to transcend the circles—to learn new ways of seeing. You keep circling back to the same old themes. I wonder if you ever reread anything you wrote.

Or could it be, Dorien revisits the gossip and the hurts because it is familiar, because somehow the process eases her pain? Franniemarie poured herself another glass of wine.

"All my life there's been a conspiracy of silence and a whispering campaign against me. I can't fight the gossip if I have to go on shadow-boxing. Nobody ever tells me enough of what's been said to let me come to grips with the problem. However, life isn't a geometric theorem—is it?"

Franniemarie was first enraged, next, tripped up by her own awareness. *Oh, crap. I'm irritated because, like her, most people seem to find me strange. I don't make friends because I'm just as paranoid as she is. For that matter, so is mother.*

"Most people are dangerous. I simply must watch with whom I make acquaintance."

Well, darlin' you probably got that right. Franniemarie turned the page.

"Sometimes I see very clearly that I am growing older—almost as if you could put up your hand and touch the change. It seems so strange to care so much about myself and my own comfort. A short time ago, I thought only of leaving the $10,000 to Dory; now that seems less important than my own comfort and convenience. Now it seems a bother to rent rooms even for a year, or six months. Now I just want to use it to pay off this place. Then no tenants would be necessary. Dory's insurance would pay for it in full and buy new furniture. I could even get a Bendix and a vacuum cleaner."

Criminy! That's just what my mother did with my father's insurance—the money mother always told me would pay for my education. When I was accepted into college, she just snorted and said she wasn't going to waste the money on anyone as stupid as I. What a shock. I didn't even know I was stupid. Guess that's the attitude their father taught them. Franniemarie turned the page, turned to a bit that captured her full attention.

"Yesterday My father's sister Aunt Fern said my father had not been such a moral angel. She added neither had Gill. I felt she thought I knew he'd been unfaithful to me. For a little while, I felt panicky and wanted to retreat into the safety of dreams. Mostly because I took a horrible chance having Nannette with us for six weeks. Nannette was only with us until she married, but she didn't have a job.

That Nannette admired Gill's looks I knew, of course; and I also knew that Gill admired Nan's pretty face and adorable figure and her pretty little ways with her hair and voice and manners. Nan has always had a great deal of looks and charm and so had Gill, and I was glad they admired each other. It was a compliment to me that each of them admired someone who was mine.

"I think if there had been any silliness between them Nannette would have told me. She'd have told me just to lord it over me. Nannette called herself a juvenile delinquent and was proud of it. I'm sorry for her. It must be a horrible thing to have on her conscience, a frightful thing to live with all her days. Imagine selling yourself to so many men that you don't know who the father of your child is!"

Franniemarie turned cold, bone cold. Even her mind seemed to have frozen, yet she read on.

"I was luckier than Nannette and Annamarie. I had my mother for five years and she made herself felt. Unlike my sisters, I've had sexual relations with only one man, my husband. Not because men were good to me, but because I had the right mother. Maybe she did scare the pie out of me with eternal damnation, either that or something went wrong in that pink bedroom—and I'd guess it was the latter, and that it was so terrible and so outraged my early moral training that I've had a feeling of insecurity with men and of a desire to escape reality into dreams ever since. Eternal damnation."

First, my mother sets me to wondering if some cousin who I've never met is really my sister, then my aunt sets me to wondering who the hell my father was. Why in hell am I reading this shit? Who in their right mind would want to know? And I wonder what in hell did go wrong in that pink bedroom? Sick to her stomach, Franniemarie drained her glass, turned off the light and went to bed with her clothes on. Her innards trembled with exhaustion, yet sleep would not come.

Franniemarie remembered the wallpaper in her mother's bedroom—the bedroom in the second-story cold-water flat they lived in after the end of WWII. The wallpaper was cream colored with a repeat pattern of white feathers, feathers that floated down in a regular vertical pattern. The furniture was all maple and curved, curved in the great round mirror that made up the greater bulk of the dressing table, curved in the headboard and the footboard, even in the detail at the top of the highboy. A small closet had been turned into a bathroom that held a toilet, a medicine cabinet, and a sink. Nannette lay on the bed reading a magazine. She was wearing a soft flowing dress that looked lovely against the cream satin bedspread. "Nan! Nan! Nan! Open the door. Nan, help me." The sun spread through the room, filtered by white lace curtains. Like a caress, the sun lit one side of Nannette's face. "For God's sake, Nan, I can't stop the blood much longer."

Franniemarie was once again an eight-year-old standing in her mother's bedroom doorway. She had no understanding of the scene before her. Earlier, her mother's friend, the one she was told to call Uncle Harry, was in the kitchen pushing down the trash. He cut his hand on the lid of a can—cut his hand to the bone, blood squirting all over—all over mother's clean dishes. Nannette said, "Oh, Harry, come quick to the bathroom." Harry, holding his wrist, went into the bathroom. Nannette shut the door with her foot, grabbed a chair, and the clothes on the chair fell to the floor as she jammed it under the doorknob, then lay down to read her book.

Franniemarie raced down the stairwell, pounded on the landlady's door, told her they needed help. Uncle Harry had hurt himself. The landlady huffed and puffed her way up the stairs. Nannette met her at the door. She smiled sweetly. "I'm so glad she found you home," she said, "We've had a bit of an accident, here. Is there any possibility you could take Harold to the hospital?"

Weighted down by memory, Franniemarie lay nailed to her bed. *Uncle Harry never returned. After mother cut me, I'm sure I ended up in the hospital. But I'm just as sure it wasn't my mother who took me to a hospital.*

In the days that followed she neither ate nor read, nor left the cabin. She didn't even answer the phone. In truth, she was so deeply buried in her blackness that she may not have heard it ring.

CHAPTER 15

FOR TWO WEEKS, Lilianna spent her spare time studying microfiche till she thought she'd go blind. She read everything she found written about her mother, but still felt she didn't know her. She'd never seen a movie with her mother in it. The disparaging manner in which her acquaintances spoke of the Tex-Mex Westerns that predated the later, and equally squalled spaghetti Westerns, left her blind to their kinder treatment of her mother's work in the film noir genre for which she was so well known. Growing up, she had shuddered with shame at the mention of her mother. Now she needed to know all she could about this woman, and the films were her last resort. During the evenings she rented videos of her mother's movies and, to her surprise, she found herself liking them.

Eating popcorn and drinking whiskey, she watched *Princess Juanita of the Amazon, The Guns of Poco Pasco, Kitty Wells,* and *Miner's Moll*. These Tex-Mex romps were totally delightful. *Mother's timing was superb. Plain as the nose on your face, these movies are a spoof on the popular Western novels of the day.*

As to film noir, she started with the *Dead of Night*. The low angles and the abundant use of close-ups were tailored to her—especially to her rich, husky voice. Lilianna ended her film festival watching *The Jewels of Cairo*, a gangster heist in which Annamarie played moll opposite Sterling Sedgwick. The fire between them blazed across the screen. *Perhaps he's my father. We, too, have the same coloring, the same fine blond hair.*

To Lilianna, the best movie of them all was *Delilah's Revenge*, a shocking spoof on Bible movies of the day that had stirred up revulsion and horror in Annamarie's movie loving fans. *What a transition out of film noir. Had mother been mediocre, perhaps they would have forgiven her. However, she was good. If you were a believer, you were going to squirm beneath the laughter. You were not going to find it funny, not at all.*

Unfortunately, the "Old Tyme Video" store did not have *The White Lily* and could offer no clue as to where Lilianna could find it. By week's end, she'd exhausted all avenues she could imagine trying to dredge up a copy. Discouraged, she poured a stiff shot of Knob Creek and settled in to see what was on the idiot box when the phone rang. "Hello?"

"Lilianna."

"Who's calling?"

"What? You don't even recognize your mother's voice."

"No, Annamarie. It's just—I was surprised to hear from you."

"Surprised?"

"We didn't end the last conversation on exactly a positive note."

"Lilianna, all families have their tiffs."

Tiffs? Is that what it was, a tiff? Sheesh! Ya could have fooled me.

"I've reserved a room at the Mark Hopkins for Wednesday and Thursday. I could take the morning flight up and we could do lunch.

"Why?"

"What do you mean, why ?"

"You're in such fragile health"

"And I'm not getting any younger"

"You rarely come to the city. Why now?"

Annamarie paused, a long pause, then spoke in her finest mortally wounded voice, "Dahling—it's your birthday. I have a present I want to bring you." In a bright rush, she added, "I know you'll truly like it. And I do have stories to tell."

Lilianna had forgotten her own birthday. *I'll bet— delightful little tidbits: who came to tea, who's doing what, what they wore, how nice they are, and their children—how successful they are, at the least the ones who followed parents into theater. Especially Johannes Sveen's wife—widow.*

Oh my God, Sveen! My father—perhaps my father. Christ, Mother, all I'd like right now is to know who my father is.

"Let me check my calendar," Lilianna found her birthday page as blank as she knew it would be. The search gave her pause. *Am I ready to see this woman? This mother of mine who may have—probably did—do my father in. If not now, when?* She took a deep breath. "My calendar is blank. Where do you want to meet?"

"It's your birthday. You decide."

"David's."

"David's. It's so, so ... how might I put it? Tacky."

"Mother, it's not tacky, it's just plain. No frills. Just good cooking. Their borsch is out of this world."

"Ah, yes. However, I was thinking something a bit more festive …"

"Since you're staying at the Mark, why not just eat there?"

"Good Idea. Top of the Mark, it is."

"And Annamarie?"

"What is it?"

"I've been watching all your movies."

"And?"

"And I think you've been the most underrated actress of all time." In a rush she added, "But I can't find a copy of the much touted *White Lily*."

"Probably because it was filmed in Sweden."

"Right."

"I take it you'd like one."

"Right."

"I'll see what I can do."

Lilianna snapped the phone cover shut. *So—stories. Is it too much to ask that the stories include the one I most want to hear?*

CHAPTER 16

A PERSISTENT LOUD rapping forced Franniemarie from her bed. In a daze, she crawled out and opened the door. Joan stood there with a package in her arm. "Geez, Frannie, what's happened to you?"

Franniemarie swallowed, hesitated, answered, "I think I've been sick."

"You poor, poor thing." Joan pushed her way into the room. "I've been calling and calling. Your stuff from the DMV came, and I wanted to get it to you." She placed the package on the table. "For God's sake, Frannie, sit down before you fall down." Joan practically pushed Franniemarie into a living room chair, got a blanket from the bedroom and wrapped it around her. After building a fire, she rummaged in the refrigerator. "Damn, this looks more barren than your mother's. Shit, even the milk is sour. I'll bet you haven't eaten in days. Don't you move, I'll be back in a flash."

Franniemarie winced at the sound of her door slamming shut. *I lied. I'm not sick. I'm just one more fuckup in a world filled with fuckups.* She started to rise, then sank back into the chair. She had no will to move. Sometime later, Joan burst through the door. "Are we in luck! Le soup de jour at the Yachats Soup n Salad Bar is chicken noodle. And they make their own noodles." Joan all but spoon fed her the soup.

And, like the sun in the morning, Franniemarie's spirits began to rise and, with them, an awareness of how disheveled she was. "Can you stay while I shower?" She asked timidly.

"No way, gotta run." Joan laughed. Then saw the look of dismay on her friend's face.

"Joke! For God's sake, Joke! Geez, Frannie, you really think I'd leave you like this?"

In front of the fire, Franniemarie toweled her hair until it felt like cool silk. She shivered. Her hair was the one thing she did like about herself. While she dried her hair, they talked about the local real-estate market and what she hoped to find. Franniemarie said, "I want a place with enough space to put in a small vegetable garden."

"Vegetable garden? Vegetables! For God sake, nobody, I mean absolutely nobody, raises vegetables out here. Flowers, yes. We even have a garden club."

"Why?"

"It's too cold."

"Gimme a break, Joanie, it doesn't freeze here five, six months out of the year. I know people who live in Zone 3 and raise all their own food. Varieties are limited, but they can do it."

"Maybe so, but out here the veggies are raised inland. Out here we have farmer's markets where they come to sell them."

Yeah, right. I'll just have to check with Ag Extension about that. "Whatever. I want a place between Ona and Driftwood Beaches."

"For God's sake, Frannie! Why?"

Franniemarie pondered an answer to the why. "I need to be near the cave." *The cave is my sacred space. I need to be able to walk to the cave. It's the most important thing, perhaps more important than a garden.*

"I mean, that's so limited. You really should consider anything between Newport and Florence. Tell you what—I have some stuff I need to pick up in Newport. If you're up for it, we could go up today."

If I'm up for it? Franniemarie had already forgotten Joan thought she was sick. Then she remembered. *How can the world be so black and evil one minute—so dark I can hardly live in it, and then in a flash it's all changed and I can hardly imagine being in that hole.* "I'm fine now. Guess I just wore myself out last week."

"That's my Frannie. You were that way even in high school. Remember when you were in charge of decorating the Armory for the Junior - Senior Prom? For weeks you cracked the whip on your crew, and in the end you must have worked alone three days straight. You never even slept for Christsake."

Franniemarie turned inward to the memory and smiled. "It was beautiful, wasn't it? Did you know I got the guys from shop to build the river bed and the bridge we placed over it just inside the entrance? And I worked with a crew digging aspens, bagging them, and setting 'em up to make a screen so that everyone would be totally surprised by the interior fantasy I'd created."

"It was fabulous. Too bad you were too sick to attend."

Sick? Oh no, I wasn't sick. I was in a place so dark, so deep, I couldn't climb out. Not to mention, I didn't have a date. "Well, now you've totally brought me back, but I still don't want a place in Newport."

"But you haven't even been to Newport." Joan protested. "They have a neat old town. Oh, not anything of the magnitude of Chicago's Old Town North, but like that in miniature. They have poetry readings, art shows, plays, quaint shops, music. All those things you love. They even have a hospital. Besides they have more places for sale there and the prices are better."

"You just don't understand."

"I guess," Joan shook her head in exasperation.

Franniemarie remembered Newport was where she needed to take her driver's exam. *This would be perfect. She could drop me off. Like the guys at the eatery on the marina said, just show them your title and your Social Security card. How absolutely fortuitous that I've never held a real job since I married! It's still in my maiden name.* She chewed her cheek. "Well, I've been told I need to take my driver's test there. If we go, could you drop me off?"

"Oh, you won't need to take the test. Just show them your Nebraska license and they'll give you a new one."

"Oh, Joan, that would be too simple. I forgot to get it renewed, so I don't even have a current one." Franniemarie surprised herself. *If I don't sound just like my mother. Guess she really did teach me a thing or two.* "I asked the desk clerk about it. She says I just need my birth certificate, Social Security number, and an address."

On the drive to Newport, a cop car raced past them with sirens and lights on full alert. Franniemarie's teeth began to chatter.

"Hey, girl, you okay?"

Laughing, Franniemarie replied, "Of course I'm okay. You know how police, for that matter anyone wearing a uniform, always scare the begeezus outta me?"

"Why?"

"Waddya mean, why? You of all people know it's always been this way with me."

"Doesn't answer my question."

Franniemarie was so exasperated by Joan's insensitive intrusion that she didn't even try to reply.

Against Franniemarie's protest, Joan left her and the car at the DMV. "No problem, Frannie, I need the exercise."

A couple of hours later Joan played tour guide and real-estate agent, starting above the ocean on the west end of town. Franniemarie was indeed taken with the vintage houses and the way they descended the hill above the ocean. On one street, a Victorian house caught her eye. A huge single-story garage had been attached at a much later date. With weeds growing through the cracks in the front sidewalk, it looked empty. They stopped for lunch at Don Petre's Italian Food Company, where they were served a good old fashioned burgundy in plain, straight-sided water glasses, a robust pasta, warm ciabatta, and a dessert of fresh apple slices with cheese.

Just before dusk, Joan returned her to the hippie house. As soon as she left, Franniemarie checked the tide table. Low tide 8:32 p.m. *I can make it to the cave before the tide turns.*

Changing into sweats and her wool cape, she drove the car at high speed to Seal Rock. When she reached the path to the ocean, it was pitch black out. By the time she'd descended, the moon was up, casting an eerie light across the beach. The waves broke rhythmically in moonlit white cascades against the rocks. She had forgotten that the entrance to the cave was strewn with large boulders and rocks. In daylight, it hadn't been a problem, but now she moved more cautiously, feeling her way across them.

Inside the cave, she listened to the sound of water trickling down the rock walls, dripping on the smooth sand at her feet. She prayed to the gods that ruled inner turmoil. *Help me to know who I am. Why I am. Bring me peace.* Then, from a place that started in the sand, sound rose through her and filled the cave, falling, rising, echoing off the stone walls and filling her bones with their vibration, her soul with their energy. When the sound found its end, the words, *"Be patient and alert,"* filled her mind, and a wonderful blend of energy and peace filled her body.

*****

The following morning was overcast and chill. Long before sunup, Franniemarie stoked the fire and curled up beside it with another journal and a cup of coffee. She waded through pages of persecution, perceived or real—in all probability some blend of each—long rants on the lack of morals of her acquaintances and, then a bit of writing drew Franniemarie into a closer kinship.

"Cleaning house wouldn't have been so bad if I hadn't started with painting both closets, the kitchen table, chair, draining and splash boards, both bookcases, back porch and all trim on the house, as well as hemming 5 double-wide curtains. It will take me two solid days to clean the house, but that includes scrubbing, scratch-coating, waxing, and polishing everything as well as all the windows and the laundry."

At least I'm not the only one to bite off more than she can chew." I hate living this way.

The house is a mess, our clothes are dirty, everything's upset – phooey! To make matters worse, Dory picked up a flea and I think it mated." Franniemarie laughed, reread the passage, and laughed again. On that note, Franniemarie closed the book, bundled herself to ward off a bitter wind, and made it to the beach before low tide.

To her amazement, a couple of kids with swinging buckets ran barefoot in and out of the ocean waves, gleefully drenching themselves. Franniemarie shivered watching them. "Aren't you cold?" she asked a robust, ruddy cheeked boy, who looked to be about twelve. "Oh, no, the cold isn't so bad after your feet get numb. Barefoot is better than shoes."

"Besides," the young girl, a slip of a child with fine curly hair tousled about her face, chimed in, "your feet are going to get wet and cold even if you wear shoes. Sandy, wet socks are really nasty."

Franniemarie found the two of them charming. "And how come you aren't in school today?"

"Spring Break, every Spring Break we get to stay at Grandma's. We're going to get some mussels off those rocks." She pointed to an extension of the rocks that formed the cave, and stretched in an arc breaking the force of the ocean.

"You like mussels?" the boy asked.

"I've never eaten them," Franniemarie admitted.

"My brother and I really like them. They're my favorite."

"I'm Franniemarie. You guys got names?"

"He's Tim. I'm Kaitlyn, but I'd rather be called Kit."

"If you like, we'll take you. We can show you how to gather them. But we better get going while the tide's still low," Tim spoke with grave authority.

At the rock, Tim pointed to the clusters of mussels in their shells clinging to the rocks. "See these huge ones? Those you don't want. They're just too tough to taste good. These...." He pointed out a cluster of smaller ones, "Now these are what you want." He began knocking off mid-sized shells with his hammer. Kit handed her a nice long thin rock, similar to one she held. "I don't bother hauling a hammer around." For a bit, Franniemarie watched her knock mussels into her pail then joined in. Soon the pails were full and the tide had changed. On their way to a higher beach, Franniemarie discovered first hand the little girl's wisdom: Wet sandy socks were indeed extra cold and gritty nasty.

"Here, you take this bucket home," Kit offered.

"Oh, no. I enjoyed learning how to gather them, but I wouldn't know how to take care of them, let alone how to cook them."

"It's so simple," Tim began a fine lecture. "When you get home, you dump out the sea water and fill the bucket with fresh water. In the morning, dump that off and fill it again. By afternoon they will have cleaned the sand from themselves. If any are floating, throw them out.

"Then you scrub them good and pull off any beards. To cook them, you just steam them till they open. Last, you eat them with soy sauce. Some people do it different, but that's the way a real Chinese man, by that I mean a man who was raised in China, taught us how when we were little. So that's why we like them that way. We remember him when we eat them. He will always be a friend."

The tide was now too high to go to the caves. Franniemarie accepted her bucket and thanked the children. "Whenever I eat mussels I'll think of you."

On the way to the car, she waved to the lady in the aqua slicker. The lady waved back. Franniemarie dutifully changed the water in the kitchen sink. *What on earth am I going to do with all these mussels? I know. I'll invite Joan for dinner tomorrow. We'll dine on mussels, salad, biscuits, and a crisp white wine. Oh, bother, I need to get flour, baking powder, butter, and the makings for a salad.* Setting the bucket on the porch, she grabbed her wallet, the bag of rocks she'd collected the day after the storm, and headed up the coast. The "open" sign was out at "Smokin Joan's" and Franniemarie burst past it.

Joan looked up from a ledger she was working on. "Frannie! It's about time you showed up, past time to change the grit in the tumblers."

A couple of customers entered.

Franniemarie held up her bag of rocks. "Any chance I can start these?"

"Long as I get half. You know the drill. All I got running right now is yours, so have at it."

The shed was chilly and the water she washed the rocks in was cold; however, it didn't take long to change the little tumbler to a medium grit and start the rest of her rocks in three of the one gallon-tumblers with the large grit. Before heading to the grocery store, she extended a dinner invitation to Joan, who beamed her back a wide smile and an affirmative nod before returning to her customers.

While at the store, Franniemarie picked up a pint of strawberries, and on the way home stopped at a chocolate shop where she purchased two dark chocolate truffles.

Before opening her aunt's journals, she built a fire, poured herself a glass of milk, sliced a banana, arranged the slices in two rows on one of her pottery squares and filled the rest of the plate with a mix of pecans, almonds, and hazelnuts. She placed her lunch on the table next to what had become her favorite chair and slipped the Polonaise into the player. Warmed by the fire, she began to read.

"For years I've dreamed of 'improving' Alameda. I used to talk of building a big park with a museum, water for boating, an indoor pool, an auditorium for concerts … everything Oakland and San Francisco could offer. I've dreamed of it since they leveled the dunes where you could lie warm and cozy sheltered from the wind and spoiled the little pools where tiny crabs hurried, killed my pink sand verbena and the long whip-like marsh grasses. I was 15 then, and I felt they'd desecrated something precious and I wanted indemnity in the form of one of the world's most beautiful miniature parks. But that won't solve anything. Clearing slums won't do that either. It's a mistake to think you can attack the problem merely from outside.

What I want is a gentle dignity. It fits the inside of me. But how to achieve that? That's my question—my quest."

Franniemarie stared into her fire. *A gentle dignity. The flames crackled and danced. A gentle dignity; she claims that's what is inside her. Here I sit in gentle dignity, but that's not what's inside of me. That's what I want inside of me. Did she really carry either gentleness or dignity inside? Or are we the same in needing the feel of grace and dignity around us—a compensation for what our innards do not own?*

"I really wasn't so fond of Dory at first, and that's the truth. How disconcerting it was when I found she was going to stay alive. Suddenly it dawned on me that I couldn't put her in a corner and come back for her sometime later when I got 'round to it."

"I was always so surprised and unprepared even though she was right there to touch. It seemed as if I had to touch her to remind myself that she was real, and then I'd absent-mindedly forget she existed and, when I remembered, the hair would rise on my scalp for fear I'd forget sometime and not remember until too late. I guess I was a very absent-minded mother."

Franniemarie's tears became a veil obliterating the page. *I tried so hard not to be an absent mother. I never forgot my children. I forgot myself in my children. But what in God's name difference did it make? Like Dory, Preston and Jacob ended up dead before their time. And God knows I wasn't much of a mother after they died. Poor Brooks had to grow up with nothing but shattered shards of mothering. He would have been better served if the mothering vessel had been broken.*

"When Dory was little, she used to pull my shirt rhythmically and steadily until my mind came back to her and my eyes would see her big patient gray ones watching and waiting for me to see that she was there. She was the most wonderful person. She still does that. She was always the most patient little tyke. It wasn't that I didn't love her, just that I didn't believe she was real. I used to look at her chubby body, big eyes, and all her lovely curls and think she might be real and wonder whose child she was, and suddenly I'd remember she was mine."

Isn't it amazing how those of us who are the least equipped are the ones who think they must have a child. Take someone, anyone, who has been neglected and abused and that's the woman who thinks she has to have a child. Franniemarie got up, washed her face, and then left the house.

Without a plan, she drove through Yachats. To the north, between the highway and the ocean, she noticed the bookstore and pulled in. "I'm looking for a book written by a local writer," she told the proprietor. "I believe it's titled something like *Murder and Madness in Oregon.*"

The proprietor's nostrils flared in disdain, "The title is *Holy Rollers; Murder and Madness in Oregon's Love Cult.* It is not written by a local. However, I do have it."

That evening, she was able to escape into a world more strange than any she'd ever lived in or even imagined. The title did not exaggerate. The book, indeed, was filled with murder, madness, and depravity.

*****

Franniemarie opened her morning with a cave meditation that streamed through her from someplace far below and grew in volume till it filled her head and came simultaneously out of her nose and her throat. The sounds rose and fell, echoing off the cave walls and back into her. When the sound was spent, she was filled with euphoria. Leaving the cave, she walked the beach absorbing the sound of the waves. The birds she could not identify, the strange flexible, yellow to orange, rope-like lengths of vegetation strewn about the beach. On the gravel bar she found a rock layered in bands of blue, white, black and grey. When she looked up, she saw a woman dressed in a yellow rubbery-looking suit and collecting driftwood on the rocks near the cliff. Franniemarie giggled with delight. *She looks like a banana. Now if I were wearing yellow with a blush of pink I'd look like a pear. In that case, I'd just walk right up to her and ask her to dance.* Turning back to search the gravel, she was yet so deeply turned in on her vision of the two of them impressing dance step patterns on the sand, the waves breaking white behind them, establishing rhythm, that when the woman stood next to her, she was startled. This young woman, a head shorter than she, was asking, "Have you a clue what that is?" She pointed at the rubbery vegetation.

"Haven't a clue. I'm not a native."

"Me, either. Where are you from?"

"Midwest. Believe me, the boring Midwest. And you?"

"Upper New York State."

"Wow, long way from home."

"U of O made me an offer I couldn't refuse."

"So what's your major?"

"Architecture."

"That's heavy."

Franniemarie opened her hand, exposing the banded stone. "Look at what I found."

"Wow, you found that here?"

"Right here. Right on this sandbar."

Simultaneously, they looked down. Soon they were moving in tandem, hands clasped behind their backs, slowly working their way back and forth across the bar.

"This beach is my favorite. I think it's those behemoth rocks. They're so powerful."

"You, too? I think they're sacred. I think I'm falling in love with this place. I'm thinking of staying." Something opened in Franniemarie, and she felt free with this woman. She had the strangest feeling of long familiarity, a sensation she had never known before. "Ideally, I'd like a place up on the cliff.

But I'm told those places are really pricey. A friend took me to Newport. We drove past a vacant building. Part of the building had a flat roof, and the other half was two stories high. I keep thinking about it and wondering if the flat roof could be made into a patio. That's really dumb. I haven't even been in the place. Don't even know if the owner would sell."

"Not dumb at all. Besides, you've come to the right person. I'm not licensed yet, but I start my first job next Wednesday. I could look the place over for you. That is, if you'd like."

In her usual compulsive, airy way Franniemarie blurted, "I'd trust you to vet anyplace I had a mind for. I'm Franniemarie Martin. You got a name?" She extended her hand.

The young woman took her hand. "Templeton. That's my only name. But you can call me Tempe, if you like."

I have a feeling everyone asks. Why? How? So why should I be any different? "So how did you come up with one name?"

Tempe picked up a bit of glitter, and asked, "This anything?"

Franniemarie looked at the smooth odd-shaped piece of clear caramel stone. "Carnelian. Sometimes it's even lighter, sometimes it's so dark it's almost rust, and sometimes you find all those variations in one stone. It's a keeper."

Slipping the rock into her pocket, Tempe continued, "First, it looked good on my drafts. Besides, who else do you know named Templeton? Truth is, my mother pasted Zelda on me because it started with the last letter in the alphabet and, as she often said, it represented the last thing in this world she ever wanted. Zelda Templeton. Dropping Zelda was my rite of passage into a world I'm making for myself."

We could have been sisters. "I have a friend coming to dinner. Why don't you join us? I'm staying in Yachats, but you could just follow me in your car."

"Not."

Oh, no. I thought we were on the same page.

"But I could follow you on my bike."

"Bike?"

"Yeah, bike, I'm on a Yamaha 750. Gets good gas mileage."

Together, they scrubbed the mussels. Tempe set the table while Franniemarie whipped up a batch of biscuits. "I've never used this oven, I hope it works. Fact is, I've been here three weeks and this is the first real meal I've cooked."

Joan, true to her nature, arrived late.

"Joan, this is Tempe. We met on the beach, she's an architect."

"Not yet, I'm still an intern," Templeton protested.

"I've told Tempe all about you, and how we were childhood friends."

The biscuits were ready the same time the mussels began to open. Tempe filled the bread basket while Franniemarie drained the mussels.

Joan raised her glass in a toast, "Long live childhood friends; they keep each other honest."

Franniemarie told them about the charming children on the beach and how they'd taught her to collect and cook the mussels. Franniemarie watched Tempe open a shell and dip it into the soy sauce. "I've never had these before."

Franniemarie held her breath. Tempe opened another.

Joan said, "The first time I ate mussels, it was in Spain. They were wonderful. I think they were served with garlic butter, but this is good."

Franniemarie relaxed and let her teeth scrape a morsel out of its shell.

"I think what I like best about the ocean is seafood," said Joan, while savoring another morsel. "Mother was a good cook. But living in the Midwest, she never cooked seafood. My first introduction was in Spain and later Italy."

"My mother didn't cook. As they say, she couldn't boil water. I paid attention to Joanie's mother."

"Weren't for my mother, you probably would have starved to death."

Franniemarie started to protest, and stopped herself. *Clarifying the merits of family dining is not her point. The point is, my mother was rotten, and there's no arguing that.*

"My mother was a good enough cook." Tempe dipped another mussel into the sauce. "However, my father ate only plain cooking. And by that I mean really plain, not so much as a dash of ginger, or pepper. He even grumbled if she used sweet basil. Mother was a strong woman, but she knelt before my father. Outside of the family, no one would have believed it. But she made sure Dad, right or wrong, ruled."

"I never thought about my mother in terms of strength." Joan broke open a hot biscuit, spread butter on it. "In retrospect, she had to have been the ultimate in strength. My dad left her to raise my brother and me alone. Up till the day she died, she worked as a secretary in a law firm. She did it all. In those days, most mothers stayed home. She was gone five days a week, and yet she did the laundry, cooking, baking, school functions, everything."

Tempe leaned back. "So you remember your dad?" She nodded toward Joan.

"Not much. He left when I was seven, and my brother Butch was five. The only thing I remember is watching him shave in front of this very large, oval, Victorian mirror. Then he'd sort of steam his face with a towel, and pat something that smelled good on his cheeks. But the most fascinating thing was this—he'd stand looking at himself in the mirror, stretching his mouth, his eyebrows, and his forehead in the strangest contortions. That was his daily exercise. I don't remember Mother ever talking about him, but sometime along the line I picked up the notion he was an alcoholic. Mom never had anything to do with men after he was gone."

"I think my dad has a good heart." Tempe offered. "It's just that he's always been king and he never needed to pay attention to other people's needs. That makes him look like an arrogant son-of-a-bitch. That's as much my mother's fault as his. However, in the few relationships I've had, I've found myself acting like my mother. I hate it. I suppose I grew up thinking that to survive you had to please and hang on at all costs. I don't seem to be able to break that mold. Piss on that."

Joan interjected. "I think everything we learn about relationships comes from family. Frannie's the only one I ever knew who was able to break that childhood example."

"So how'd you do it, Frannie?" Tempe asked, as if she really wanted a serious answer.

"Lot of men drifted through my mother's life. She used them like paper plates—mother's disposable men. When they leered at her, she had a way of lowering her eyes and sucking in her breath that made their knees buckle. She would reaffirm and reinforce their political, moral, and religious persuasion in a way that made them feel powerful and invincible. In return, they bought her flowers, candy, dresses, furs, cars, trips to Europe, and even houses. She did well. I might have done the same, but I loathed her slimy men. They were pompous, rich, butt-pinching assholes with egos that begged stroking. She always said she never slept with any of them. If that's really true, I say, more power to her.

"I chose to give it away. If I was attracted to a man, I took him to bed—always thought, 'just get it over, get past that infatuated attraction. Then decide whether or not you want to be friends.' *I can't believe I said that. Well, it's true.* Franniemarie stood to bring the strawberries and sliced truffles to the table.

"And your father?" Tempe nodded to Franniemarie.

"Oh, him. When I was very, very young Mother killed him."

Laughter filled the room, Franniemarie joining in. *If you only knew.*

Laughter filled them, like the strawberries and chocolate, with a richness that lit their dark interior shadows.

CHAPTER 17

EYES CLENCHED SHUT, Cricket screamed, "Christ, disconnect me. Let me go. I have a will, a living will, just let me go."

Then he felt his son's fingers stroking the back of his right hand. "Dad, it's okay. You're going to be okay, Dad. You're not on life support. You're in the Nebraska Medical Center. I've rung for a nurse."

On hushed shoes a nurse, who was a bit long in the tooth, entered briskly. "How are we feeling?"

"Died and gone to hell! Ma'am."

"We can do something about that." She tweaked a drip-line valve, watched it for a moment and then disappeared as quickly and silently as she'd appeared moments before.

Brooks continued to stroke his father's fingers. Slowly, the pain slipped off.

Cricket opened his eyes and stared into Brooks'. For a moment he felt as though he'd floated into Franniemarie's. "How bad's the damage?"

"Concussion, three broken ribs, ruptured spleen, and one crushed hip."

"I meant the tractor."

"Tractor's fine. We winched it up. It's in the shed. What happened?" Brooks asked the question primarily because he did not know what to say and wanted to avoid that which needed saying.

"It's the hill. That damn hill. Frannie's been at me to quit farming it for years. She always said it was going to be the death of me. Last I remember it was getting dark. I thought I'd make just one more pass, then I felt a wheel sinking in a soft spot and the tractor went tilt. It was like being bucked off. One minute I was on the ground, next the damn tractor was on top of me." Cricket began to sweat.

"Dad! Dad! Take it easy." Brooks squeezed his hand and held it for the longest moment. At last he spoke his mind. "Now you're awake you're going to have to talk to someone about the accident."

"Let it wait. At least don't send them in till after you leave."

Brooks stayed when the surgeon came in. In less than ninety seconds the doctor had announced that reconstruction surgery went well. Cricket could be expected to be released in ten days. And no, he would not be able to drive the tractor at that time. Therapy alone was going to take a minimum of six weeks. It would be summer before he'd be healed enough to be sitting behind its wheel. A nurse entered as the doctor left. "Time for you to become mobile." Her voice was all smiles. Her eyes told another story.

Cricket shook his head. "Can't do it."

"Of course you can. It's been twenty-four hours since you came out of surgery. You only have to go from your bed to that wheel chair waiting in the hall just beyond your door. We'll give you a ride back."

With the nurse wheeling the IV on one side and Brooks on the other, feeling weak and exposed, Cricket held himself up by pushing a walker all the way to the chair. By the time he made it back, the bed had been stripped and remade. The blankets could not staunch his shivering. After readjusting the IV and the heart monitor, the nurse fetched a warm blanket. He fell asleep before she'd finished tucking him in.

Brooks was still with him when he woke to the clatter of lunch being served. Cricket wasn't hungry. "Come on Dad, you've got to eat something."

"I said I'm not hungry. Brooks, what in hell am I going to do?"

"Get well. That's what ya gotta do. That's your job now."

"Hell! I'm talking about the farm. This accident is going to cost us the farm. Even if you get the crops in for me, which I'm not asking, it's still going to cost …"

"Why aren't you asking?"

"What the hell's that mean?"

"For Christsake, Dad. Who would you ask but me? I'm your son. You're supposed to ask me."

"I take it you're willing to take it on."

"Hell, yes. That's the least I can do. 'Sides we'll just put it back to corn and soybeans, same's I'm doing Aunt Pru's." Brooks poured broth into his father's cup and held it to his lips.

"Franniemarie's broth would mend me. When she gets here, I'm going to ask her to bring me some of that fine broth she makes with beef. That'll pick a man up."

Brooks could not check the stricken look that flashed across his face.

"What?"

"I don't know how to tell you ..."

"Christsake just spit it out."

"I came looking for you day before yesterday. No one was home, the car was gone. Charlie called, said you were supposed to meet him at the café and you didn't show. So I went looking for you. That's when I found you under the tractor. I didn't feel a pulse. You were stone cold and I couldn't even tell if you were alive. I called an ambulance, then Charlie. We got you out. Far as I can tell, you must have been out there all night and half the day. The weather turned cold—I guess it kept you on ice. Guess that's what made it possible for you to live."

Cricket watched his son intently.

Brooks could delay no longer. "Dad, we can't find Mom. The cops sent out alerts and she hasn't turned up." He blinked back tears.

Cricket reached for his son's hand and gently squeezed it. "It's okay, son. She's with us."

Puzzled, Brooks shook his head. "What?"

"Sometime after the tractor pinned me, I heard the Chevy—you know that certain sound she makes, and then I heard her calling me. 'Cricket! Cricket! Cricket! Can you hear me? Cricket!' Her voice came to me from some far place. You know your mom has always been fragile, even before we lost your brothers. Runs on her side of the family. I tried to make her stronger, to see life in a more useful way. But I never could. She's run away." Cricket saw huge question marks on Brooks' face. "She's always needed me. She just couldn't face another funeral. A life without me. Oh, Brooks—she loves me that much. But I know my Frannie. When she gets herself together she'll be back."

CHAPTER 18

TEMPE AND FRANNIEMARIE cruised Newport, looking at the buildings in the area west of the main street thoroughfare and down the hill to the waterfront. When Franniemarie saw the building that had caught her attention earlier, she pulled up to the curb. Wordlessly they got out, looked through the ground floor windows, and walked around the structure. In the back, a parking area opened to a large garage type door. "What do you think this was?"

"Maybe someone's auto-repair shop. It looks like some type of retail or office was in the front where the big window is, but this room is cavernous. It looks like a huge display window. But what would a mechanic be displaying?"

"Whatever it has been, it's obviously empty now. But there's no *For Sale* sign and it looks a tad neglected."

Templeton was poking around the edges of the foundation. "This end is on a slab, looks like the other has a basement beneath it."

"Maybe we could talk to the neighbors and find out."

"How about we go to the courthouse?"

The clerk at the Clerk and Recorder's Office was cheerful, friendly, helpful, and even better, she knew someone who knew the former owner of the building, that owner having passed away. Within the hour that someone was turning the key to the flat-roofed extension of the building. "Joe was my best friend," the old man explained. They'd grown up together. He'd gone off to dental school; Joe stayed home and worked with his father. His younger brother Don bought that building over on North Third & Coast where he and his wife now run an Italian restaurant with food so good some people ate there almost every day of their lives."

I'll bet that's where Joan and I ate.

"Believe me, best Italian food you ever ate. The folks there are getting on, but the food is just as good as ever.

"Let me tell you, they were the finest mechanics in the business," inside he spread his arms. "Back in the fifties, they turned this part of the garage into a showroom. For about twenty years they were the local Pontiac dealers. Sold 'em and fixed 'em."

While he rambled, Templeton studied the girders in the ceiling, "They must have added this on in the fifties."

The old man scratched his bald head, walked them to the back of the room, and rolled up a twelve-foot-door revealing another room as large as the first. "This was their shop. It was a shop before Joe and I were born. They added the showroom after we graduated from high school."

Templeton chewed her cheek. "But the girders, they run through both rooms. Did they replace both roofs?"

"Golly, I wouldn't know about that." Together they retreated into the showroom where he unlocked a door. "This was the old man's waiting room. In the back's his office." Inside the original Victorian portion of the structure, a stairwell divided one end of two rooms. The space below the landing, where the stairwell doubled back on itself, served as a small storage room. Across from the stairs, the rooms were divided on the other side by a bathroom.

In the waiting room, tall old-fashioned double-hung windows looked out on the street. The door to the stairway, like the window treatments, was oak and still wore what was left of the original varnish.

Franniemarie couldn't wait to see the upstairs. However, Templeton insisted they go down to the basement first. Toward the back of the office, an exterior door led into a shedroofed porch. They worked their way through boxes and trash to another door that led to the basement below.

The basement was dark, musty, lit by two bare bulbs, and cut up into smaller rooms defined by warped sheetrock. One of the smaller rooms looked to have once served as a vegetable pantry; another was a dingy bathroom with a rusted-out shower. The largest area was filled with an aging furnace, what looked to be a burned-out water heater, as well as an ancient washer and dryer. The outer walls and floor were made of some kind of mortar mix and stone. Templeton seemed fascinated. She spent a good deal of time feeling pipes, digging in the rafters, digging in the walls and the floor. By the time she was ready to leave, Franniemarie practically raced upstairs.

"When we were kids, the kitchen and dining room were downstairs in the back. Of course, in those days, the waiting room was the living room. When Joe's little brother Don left, they moved upstairs so they could expand the business."

The treads on the staircase were worn, and the paneling scarred, a testament to years of use. Above the landing, Templeton spied a trapdoor stairway. In a flash, she'd pulled it down and disappeared through the hatch.

Three doors opened off the upper landing. Straight ahead, a door opened to a bathroom. The bathroom was finished in coral, aqua and black tile and was set off by cream-colored walls. It wasn't a Victorian fit, but never-the-less it was arresting. Towards the back of the bathroom, another door opened to a bedroom.

The door to the right led to a small living room graced with two windows, streaked and peeling ivory on parchment brown wallpaper, and a cabbage rose wool rug. The east window opened to the street, the other looked south across the tarred roof above the showroom and neither was trimmed in oak. They were plain and painted a yellowed white.

From the landing, looking to the west, through the dining area, through the windows, across the rooftops, waves crested and fell beneath an ocean blue sky. The dining area was as big as the living room. Walking in, Franniemarie was taken by the light, two banks of windows, one facing west, the other to the south. To the north, the kitchen was closed off from the dining area by a cheap, painted pocket door. The paint was worn and grubby. The kitchen, as large as the dining room, had only one small north window above an old gas range. The linoleum was long worn out, the cupboard doors hanging from their hinges. In the least, it was a disaster. Too late, Franniemarie had fallen in love.

Templeton returned and proceeded to peel back the carpet and bits of hanging wallpaper.

Franniemarie asked, "Do you think the guy who owns the place would sell it? How do you get hold of him?"

"Hold your horses, lady. Far as I know, the property is still in probate. I haven't a clue what little Joe wants to do with it, but he hasn't been home much these last thirty some years. He's a big shot civil engineer in Houston."

Disappointment clouded Franniemarie's face.

"He asked me to look out for it, as I just live a few blocks down the street. After all, I was his dad's best friend." The old man spoke gravely while watching Franniemarie intently. He stroked the stubble on his face. A twinkle came to his eyes, "However, I could give you his lawyer's number. With him, you could better find out how it stands."

Franniemarie practically knocked him over with her profuse thanks.

Templeton wrote down the attorney's number.

Abruptly, Franniemarie said, "I think you should grow a beard."

The old man returned his hand to his face, "You think so?"

"Yeah, I really think so. I think you'd look really distinguished wearing a beard. I've always admired a man in a beard, especially a bald man with a beard."

Templeton had the presence of mind to take down his name, address, and number before they took their leave. Outside she turned to Franniemarie and asked, "Whatever made you blurt out such a personal comment?"

Franniemarie shrugged, "Sometimes it just happens. Hey, Tempe, I know where that Italian place is. How about I take you to lunch?"

Over pasta and wine they discussed the merits of the building.

"Can I make that rooftop into a patio—a patio with wind-breaking windows on the west side? I have to at least have a small garden."

"It won't hold soil, if that's what you're after."

"If I could use big pots, that might make do. And maybe three foot tall planters sort of like a railing around those three open sides. That would do. I think, if I added potted plants and furniture, it would be wonderful. Well it needs something different than tar on the top. Of course, I'd need doors out to it."

"Doors and an outside stairwell? That place could be a deathtrap without one."

"Ya think?"

"I know."

"I know it's a bit of a mess, but is it solid?"

"Oh, its structurally sound all right, the girders are good. I'm worried about the basement. That end of town slopes toward the sea. I could see a potential for problems, but the walls are original, and they're solid—no cracks in the floor either. That's pretty amazing considering its age. I think it's survived so well because the block it's on and the one above it are on relatively flat ground."

"What about the roof? It looked like water streaks down some of the upstairs wallpaper."

"It's leaked, but that roof is metal and it's not old. When I peeled back the paper, I got wood—not plaster. From the attic, the wood looked good—that is, I didn't find any rot. The paper looks like it was pasted right on tongue and groove."

"So it's good?"

"It doesn't have a lick of insulation. And the wiring needs to be completely redone."

"And the plumbing?"

Templeton waggled her hand. "It's a mix, but I think you could live with it."

"Oh, I hope they'll sell it. And I can afford it!"

"If it's tied up right now, you might see if they'll rent it to you with an option to buy."

"After I take you back to your bike, I'll go to that attorney's office."

"And you'll call me tonight."

"Right, I'll call you tonight."

Driving back to Yachats, Franniemarie could hardly contain herself. *That attorney, that wonderful attorney, he liked my idea—well Tempe's idea. He said to bring him an offer and he'd talk to Joe about it. I wonder how much those bonds are worth today. It's strange, I never wanted to know. And I need to know what I should be offering. Oh, I hope I have enough to buy it outright. No one would give me a loan. I don't even have a job. I've never had a job. My resume reads ex-ranch-wife, can cook, clean house—windows and toilets, no problem. You got a cow in trouble and calving? Not to sweat, she'll hook the birthing chain around that calf, make the attachment to the tractor, hop on and ease that puppy, all steaming and snotty, into this world. Yeah, right.*

But I might be able to rent out that downstairs to a retailer. Na, that stairwell would be a problem. I can see making that apartment into something sweet. I'd start by ripping off those cabinet doors in the kitchen, rip up that dead linoleum. It would be wonderful if the flooring under it was wood. I'd just paint the cupboards and refinish the floors. Maybe I could take out the wall between the kitchen and the dining room. Maybe I could even put windows on the west side of the kitchen. That would really let the light in. Oh, my, I'm beginning to think like Aunt Dorien.

*****

From beneath her bed she retrieved the tin box she'd carried from Nebraska. She lifted the lid to her cash cache. On the top, a layer of rumpled bills covered bundled packets, ranging in denominations from one to twenty, held together with rubber bands. She counted the money three times. Each time she arrived at thirty-seven thousand, three hundred dollars and an additional sum that varied between twelve and forty-six dollars. Math was not her strong suit. The bottom of the box was lined with a leather jewelry case and a thick packet of government bonds, Franniemarie's inheritance from her paternal grandmother, Mari Martin. She remembered meeting once when she was ten. On their face the treasury notes, EE bonds purchased in the late 40's and early 50's, were worth $26,000. *I'll have to call a bank to figure what they're worth today. Right now this is one meaningless mess.* She opened the leather case. Picked out a diamond tennis bracelet and let it ripple through her fingers. *Who would wear something like this on a tennis court? If the bonds don't amount to enough to purchase my building, perhaps the jewelry could make up the difference.*

Tempe shared her excitement over the progress on the status of Franniemarie's building and suggested she make an offer of at least $100,000, adding, it would take at least that much more to bring it up to snuff. However, she hadn't a clue about the worth of either the bonds or the jewelry. "I'm the one holding $30,000 in student loans. How money smart is that?" Before disconnecting, Franniemarie promised to keep her posted.

Franniemarie picked up another of her aunt's journals, noticed the *Love Cult* book, made the trade, snuggled under her comforter, and returned to life in a distant world.

*****

Her morning calls revealed that her bonds had an after-tax worth close to $154,000, Tempe was out of her office, Joan wasn't answering her phone, the attorney could meet with her at nine thirty, and the author, who 'is NOT a local Lady', lived eight miles north of Yachats in Waldport. However, her co-author did live in Corvallis and that was certainly not local. Theresa McCracken would be delighted to meet her for lunch tomorrow and sign her copy.

Franniemarie packed a lunch and grabbed her warmest jacket before heading to the lawyer's office in Newport. Her offer of one-hundred and twenty thousand dollars was drawn up in fifteen minutes, and faxed before she was out the door. All she could do now was wait. Twenty minutes later, she was scrambling down the steep rock-strewn path nearest the Seal Rock cave. Today she found herself immersed in a joyous exchange of sound between herself and the rocks, an exchange of praise and thanks that connected her core to something universal—and it returned to her a sense of both energy and peace.

Outside, she was met with a cold brilliant sun dancing on surf. To her surprise, Tim and Kaitlyn were in the ocean and splashing water on each other, knocking each other down, and teasing like a couple of river otters. Through it all they screamed and giggled. And when a large sneaker knocked Kaitlyn down, her brother was quick to her rescue, reminding Franniemarie of her own children. *Like them, my boys teased and wrestled, fought and tumbled, made a lot of noise, and like them they were not mean. They were buddies.*

The urchins spied Franniemarie on the beach and came running. "Did you like the mussels?"

"Indeed, I did. I shared them with friends of mine. Thanks to you, we had a wonderful meal."

Franniemarie shared her lunch with Tim and Kit, and they introduced her to sea anemones swaying in the pools of low tide water caught in pockets created by huge rocks and sand.

On her way back to the car, she saw the woman in the aqua slicker. They nodded in passing.

Later, warmed by her fire, she began jotting down thoughts for a poem. ROCK POEM When I was Rock I came closest / to understanding God / nestled in sun warm grasses / his breath passed over / and the grasses whispered the name / vaporized volcanic ash / I transcended rockdom / [charged radiated atoms] [radiation atoms] [charged / infused] [freedom to transcend rockdom] / fascinated with that earth I came back foraging / cold-blooded killing, long time decaying / a rodent fragile trembling / returned as a tree / burned and decayed, / sentient and ready I became dolphin / singing songs, telling / stories, meeting man / I became man observing / I came back a rock

Setting aside her scratchings, she returned to her aunt's legacy.

"When you were little you had love to spare, and picked me out to give it to you, the way you pick me wild flowers in vacant lots. Then suddenly you got temperamental. For a while you were so mean to me I thought you hated me. I tried spanking you until I was at nerve's end with shock and unhappiness, and then I learned that loving you worked better. I'm still not as good at that as you are."

Franniemarie stood, stretched, and made a pot of tea. While the water heated, she sliced a pile of carrots and placed them on one of her pottery pieces. *Mother used to take a plate of carrots to bed and the two of us would lie there eating carrots and reading. That's my favorite memory of my mother.*

"There's a V-shaped lot, the land slanting a bit to the water, with a view of the San Leandro hills and the airport and I could paint it someday. The changing light on the Bay, the slight rippling lap of water on the sand, is beautiful. There is a railroad-line on the hill where I saw freight cars and that made another beautiful picture. The quiet colors of sky, hills and water, of red-quarried hillside, of freight trains and industrial buildings and homes, a future of industry and transportation in an urban community. This world has all the beauty, thrill, tempo and color of achievement. And there was a white boat in the foreground that spoke of pleasure and relaxation. However, I can't afford it. There's no use being silly about it. Oh, phooey! I've a notion to buy rose-colored mohair and do the room in aqua.

"Talk about gracious living. That was Monday afternoon at Anita Z's—everything so pretty and clean, flowers, pretty dresses, good food, a silver tea service and nice china. Oh, my, that's so how I want to live".

Chewing on a carrot, Franniemarie stared into space. *Me too! I do hope I can afford this place—this place of my dreams. Oh, to live quietly and elegantly—that's what I've always wanted.*

I'm so like my aunt in my desires. Except for pretty dresses, I don't give a fig for pretty dresses.

Franniemarie set aside the writing, took two aspirins, brushed her teeth and went to bed. *I wonder if Kit and Tim will be at the beach tomorrow. If I meet them, I'll ask them if they'd like to go to the cave. And, if they want to, I'll teach them to howl inside the rocks.* She woke to the phone ringing. *Oh, my, could it be the attorney?* Breathlessly, she picked up the receiver. It was the attorney, but the news was not what she expected. No, Mr. Rossi did not want to sell the building; however, he had talked with his father's old friend Willis Milner and the old man convinced him Franniemarie would be a good bet to fix the place up. "Here's the deal," the lawyer said. "He'll trade you a place to live in exchange for renovating the building— the apartment upstairs, the ground-floor to accommodate a business. And he'll pay you to manage the building as well as cover the costs of renovation. I know that's not what you had in mind, but you might want to think it over."

"No. I mean, I don't need to think about it. That would work for me, provided we have a contract guaranteeing my place there for a decent length of time and the right of first refusal should he decide to sell."

"I'll talk to Mr. Rossi and get back to you."

On her way to the cave, Franniemarie passed the lady in the aqua slicker. Neither acknowledged the other. The children were not at the beach. Today, her cave meditation was a plea that Mr. Rossi would not change his mind.

At noon she met Theresa McCracken, the published author, at a small café in Waldport. Over a crisp salad they talked writing, books, and the strangeness of truth. Before they parted, the dark haired, engaging author had signed her book. Franniemarie wondered if the self-assurance and ease with which Theresa held herself came from being published or if she'd always been that way.

Feeling empty, Franniemarie drove to SMOKIN' JOAN'S. As usual, the shop was buzzing with customers. Joan greeted her with a smile. "Bout time you showed up. I've been calling you for two days."

"Not like I haven't called you."

"Hey, girl, check out your rocks, then we can catch up.'

The rumble of the tumblers greeted Franniemarie before she opened the garage door. She washed the bag of rocks she'd collected since she last changed out the canisters, placed them in a new canister, dated the tag on top and then added it to the cans rolling on the belts. *Four more days and I'll be able to take that first batch out."* Anticipation of the pleasure that she would find in looking at the finished rocks filled her body with a smile.

When she returned to the shop, Joan was yet in the midst of talking to her people. "I'll call you tonight."

*****

Before the sun rose to welcome a new day, anxiety woke Franniemarie. *I need to go to the cave. But if I go to the cave, the lawyer might call. And if he called, then I'd miss him. If I go to the cave worrying about missing this call; going to the cave will bring me no peace.*

Slipping out of bed she headed for the kitchen, bare feet complaining all the way. The floors were cold. She checked the tide table: low tide 8:20 a.m. The clock on the stove read 6:34. *If I leave now, I can be back before 8.*

Under a cold, flat grey, predawn sky Franniemarie scrambled down the short path. In the distance the ocean called, and the nearer she came to the beach the faster her heart beat—beating beneath the waves crashing against her beloved rocks. By the time she reached the cave, she welcomed its coolness.

Breathless, she hardly knew where to begin, hardly knew what she wanted. *Please, oh please,* she began. *I need this place. I need a place I can make my own. I need to live in my color, in my cherished music. I, like my aunt, need a place with color and sound, a space that speaks of grace and beauty. Only there can I find peace enough to still the inner noise that drowns out the voice in that part of me that can tell me who I am—why I am. I need to know that place won't be taken away from me, at least not because of human vagaries. Oh, please, let me have this one thing before I die.* Tears, first formed in her heart, coursed down Franniemarie's cheeks as she began a sound mantra that transported her on an inner journey through the ocean, past the sea lions, whales, porpoises, giant squid, schools of fish and islands of plankton, then deeper and deeper until she slammed into a wall so dark it blinded her, then shot her to a place as calm as the eye of a hurricane.

Driving back to the cabin, she felt more blank than empty, as if erased. She did not return to her aunt's material until after she'd made a pot of tea and eaten a light but leisurely breakfast. And when she did, she did so reluctantly.

"There is, of course, that peculiar glandular imbalance that impels me to "save the human race". It is, I am sure, accentuated by emotional disturbances that tend to increase the glandular misbehavement. I've known rare brief intervals of peace of mind and emotion. Once, I took thyroid extract and became sleepily disinterested in anything but sunshine and myself. Had I felt emotionally secure and well liked, I wouldn't be emotionally disturbed and insecure.

"My family started saying I was crazy when I was six. My aunt dumped her responsibility for me on that theory, instead of facing squarely the fact that she was so lazy she walled me up by punishing me for the slightest sign of temper without discovering or addressing its cause. I claim that I am not crazy, my people are vicious. I am not insane.

"If I can get some of the troubles that distress me into the form of sensible questions, I'll find a reliable psychiatrist and I'll go until I get this thing straightened out. The next one won't tell me I'm normal and need to get away from my family and marry. I'm in serious trouble, as serious as if I needed surgical care."

Oh, Auntie, poor Auntie. Auntie.

"I suppose I would have killed Gill eventually for insisting he'd prevent me from divorcing him, but at the time it seemed easier to fix up the house on Walnut St."

Be that as it may dear, it appears to me, you still felt the need to have him put down. Franniemarie paddled into the kitchen, scooped out a cantaloupe, arranged it in bite sized pieces, then served it to herself with green tea. Sipping the tea, she read on.

"Maybe, after all, I don't need a psychiatrist. Life makes a series of interlocking patterns. Begin with my father whom I have always pretended to love, I disliked him because I felt that he had done me injury... a graver injury than my poor heart yearning for pinks."

"In my voice the hysteria is there all the time—and a panicky sense that I can never make myself understood. The quiet low tones of my voice are really a tense, desperate, attempt to control my voice. Sometimes I slip and the hysterical panic lifts my voice until I grab at it and stop. Actually breaking off in the middle of what I'm saying— snatching at a place in the sentence that could sound like a period. So the sentence sometimes is very different than what I was really saying. The sentence ends, snapped off short without a lowering of my voice."

Oh Auntie, perhaps I'm like that, too. Sometimes I'm out of control. For me it happens most when I find myself talking, and I am too loud and I've gone on past the listener's tolerance. I can't seem to stop myself. And, like you, there's that something else, some blame laid against the world for everything that happens—some refusal to take responsibility for my role in shaping my life. There are times when I think someone has done me an evil and I stew and stew and stew over it.

The sun cast low, slanted shadows through the west window. Franniemarie took the dishes into the kitchen and checked the time, 5:10. *Another day, another no call, another Friday night. I'll bet the Triad Gallery is still open.* She dialed Joan's number. No answer. *Oh, well.*

*****

When Franniemarie drove up to the gallery, to her delight a large sandwich board proclaimed the opening of a Kirk Jonasson show. Inside, the building was as exciting as its exterior. The undulating walls provided wonderful space for a wide variety of art forms; fine jewelry, Shaklho's sculptures fabricated out of pleated, pinched and stitched hand painted silk and window screen, bronze sculptures, sculptures made of seaweed and beach driftwood—huge organic structures that both stimulated and soothed—and more, so much more. *Bull whip kelp! That's the stuff neither Tempe nor I knew. Thank you, Ursula Dittl. For all I know, I could have spent the rest of my life with that slice of unanswered question lurking in the dark recesses of my mind. I can't wait to tell Tempe.*

Franniemarie accepted a glass of red wine, and then placed a few grapes and water crackers, topped with squares of cheese, on a napkin. She overheard a couple of fellows bemoaning the fact they couldn't find space to build a pottery. Franniemarie excused herself and asked how she could reach them. She told them that she might know of a place in Newport that might be available in a couple of months. She promised to let them know if her desired transaction was successful, then turned to Kirk Jonasson's work. He was an artist using a camera for brush, and trash as his model. Franniemarie was fascinated by the transformation of his subjects from objects abandoned in disdain into objects of drama and beauty. In one piece, the sheer power of a centered, rusting-red door on an aging white boxcar sidetracked beneath white clouds floating across a blue sky held her captive.

A fine guitarist playing cowboy tunes drew her into another room. When he began to play *I Ride an Old Paint,* Franniemarie could not resist singing along. Soon a slender woman with black hair down to her waist added her voice to the mix. Behind her a full-throated tenor joined the chorus. At song's end, the room erupted in a cacophony of clapping, laughter, cheers and calls for more. Franniemarie turned to the tenor and was taken aback. Yves was smiling at her. "It would appear we have more in common than a delight in rocks and poetry."

The woman with the hair tapped Franniemarie on the shoulder. Yves stepped back in a move that welcomed her, and set Franniemarie at ease. "You guys are great."

"You're not so shabby yourself," Franniemarie replied.

"Hey, we're casting for a show at Newport. Why don't the two of you audition?"

"I haven't done a play in years."

"Ditto, the only play I was ever cast in was *Our Town* … High school … Bit part," Yves took on an "ah shucks" attitude.

"I'm Terry Schmittroth," the woman swung her hair over her shoulder as she extended her hand to Franniemarie. "But everyone here calls me Sweet Cakes. Old theater major, aren't you?"

"How'd you know?" *Theater was so long ago, another life, really, hardly an option for a woman on call for pulling calves and hauling grain.*

"That old *je ne sais quoi*." Turning to Yves, she gushed, "And you, what I wouldn't have given to play Emily to your George."

The twinkle Franniemarie saw in his eye when she'd turned around was gone.

"I played the milkman."

"Whatever," Sweet Cakes rummaged in her purse, "Here's my card."

Yves looked at Franniemarie, raised an eyebrow, "Interesting proposition, that."

"Have you seen Jonasson's show yet?"

Together, they refilled their glasses and walked into the next room.

"It's amazing how much energy that man pulls out of decay," Yves opined.

Franniemarie nodded, "He extracts color and line in a way that reminds me of something Oriental."

"Speaking of Oriental, there's a fine Japanese Restaurant in Seal Rock. Want to go?"

His question woke a conflict in Franniemarie that left her speechless and light-headed.

"It's just supper," Yves gently reassured her.

For God's sake, Frannie, like he says, it's just supper. What the hell's wrong with me? My car is here. I have to drive it back. Why this displaced tangle of fear and longing?

"I've never eaten Japanese. I'd like that."

They were seated in a private space, all burnished wood turned golden by the light of a paper lantern. Yves selected their supper and ordered a bottle of plum wine.

Franniemarie began to relax.

"So, why have you been avoiding me?" Yves' smile was pleasant indicating the question was straight and not complicated by overtones of accusation or prejudgment.

Franniemarie could think of no reasonable explanation. She countered, "What prompts you to care?"

"There's an aura about you that fascinates me. I'm intrigued. I'd like to know more."

"You may not like what you find."

"Perhaps, however, isn't that the chance the adventurer takes, walking into uncharted tomorrows? And I suspect you are also an adventurer."

"Perhaps, however, my adventure is mostly an inward journey. I keep trying to keep the exterior under control. I don't think I can manage both."

"I won't hurt you," he said.

"You can't know that."

"I can promise. And I keep my promises."

"Only a fool makes promises."

"God forbid I be a fool. I take back my offer," Yves poured more wine and proposed a toast to a tomorrow without promises.

Between bites of foods, like none she'd tasted before, they explored bits and pieces on the surfaces of their lives. Yves had been a biologist in a lab in California. His life had become so damned predictable it was deadly. Four years earlier Yves quit his job, headed for France and ended up spending two years living with relatives on his mother's side. After the war, his father had married his mother in Lyons and brought her back to the States. She would never talk about either the Continent or her family. "She would never even speak French. So, of course, anything French captured my imagination. I studied it in high school and college. When I got to France, no one understood me. It took two years of immersion just to be able to get by. Even now I couldn't carry on a philosophical conversation in that language."

Franniemarie talked about her days at the University of Chicago, where she majored in theater and literature. She did not tell him she'd killed her husband, didn't even mention she'd been married. And she was glad he hadn't asked. For all she knew, he'd had a wife and killed her.

Between them lay two unexamined lifetimes, yet when their fingers met on the surface of the table, electricity visibly snapped—streaks of neon white, aqua, red, and green conjoining feminine to masculine.

Before she entered her car, she turned to him and they came together pressing their length against each in a mindless aching passion that burned the chill off the night. Wordless, they broke away and returned to their respective worlds.

CHAPTER 19

WHAT THE DOC could not have known was that Cricket would develop an infection that he'd have to beat before he could see his way home. Ten days would turn into weeks, and the weeks would turn into months—nearly three months mending in Mother Hall's Rest Home in Kearney. What Cricket could not know was he'd spend the greater portion of that time chained to a kid younger than his son, one Private Peter Whitaker. According to the private, he was "Ace" to his friends, and Cricket was no friend of his. This whining army grunt was laid up with God only knew what. Claimed his legs wouldn't hold him, that the fuckin' military put him here, a flaming liberal who seemed to think he could change the world by shouting at the radio, hollering at the TV. Worse, the damn kid held the controls and was not about to give them up without a fight. No folksy farm and ranch programs, no fine country western music, and definitely no more Rush in the morning for Cricket.

PRESIDENT BUSH SAYS HE WON'T BE SUCKED INTO A CIVIL WAR IN IRAQ.

"Damn right you won't, Lard Ass," Peter Whitaker shouted at the radio.

BRUTAL REPRESSION OF THE KURDS.

"Got his fuckin' oil tied up when we kicked ass in Kuwait. We don't give a rat's ass about the Kurds."

A holding pen. This place is nothing but a goddamn holding pen. Ten days in the hospital, and now this. Bad enough Frannie's gone. Pru Ellen? Off on some damn cruise with her tap-dancing troupe and never even mentioned it before she left. Brooks says she told him, but she didn't tell me. It's the shits when dames old enough to be your mother start acting like teenagers. AUDIT UNCOVERS SUPERFUND ABUSES.

"Take note, old man, Bush don't give a fuck about that."

… THE GOVERNMENT MAY BE REIMBURSING CONTRACTORS FOR MILLIONS OF DOLLARS IN QUESTIONABLE EXPENDITURES.

"Count on it. The rich get richer and the rest of us are just a bunch of lazy cruds."

Beyond worse was Cricket's inability to control his life. His hip lay limp while he waited for the infection to respond to the antibiotics, waited for the healing to begin. And his room-mate, the SOB, no 5 a.m. weather report for him, no, he had to listen to the *World News and Report* on NPR as if the BBC were privy to information KRBN didn't have. He could handle the classical music all right; living with Franniemarie, he could hardly escape it. But this guy listened to opera, listened to opera on Saturdays *and liked it*.

… TO PRESSURE COL. MOAMMAR GADHAFI TO HAND OVER SUSPECTS IN THE BOMBING OF PAN

AM FLIGHT 103. COL. GADHAFI REPLIED. LIBYA KNEELS TO NO ONE BUT ALLAH.

"You tell 'em Gadhaf'! See where it gets ya!"

CLINTON RECEIVES AFL-CIO BACKING. PRESIDENT BUSH, ON VACATION IN WEST VIRGINIA, TAKES A POWER WALK.

"That murdering bastard."

"Why do you listen to that crap? Just sets off your mouth, not to mention what it's doing to your body."

"You just don't get it, old man. He's our Commander in Chief. He didn't just nuke the enemy; he nuked our own troops."

"For Christsake, Whitaker, just shut the damn thing off. Tune to something a little lighter. Try Country Western."

The room went silent, momentarily stunning Cricket. *Actually Frannie would like this crazy ranting guy who lived on a steady diet of highfalutin clap-trap and la-de dah music. She'd find him exotic with his dark skin and strange tastes. If Frannie were here, she'd pump him for all he'd seen serving with the military. She wouldn't let him go off on his indecipherable tangents. No, she'd make him slow down and fill in the spaces. By the time she was done with him, he'd damn well know what the hell was wrong with his poor body, and his mind would have been pushed through a wringer.*

God, I wish she'd come home. What she doesn't know is, I do know all about her. I wish we'd talked. I always shied away from her when she started to bring up her past—who she was before us. I knew it hurt, and I knew she didn't understand. Ah, hell! I didn't understand, so what good would jawin' about it have done. I need her now. All those years she needed me, now I need her. Shit! Get over it. The whole family's crazy. She thinks I'm dead. She's gone.

"What you don't understand, old man, is this, Kuwait is nothing but sand and oil. Desert Storm was nothing but oil. That and the sea ports had everything to do with Iraq's invasion. Hell, Kuwait was once part of Iraq. It was all about the oil and the money for Saddam. It was all about oil and money for Bush and his cronies. They'll make it big so long as the good ole US of A controls it."

"Cut the crap, Whitaker. It's not all about Bush. He had a Congress behind him. He had Europe behind him. If it's all about oil, what did they have to gain? I don't give a rap about your being over there. Would have been better if you'd have stayed home and grown up. Would have been better if you understood what a great country you were raised in." Cricket turned his face to the wall.

"Sorry, old man, it's just—today all I see is the children, all those dead children—them and my own deformed son. If I hadn't been there, my head would be where yours is."

Nurse Marjorie came in dispensing meds and forced good cheer. "Quicker you mend, quicker we can get you on your feet."

Cricket stifled a groan. *What would this peaches and cream lady with her fine-fresh-from-the-beauty-parlor hair and manicured nails know about mending? Any other year, by now Frannie would be all tan and tangled hair from working the cows and planting the garden. Now that's a sight that could mend a man.*

CHAPTER 20

THE MORNING DAWNED bitter cold. Franniemarie would have called Joan and Templeton, but she did not want to tie up the phone. *Cricket would have said, "If it's important, they'll call back." He's right. Eventually they'll call back, but I want the information as soon as possible. Cricket always said I had no patience, and again Cricket is right. Patience, like compromise, are two notions I haven't a use for. The act of being patient leaves my mouth feeling full of sawdust, and compromise guarantees everyone's dissatisfaction. The only solution is to find a pail to jump in that pleases both parties.*

She gave herself up to hot chocolate, warm fire and her aunt. "I know my father is associated with what happened so long ago that I don't remember completely, but I do remember that I was belittled and shamed—I remember that I could understand what they said, but I hadn't words to defend myself."

Franniemarie heard Yves loading her box with wood. For a moment she hesitated, but then she opened the door. "Hello Yves."

Yves smiled and turned to bring the extra armload of wood he'd been leaving her each morning.

"I really appreciate the extra wood. Do you have time for a cup of coffee?"

Yves kept his distance. "Not today. Weekend guests are already arriving. Today I work late. Perhaps tomorrow."

"Perhaps tomorrow," Franniemarie went inside. Shaking, she leaned against the door. *For Christsake, you old fool. This is not a time for such nonsense.* Disgusted, she plunked herself into her chair and resumed reading.

"Dad refused to buy me a tricycle; I was taught to sew instead. I couldn't make a fuss about it because I learned early I would never get anything at all if I didn't accept no.

He refused to buy me a nice doll, although I asked Santa Claus for it every Christmas for 5 yrs. He always bought me a celluloid doll for one dollar on the grounds that he was always going to treat all three of us alike. He wouldn't buy me skates because my ankles were so slender—he said he was afraid I'd break them, but he didn't worry when I climbed on garages and tall fences. He wouldn't buy me a bicycle for the same reason as skates."

I remember, I must have been five or six because we were still living in the back of Mrs. Riggs' house, I don't remember what I'd done, but Mother said, "You've been so bad I'll show you what you're not getting for Christmas," and I remember the beautiful box she opened and the doll with real hair and eyes that opened and closed and teeth that looked like real ones. I remember the doll's perfect fingers and black patent leather Mary Janes. She was so beautiful in her pink organdy dress and white stockings; looking at her, I could hardly breathe. That Christmas I was given a plastic doll that was so ugly; come Spring, I buried it in Mrs. Rigg's flower bed.

"For six months I saved dog care articles out of the Sunday School paper and pasted them neatly with pictures in a pretty scrapbook and put in extra pages for pictures of my dog. But when Christmas came, there wasn't any dog. Instead, I was given a canary in a cage, and I was glad when it died."

When I was ten I asked for a dog and got a stuffed one. In all fairness, we were living in an apartment building. A dog was out of the question. Someone did give me a Guinea pig. I had it for over a year. One day, I found it was missing. I'm not sure why, but I always suspected mother killed it. Perhaps because it happened not that long after she'd locked Harry in the bathroom.

"He bought me a sewing machine, but never noticed that I needed glasses. He was always talking about getting me through school fast so I could teach and put my sisters through college and then we'd all work, and vacations we'd go on to Europe. He was always talking about how much he'd sacrificed for us, but he wouldn't put me in an orphanage as I asked him to do. My sisters wanted to go too because we were always changing housekeepers, and we never got along with any of them."

I wore hated, brown laced shoes. In my case, it was because my ankles were weak and my feet pigeon-toed. Strangely, my mother would buy expensive shoes for herself, but wouldn't pay for braces on my teeth. Beyond those hideous shoes, all the money my mother spent on clothes didn't put any on my back. By fourth grade I was already wearing her castoffs, and on those occasions that she did buy anything for me then she bought it in sizes so large I threaded twine through the belt loops to hold up the pants, and by the time I'd grown into them they were nearly worn out.

But I did save half the money for a bicycle from little jobs I did for an elderly couple who lived two doors down. And she did pay the other half. Her lovers bought me skates, and sometimes nice clothes.

"He'd get mad just before dinner and wouldn't come to the table until he was coaxed and the food was cold. He did it again on my birthday and I said to my sisters; 'I'm hungry, let's eat.' So we did and he came fast enough."

My mother did weird things. Once, in junior high, I took a sewing class. For the class project, I bought a pattern and aqua corduroy for a circular skirt with money I'd earned babysitting. When she saw it, she screamed at me, "You dumb little bitch! You don't know shit about sewing. What a waste of money." And all the while she was screaming, she was ripping the fabric apart. I remember I had to buy more material and didn't have enough money to make the circular. I ended up making a straight brown twill skirt and I always hated it.

How could we have had so many similar experiences? Excepting for the sexual abuse. After all, I was never abused like that. But the rest? We're a generation apart and I certainly never grew up knowing her.

"He was always saying he would never marry and how he and I would always be pals. I'd teach and we'd travel. So I promised I'd never marry."

Not one of Francis Tourneau's girls had any business reproducing. Not them, nor I.

Franniemarie pulled out her notebook and began. POEM: Forget time travel / Find air streams / where bone brittle / leaves bruise. / Fearlessly face ice / banks—ice ridges. / If ice shards skin, / float on blood. / blood will nourish / skin will heal.

INDULGING: As if by this excess feeding / I can fill the void / A frenzied lifetime / feeding, foraging / tokens of love.

Cumulus City in the Sky, random patterns moving toward order, order is good, we yearn for predictability, the unpredictable rejuvenates, the angled spar propels us into the color of our perception. Cumulus City / painted sky dream, / brilliant white, day dream / illuminating night.

Franniemarie ripped the pages, crumpled them, fed them to the fire, and went to bed only to wake at 4 a.m. Unable to go back to sleep, she gravitated to the kitchen, took note that morning's low tide came at 10.48 a.m., flipped a Chopin CD into the player, heated a cup of milk, added a dash of nutmeg, and then restarted the fire. *If I leave by nine then I could make it to the caves before low tide. Yesterday I stayed home listening for the phone that never rang. I can't spend my life that way.* Knowing sleep wouldn't come, she returned to the exploration of her aunt.

"At least, I am getting some of the threads untangled in my mind. Why didn't my father sue those women who accused me of being my father's mistress for slander?"

The sound of Yves loading Franniemarie's wood box gave her pause. *I will not go out and make a fool of myself again. Blame it on the plum wine. Plum wine be damned.* For all her bluster she could only stare at the page without comprehension. When he knocked on her door, she needed to steady herself before rising. She had no will to stay his call.

"You'll have to come back later." She tried to act casual. "The coffee isn't ready yet."

"Actually, I was hoping you'd allow me to take you to Huckleberry Hill. It's going to be a beautiful day, and the agate hunting should be splendid."

"I thought you had to work today."

"That's what's on the schedule. However, I'm not the employee in charge here. I traded six hours out of the middle of the day so we could be on the beach during low tide. It's not eight yet. I don't have to be back until two. I didn't say anything yesterday because I wasn't sure I could make it happen. Do come. We can pick up my dog on the way over."

Franniemarie threw a couple of apples, a block of cheddar cheese, and a small box of crackers into a canvas bag, grabbed her windbreaker, and was out the door before Yves finished putting away the wood wagon.

Both paths down to the ocean from Huckleberry Hill were steep. Yves suggested they take the northern route. His dog Fang, an ancient Manchester terrier, zipped on ahead. Yves frequently turned to Franniemarie, extending a hand whenever the path became rugged. Below, fingers of rock laced the beach, black on tan. On the beach, the sand was hard and walking easy. Yves pointed to a massive ocean-pummeled outcropping. "By the time we get there, the water will be low enough we can hunt the mighty agate."

Dodging outcroppings, they worked their way swiftly across the beach. On reaching the near side of the rock, Franniemarie began the hunt darting in and out of waves, snatching treasures from the ocean when she could, while Yves took a plastic sour cream container out of his backpack and filled it with bottled water for his little dog companion. Soon Fang joined Franniemarie, grabbing rocks and dropping them on high ground. Amused, Yves watched the two of them. Then he calmly stepped into the pool and picked up a beautiful green rock that looked more like jade than jasper.

Three hours later, halfway up Huckleberry Hill, on a massive flat rock they sat listening to the ocean, Franniemarie feeding Yves fruit, cheese, and crackers, while Yves fed her bottled water and chocolate. Exhausted, Fang stretched out beside them. Franniemarie intently watched the ocean where not an hour ago they had played. It was as if that place had never existed. Then she felt Yves looking at her and became self-conscious. She turned her head, "What?"

"You're a beautiful woman Franniemarie Martin."

"Oh, Yves, what good is that?"

"The good is in the pleasing of the eye. Isn't that good enough?"

Franniemarie stared at Yves' long slender fingers. They were restful, and she found them beautiful, and she wanted to pick up his hand and wrap her mouth around each finger, one at a time. Smiling, she stood. "Well, it sure isn't enough to keep me warm. Race you to the car."

Yves turned up the heat, dropped off the dog, and let Franniemarie out at her cottage, but not before he'd turned to her, slipped his long slender fingers along her chin and tipped her face toward his, not before their lips met in a kiss so tender that Franniemarie held back tears.

Jesus, Martha, he's almost young enough to be my son. What in hell am I doing? Clutching a jade jasper, she watched Yves drive away before she entered the cabin. Absentmindedly, she pulled up another journal and sank into her favorite chair.

*****

"I think they are gossiping about me. She keeps answering all my questions with a parrot-like response, "Nobody told me to say it. Nobody told me to say it." But she's saying things she never learned at home. Things she's too young to know. Putting words together she's too young to understand."

At least Brooks is normal, seems normal anyway. Bad as I was, he doesn't seem to have suffered so much as Dorianna, my aunts, or me. I think that's only thanks to Cricket. Feeling estranged, Franniemarie put the piece aside and spent the rest of the evening chatting on the phone with Tempe. Tempe planned to visit her the following weekend. Franniemarie talked on and on about poetry, her aunt, the rocks, and the ocean. She did not tell her about Yves.

Sunday morning, at 6 a.m., Franniemarie woke. *Too early for the beach, Too late too for sleep.* She snapped on the bed lamp and curled into another of her aunt's journals.

"Now that I've written down all these things, I'm beginning to forget them. They grow fuzzy at the edges and then they slip out of my mind like the dates for luncheon and people's phone numbers and the due dates on library books and addresses. Maybe, after a while, I won't remember any of the ugliness.

I wonder if the police would be able to catch a person who murdered me. Not if the neighbors protected the murderer. But the person most likely to benefit from my death is the person whose secrets I've kept. It's dangerous to keep secrets.

Over and over and over again people have said I'm crazy, or threatened me with incarceration. So I built a sanctuary of dreams, of the flittering turn of the leaves on the trees in the wind, the mellow color of a house wall, blue sky and the shapes of clouds and the soft diffusing that delicately transmuted the landscape."

The phone rang, startling Franniemarie out of her aunt's world. Eagerly she jumped up to answer, only to discover the caller had a wrong number.

"Father's sister, Fern, asked, 'How could it hurt Dory if you were talked about?' Good Lord! I won't have her in my house. She said Dad slept with his housekeepers. I could forgive what she said about me and her husband on the ground that he is a conceited fool, but when she inferred that my relationship with my father was the same as with her husband, I was just a child at that time, well that's too much."

Franniemarie heard footsteps on the porch. Quickly she slipped on her shoes and opened the door. Disappointed, she smiled and wished the young teenager who was filling her wood box good morning.

*****

Hunched against a cold wind, Franniemarie walked from Ona Beach to the cave. Beneath overcast skies the birds gathered and flew just as they did on any other day. At last, Franniemarie stood inside the cave, calmed by the sound of water dropping down its walls. *Why don't we take responsibility for ourselves; why don't we see how we push our fate onto the actions of others?* Franniemarie's song was stronger than the wind, louder than the waves, more rhythmic than the phases of the moon. The silence after her song ended was filled with an understanding. *For some, to recognize one's hand in their fate leaves them with no way out. For some, a second step that might lead to a stable life of some mental comfort is inconceivable. In that case, the only way out is suicide. Aunt Dorien chose life.*

The wind pushed against her all the way back to Ona Beach, but she didn't get warm till after the car engine heated and she had turned on the blower. On reaching Waldport, she drove to "Smokin' Joan's", washed her first batch of rocks, and put them in the tumbler for their fourth and last tumbling with soap. Today the shop was quiet, offering the two friends a chance to share a cup of coffee and visit. They talked of the rocks in the soap tumbling that would be finished tomorrow, the tobacconist's business, of Franniemarie's hopes for the property in Newport, and of days long past. Joan said the next day they had an invitation for lattés at the home of a friend who lived near Ona Beach. Franniemarie did not mention Yves.

That evening, she wrote *A Poem For Living*: Carrion clings like mistletoe / to deadwood thoughts of virgin snow / Narcissus flesh of twilight lingers / despite decay's effacing fingers. / And moonlilies 'neath a midnight sky / ride truth so charged it's changed to lie. / While doctrine hunters scavenge bone / like waters rippling over stone / Dharma's green-leafed truth makes sorrow / health begins in bitter yarrow. / So rookery rascals take ye heed / this sun's but painted golden weed. / Before death makes my head a pillow, / I'll carve my flute from fruit once willow.

Franniemarie woke, hungry, cold, stiff—cramped in a tightly coiled fetal position on the couch. When she turned on the table lamp, she noticed her notebook and pencil on the floor. Puzzled, she picked it up and read the poem she'd written hours earlier. She did not remember writing the poem. In fact, the last thing she remembered was leaving

SMOKIN' JOAN'S. She reread the poem. *This is strange. It's my handwriting, but I don't write that way. I never write in rhyme. I strive for rhythm, but never so formal. So what did I do, besides write this atypical poem?*

Sometimes, post adolescence, Franniemarie would become lost and then, usually some hours after she was supposed to be at a specific place, she'd come into herself. Often it was something as simple as having promised to meet a friend in the morning, then losing the memory till afternoon. Her friends found it disconcerting, especially when they'd talked to her as recently as a half hour before they'd agreed to meet. Everyone, including Franniemarie, chalked it up to being absentminded. After all, she could always remember what she'd done between times. This was the first time she was aware of not knowing.

4 a.m. Franniemarie yawned, spread tuna on a piece of whole wheat toast, sliced an apple, poured a glass of milk, ate, brushed her teeth, and crawled naked back into bed.

9 a.m. The ringing phone brought her to her feet. Grabbing her robe, she raced into the kitchen. It was the lawyer. Mr. Rossi was willing to make his offer contingent on a five-year exchange if she was still interested.

Shit! "Yes. Yes. I could be there by ten. Eleven would be better. Good, I'll be there at eleven."

Joan called before she'd climbed into the shower. "Just to remind you we've a date this afternoon."

They agreed to meet in the Ona Beach parking lot at two o'clock. Franniemarie promised she wouldn't forget. Drying her hair, she wondered how she, absentminded as she was, could promise anyone anything. As quickly as the thought came it was then gone. Minutes later, while headed out the door, a piece of paper placed between door and frame fell.

She picked it up, walked to the car unfolded it, read it while starting the car.

Dear Franniemarie,

I'm so sorry to have missed you last night. I waited till after seven, then went to dinner with friends as we'd planned. They were disappointed not to meet you.

Until I hear from you.

Sincerely,

Yves

Franniemarie looked around. She saw neither Yves nor his car. *Shit! Well at least I know where I wasn't last night.* With an angry flick of her hand she dismissed her tears. *You haven't time for this crap; you're an old woman, not some teenage bimbo.* When she glanced in the rearview mirror, the face she met was hardly that of an old woman, but then it wasn't the face of a bimbo either. She smiled. *It's the face of a woman about to acquire a place of her own.*

CHAPTER 21

LILIANNA FOUND HER mother at the bar, trim, aging, but beautifully coiffed. "Sorry I'm late."

"When were you ever on time?" Annamarie's voice carried the mute of alcohol across her tongue.

Oh, boy. Lilianna followed her mother to their table. *Not to despair, the juice might just loosen her lip.*

Annamarie ordered them each a sherry, leaned back, and launched into a rapid patter about the flight, and the friends she left behind.

Lilianna interrupted. "It's my birthday, Annamarie. Just once, I ask you to give me what I want."

"And what might that be?" Annamarie asked with mock amusement.

"Look. I know about you and Johannes Sveen. I've read all the news reports. They're leaving something out."

"What makes you think so?"

"For one thing, you could handle any wheel. The papers say you couldn't and that's how he went over."

Annamarie, snorted. "Damn little you know about it. In a squall like that many a hardened salt has lost the wheel."

"That may be true, but you let them think you knew nothing about sailing. And that leads me to wonder what really happened."

"Well, aren't we the little detective?"

Lilianna did not respond.

The waiter brought in plates of lofty chef's salads and an Iron horse white wine that Annamarie had ordered. Lilianna began to eat. Annamarie sipped her wine.

"On board, Johannes Sveen always treated me as if I were a moron. He had no idea I knew a thing about sailing. That afternoon the ocean was fairly calm. We were drinking gin and tonics, and Johannes was happy playing seaman when a stiff breeze came up across the starboard bow." The room disappeared as Annamarie became lost in her story. "In the distance, the sky was dark and squally. You know how hard it is to judge these winds. Anyway, we watch the storm and of course Johannes, big shot that he is, dallies overlong, testing the *Lyckodam*'s agility. Then, *wham*! It's upon us. Johannes orders me to hold the wheel. Grinning, he says 'Just keep us on course.'"

Annamarie sipped her wine. "Of course, I smiled to cover my irritation. I did know how to trim a sail, still do. However, I'd be damned if I'd let him know. You better believe, I had one hell of a surprise in store for him. I held that wheel steady, holding on a starboard tack and watched the wind separate his fine blond hair. The *Lyckodam* shuddered, and so he jumped up on the cabin trunk to loosen the main halyard and let the mains'l down part way. The wind was stiff and I held tight, one eye on the compass and the other on him. In no time, flat he jumped down, tied off the reef points, and leapt back on the cabin trunk to winch down the halyard and tie it off. He was fast, fit, and handsome. Next, he headed for the cockpit and reset the mains'l, and I was honestly fighting to hold the course. In spite of my effort the *Lyckodam* began to spin, and the squall was upon us. We had too much sail. The wheel had become most ineffective. It knocked her over and, when she bobbed up, the wind spilled out of her sails. Johannes was screaming. "Hold the course, damn it! I gotta douse the genoa, put it in the bag. Put up the working gib."

Silently the waiter refilled Annamarie's glass. "He maintained a precarious balance on the bow, had the genny about a third of the way down when I let her fall off to port. He swore at me, a glorious gust of wind hit and then she heeled over. Johannes lost his balance." Smiling, Annamarie closed her eyes. "I do believe I heard his skull crack when he went down." She lifted an eyebrow. "Well, perhaps that's only in my imagination. What I probably heard was the sound of Johannes' cursing. I corrected her course, obediently she hardened up, and we sped on by."

"We sailed, the *Lyckodam* and I, for what seemed quite some distance. The squall had blown through, leaving me exhilarated. Now it was just the sounds of the ocean, the genoa luffing in the wind, and me in charge. I thought I might tie off the wheel and handily reduce sail. I thought, 'I'll tie a line to the wheel, release the main sheet and let it go slack. She'll wallow in the water and I can go forward and finish hauling down the genoa. But no, I corrected my thought, then they'll suspect I know something about the task, they'll know I am responsible. No—better to continue driving on the mains'l till we reach the ship channel. Sometime later, I threw out the ring-buoy—it tracked behind like a faithful friend."

Annamarie returned to the present, looked at Lilianna with surprise, as if she'd just appeared. Sipping her sherry, she continued. "I remember thinking I was glad he didn't let Herreshoff put in one of those new-fangled radios. Even if he had, even though I can sail, I probably couldn't have operated it."

"The papers reported you were picked up by a fishing vessel. You lit a flare. Yes?"

Annamarie laughed. "They always said I was at my best in *The White Lily*—little do they know."

Annamarie began eating with relish. "You're the only one who ever figured it out, the only one who knows. Well, except for Solvieg. When she confronted me, asking how things were with myself and her husband, I told her I was pregnant, that I had asked Johannes to make it good, that he'd laughed at me. He said I could never prove it. She knew him. She knew that was the sort of stance he would take. She offered me a good sum, as well as her personal doctor, if I'd get rid of it. That's just what she said, 'get rid of it'. I got hot under the collar and gave her what for. She had the gall to say, 'so what's the problem? It's not as if you haven't done it before?' I let her know I wouldn't have done it if the studio hadn't forced me. They insisted, even though Sterling wanted to marry me, Sweden was their idea not mine. Then Solvieg smiled and said, 'I understand you can sail. Perhaps we could help each other.'"

"So you killed him."

"Hardly. He killed himself. He was the one playing big shot, toying with the wind when he should have been trimming the sail." I'll admit I didn't help him out of the mess he made for himself. The waters were cold and he had been drinking, and I didn't throw out the life preserver until I was miles away. However, he chose to drink and play the smart guy. No, he has no one to blame but himself. Lilianna, he was the only man in my life."

"And Sedgwick?"

"Sedge was a damn fool. I don't know what I was thinking. He was nothing. Believe me, Johannes was the only man I ever loved. Oh, in high school there was David. He was my first fiancé. Of course, I've always known it was his good grooming that made him attractive to me. That was before I knew what he was like."

"So you used me to blackmail her for more."

"Lilianna, I did no such thing! I was 29. This was my only chance to have a child. Dorien and Nannette both had children, and they were raising theirs alone. So why shouldn't I? Solvieg seemed to agree with me. She promised to split the estate if I never told a soul you were his child."

Annamarie signaled the waiter to remove their plates. "I'm curious, when did you become so sure he was your father?"

"When I saw his picture in a news clipping."

"Oh, my, yes. By the time you were two and a half, or maybe three, it was obvious. Solvieg insisted it would not be prudent to have you around. That's why she paid for all those fancy private schools and camps you were so privileged to attend. She was bound to keep the gossip away from both you and her boys".

"Did Dorien kill her husband?"

"Oh no! She'd never do that. Much too timid. No. She got Clay to do it. She was just nuts about Clay, and he was keen on her. But after, he never wrote and when he got home from the war—he hardly spoke to her. In less than six weeks he'd married some vixen. You know the type, brassy-cute today, frumpy-dumpy tomorrow. Broke poor Dorien's heart." Annamarie tried to catch the attention of their waiter. "Would you like an after-dinner drink?"

After dinner drink? Sheesh it's lunch. Lilianna shook her head. "And what, pray tell, prompted you to name me Lilianna?

"I named you for my mother, whom I never knew and always longed for, and for myself in hopes that you would make me whole—because I loved the idea of you, and I wanted something of me to live on long after the canisters of film rotted. Besides, I was sure you'd be whole and healthy as all the rest of us weren't."

"Enough." Annamarie snapped her fingers and ordered chocolate silk for dessert. She fished a small box, embossed in gold foil and beribboned, from her purse. Intently, she watched her daughter slowly and carefully unwrap her gift.

On opening the box, Lilianna sucked in her breath. There lay a pair of earrings, diamonds set in platinum. Not just any diamonds. Each earring held three magnificent stones, a white half karat hugged the ear lobe, followed by a yellow three-quarter karat. A bold, sparkling, brown full karat weighted each bottom. They were set in a linking platinum rope that allowed them to swing like pendulums.

"Are you going to put them in your ears, or are you planning to spend the afternoon staring at them with your mouth open?"

Speechless, Lilianna slipped off her plain gold hoops and threaded in the diamonds.

"Ah, that's more like it. They suit you well, Lilianna. They were meant for you."

"Mother, you've always given me lovely presents. But this—this sharing." Tears coursed down her cheeks. "First, the truth about my father—I no longer know why it became so important to me. But it was, and now that I know—it's not—Annamarie, I recognize the earrings. I never saw *The White Lily*, but I did see the advertisements for it. You were wearing these earrings!"

"Yes, I was." Annamarie looked distant and dreamy. "Johannes gave them to me on my birthday the year we met." She looked across the table at Lilianna. "Now I give them to you."

"Forgive me, but I can't help asking—why? Why now?"

Annamarie took a deep breath. "Over the years, I've talked to Nannette. Not often. Just enough to reassure myself that, in spite of the many things I've done, I really wasn't like her—just enough to know the shameful way she's treated Franniemarie. I came to the understanding that it is not right to keep secrets from you. Unlike my sister, I didn't keep my secrets because I knew there is no statute of limitation on murder. I did it because I was afraid of you. I did it because I didn't want to lose your love."

Lilianna reached across the table and gently squeezed her mother's wrist. "Isn't it in the Bible, 'and the truth shall set you free'? Annamarie I shall never stop loving you." She did not add that she never knew she'd loved her mother till this moment.

Annamarie smiled. "Just remember you can't prove a thing. Just your word against mine, and we well know who'd win that one."

CHAPTER 22

WHEN FRANNIEMARIE SIGNED the papers at the lawyer's office, the lawyer told her Mr. Milner had agreed to work with her. Mr. Rossi had added him to his payroll. She needed to pick up the keys from Mr. Milner. Mr. Rossi's attorney walked her to the door.

Franniemarie ran up the steps to Mr. Milner's house. Breathlessly, she knocked on his door, waited and then knocked again, and again, and again. She walked around the house, peeking in the windows of his garage and his greenhouse. Mr. Milner was not home.

Deflated, she drove the main street, wandered into the "Ben Franklin" store. There she found a heavy, tall, cylindrical glass fish bowl. *Perfect for my rocks.* Before leaving Newport, she went back to Mr. Milner's house. He had not returned. She spent a couple of hours at the library, checked on Mr. Milner one more time, then headed to the Ona Beach parking lot to meet Joan.

High above the ocean, Franniemarie sat in Joan's friends' living room sipping a latté topped with whipped cream and eating a chocolate dipped biscotti that not one of the persons in that room had any business ingesting and not one of them had the moral fortitude to refuse. For a couple of hours she watched the waves, intrigued by the kaleidoscopic changes in light and motion. Behind her, Joan and three couples passed the time talking about a cruise from hell and the status of traffic ticketing on 101.

"You sure were quiet." Joan parked next to Franniemarie's car. "I understand your disappointment over the keys, but this really isn't like you."

"Joanie, your friends seem like very nice people. It's just— just I don't know how to talk to them. I've never been on a cruise, can't even imagine myself on one."

"You could have told them about your new place. They would have enjoyed that."

"I don't know. I'm sure you're right. I'm just in a strange space right now."

"Right now?" Joan laughed, "Try, when aren't you?"

Franniemarie laughed dutifully. "In that case, why are you surprised?"

Following Joan's car, she wondered how she could explain to Yves how she'd not only forgotten their dinner date, but she couldn't remember his asking her. When she reached Seal Rock she pulled into the Japanese Restaurant parking lot. Without deliberation, she purchased a couple bottles of plum wine at what she thought was an outrageous price.

Joan was in the garage when Franniemarie pulled up. Joan didn't ask her why she'd taken so long to get there, and Franniemarie was relieved not to have to explain herself.

Together, they pulled out her agates and marveled at their beauty.

When Franniemarie parked her car she saw Yves digging a flower bed across the green from her cabin. *Okay, lady, this is it. Be responsible. Do the honorable thing.* Walking toward him, she delighted in the quiet strength and simplicity of his repetitive motion, his total immersion in the act of setting his spade into the ground. His words echoed in her mind: "The best part of working here is that I'm always outdoors. I hope never to work inside again."

When she reached him he looked up and smiled, but he did not break rhythm.

"I'm sorry about last night."

Yves did not pause.

"Please, come see me after work. Please, let me explain—at least try to explain."

"I'll come. But I must warn you, I'll be hungry."

"I'll see what I can dig up." Franniemarie felt tears well, willed them back. "Thank you."

Yves nodded and kept on turning over the soil.

That evening, she shared with Yves the beginning of her polished rock collection with which she'd filled the bottom of her aquarium, shared with him peanut butter sandwiches, sliced apples, plum wine, shared with him what she knew of her aunt, her family, her fears and her search for understanding. That night she confessed to him her lapses—lapses she did not understand.

"Fugue state!" Yves interjected. "What you're experiencing is not related to memory or lack of it."

"Fugue state? What in hell's that?"

"A defense mechanism. It's related to multiple personality and split personality. It seems to be found in persons who have been battered, especially at a time before language is well developed. The abuse is usually sexual," he added softly.

Franniemarie bristled, "I've never been sexually abused. Never! However," she added, leaving off her hostile stance, "my mother did once cut me and leave me for dead." She refilled their glasses. "How do you know about this fugue state stuff?"

"My first lover, after his therapy sessions we would talk for hours. We shared so much: poetry, art, theater, hiking, and boating. We laughed at the same jokes, made fun of the same politicians, cried over the same movies. Most of all, we took care of each other. I think, if he had made it through his nightmare, we would still be with each other. It ended when he killed himself."

Franniemarie kissed the back of his hand and held it with both of hers. "I'm so sorry, Yves."

"That was a long time ago."

"I know about old wounds. Sometimes the pain returns as fresh as yesterday."

"After Alex, in my subsequent relationships, whether with men or women, something was always lacking. I guess that old saw 'you never forget your first love' holds."

Franniemarie opened the second bottle of plum wine. By morning, she'd confessed she was either married or a widow; however, whatever her status, she was determined not to return.

Yves promised he'd see her soon in Newport.

CHAPTER 23

"Dad. Dad." Cricket woke to his son's soft voice. "Sorry to wake you, but I had to come to town to get another bearing for the corn planter. Don't have much time, and I wanted to talk to you."

"Shoot."

"Last time I visited, you seemed a bit down."

Cricket sighed. "Well, what do you expect?"

"Got to thinking, we should try and figure out where Mom might be. I thought she might have gone with Aunt Pru. So I tracked her ship down… managed to get a call through to her. Aunt Pru said Mom had been talking to her cousin. She thinks Mom might have gone to California, gone to see her cousin."

"Lilianna?"

"Yeah, her. Aunt Pru said Mom had been talking to her not long before you went down. What do you think?"

"I try not to."

"Daad!"

"Could have."

"Where do I start?"

"Hell, I don't know. She probably found her in the Bay Area. She'll be back when she's ready."

"How do you know?"

"I know her, you're here. She'll be back to see you."

"We were never close. Not like she was with Preston and Jacob."

"Don't even go there, Son. She was never the same after they died. Had it been you, the results would have been the same for the ones left behind."

"Nothing personal, huh?"

"Ah, hell. Every thing's personal. It's just a fact. Your kids aren't supposed to die before you do. It turns everything upside down. And you, Brooks, you weren't exactly easy. After Pres died you wouldn't let either of us hold you. It was hard. Not so bad for you and me 'cause we could work together. Man you used to follow me around like a little shadow." Cricket looked into his son's face and, to his surprise, saw tears coursing down his cheeks. He reached out and clasped his arm. "What?"

"I always thought everything would be okay with you guys if it had been me instead of either of them."

"Brooks. You're what made life worth going on. You did that for both of us. Only I know, your mother thought everything would have been better if the death were hers."

"We're one messed-up family."

Cricket grinned. "You got it."

"Back to Mom. I want to at least try finding her." Brooks held up his hand. "It's not just for you. I need to talk to her. Since she's been gone, my head's become a wastebasket filled with crumpled paper and on each sheet is a question.

Questions I never knew needed answering. "Do you realize I don't even know her cousin's last name?"

"It's Tourneau. Lilianna Tourneau."

"Tourneau? That's her mother's maiden name?"

"Yeah. I don't think she ever married."

"I thought she was an actress."

"Yeah. Probably still is."

"You'd think the world would know."

"Maybe she wasn't that great an actress."

"Thanks, Dad." Brooks turned to leave, but then stopped. "Anything I can get you?"

"Next time, bring whisky."

Brooks laughed, "I'd probably have to smuggle it in."

"So don't be a candy ass. Do some smuggling."

Supper came clattering. The aide that brought it was perky, young, and healthy. Cricket had the strongest urge to reach out and squeeze her butt; however, he refrained, but took his pleasure in watching her leave the room.

As if reading his mind, Ace said, "Nice ass. Huh?" He did not turn on either the radio or the TV. The room seemed strange and silent but for the clicking of the utensils on their plates. "I wasn't sleeping. When your son came in, I wasn't sleeping. That's a tough one. You know we get so caught up in our own sorry-ass stories, that's all we see. I'm pissed because my son is deformed and I believe the army caused it. I'm pissed because I can't screw my wife because now my jiz burns her insides, and I believe the army's the cause. At least I can hate the government. At least I have that."

CHAPTER 24

B Y THE TIME Templeton arrived on Saturday, Mark Dykstera and John Wheland, the two potters Franniemarie met at the Triad, had cased the garage and, in consultation with Franniemarie and Willis, had drawn up the pottery plans. Franniemarie and Willis had the upstairs all torn to hell. Willis Milner was running new wire. Franniemarie had ripped out the wall between the kitchen and the dining room, removed the doors from the kitchen cabinets, and stripped the outer wall coverings from all the apartment rooms except the bathroom. That was the only room that neither Franniemarie nor Templeton wanted to change. Willis grumbled about having to fish all the new wires into that space, and he grumbled about the lack of insulation in the outer wall. Templeton suggested they pour insulation between the studs after he finished rewiring. Franniemarie just smiled. She'd watched him fish wires on all the interior walls, and knew he was getting a kick out of giving them a hard time.

Franniemarie, camped out downstairs and was eating take-out, glad there was at least a mattress on the floor. Templeton tossed her sleeping bag next to Franniemarie's nest before pulling out the drawings she'd completed since their last conversation. She'd redesigned the staircase, for the most part reusing the existing materials. Basically, she'd turned the landing so that the entrance was now off the back porch. She'd also drawn up plans for the rooftop patio, with a full light access door from the dining room. By noon, they'd measured and ordered the door as well as new windows to cover the western kitchen wall. By midnight, they'd cleared out the back porch and a good portion of the basement, and she'd told Templeton about Yves.

By the first light of morning, Templeton was up and itching to get back to the basement.

"But Tempe," Franniemarie protested, "that's hardly my first priority."

Her friend would have none of it. "Look, Frannie, how about I make the basement my project. Just help me clear it out and I'll come on weekends and take care of the rest. Trust me, when I'm done you're gonna love it."

By one in the afternoon, they'd hauled out the rotting sheet rock and were ready to call it a day, when curious Franniemarie pried open a warped door off the large utility room. The room was stacked full of beveled glass-leaded doors. "Look Tempe!" She carefully disengaged the nearest and carried it into the greater room. I think these will fit the upper kitchen cupboards. The filth that covered the door could not conceal its beauty. It took three hours for the two of them to bring the treasure up and stack it on the back porch. Then it was time for Templeton to leave. "I'll be back next Friday night," she promised.

Willis teased Franniemarie, "I see you finally met someone as hell-bent on self- destruction as yourself?"

Franniemarie did not find it amusing. Each day she woke by 6 a.m. Each day she worked till one or two in the morning, and nothing could slow her down. On Mondays, when Yves came on his day off, he joined her in sanding, painting, setting tile—eating fruit and nuts and drinking milk on the fly.

By the end of six weeks, the upstairs wiring was finished, the structure insulated, the windows and patio door installed. By the end of six weeks Templeton had transformed the basement into a spa-like spot, complete with sauna. By the end of six weeks, Franniemarie had taped, mudded, and painted the kitchen and dining room; hung the cleaned leaded doors on the kitchen cabinets; stripped the linoleum off the floor; and joyously sanded the maple flooring she'd uncovered. By the end of six weeks, the cough that started two weeks earlier had progressed into a crackle.

Willis worried and nagged, "I don't like the sound of that cough, Franniemarie. You need to see a doctor. You're going to kill yourself working this way." Still, she would not quit.

Before Templeton left for Portland, she ordered Franniemarie to lie down. "You're not just pale, Frannie, you're grey." However, she knew for sure Franniemarie was terribly sick when she followed her orders. Before leaving town, she called Yves. "She sounds terrible," she said. "I don't think she should be left alone."

By the time Yves arrived, Franniemarie was too weak to rise. "Frannie, oh Frannie, what have you done to yourself?" Yves picked her up, carried her to his car and took her to the hospital. There, the admitting physician diagnosed her condition as acute double pneumonia, and set her up with oxygen. Yves told the staff that he was her brother. He stayed the night, sleeping in a recliner next to her bed. Mid-morning, he called SMOKIN' JOAN'S, told her how ill her friend was, and muddled through an awkward self-introduction. Joan said she'd be there to see her Tuesday afternoon. Days, Yves worked in Yachats, nights he slept in Franniemarie's room. With each breath she took, Franniemarie's lungs crackled like cellophane.

When Joan arrived, she hardly knew what to say to this friend she now felt she hardly knew.

"I'm so sorry you have to be here."

"Sorry? Why?" Joan's comment baffled her.

"You know. Hospitals are so awful."

"Awful? Oh, no, they're wonderful." Franniemarie gasped. "All the nurses and doctors in their wonderful white uniforms." She wanted to add, *These white walls are wonderful. It's safe here. These people take care of you. I'm safe here."* But she was too weak.

Sometime after Joan left, she woke with a start. *White uniforms. I'm not afraid of white uniforms. White uniforms are safe. I'm not afraid of all uniforms. Just—just what?* Franniemarie shook with a chill that was not made of pneumonia. Helpless, Franniemarie slipped under the embossed sheet of iron before it crashed.

She stood, her back pressed against the closed door, trembling like the rabbit thrust into an anaconda's cage. He, his hair cropped so short it almost wasn't, his face clean shaven, eyes dead blue, sat in a chair. Sat dressed in an olive drab uniform, a crisp olive drab uniform with ribbons and medals on its jacket. Sat with his legs crossed, and smoking a cigarette. "What a pretty little morsel." He smiled, ran his tongue across his lips, then stubbed out his cigarette. "Come here. Don't be afraid. I won't hurt you."

"You be nice." Nannette spits the words through clinched teeth. "You be nice." Over and over and over, Nannette's voice hisses through her. But she isn't there. Dutifully, Franniemarie walks across the room and stands before him. Her head barely reaches above his knee. She does not struggle as he places her on his lap, places his cheek next to hers. His cheek smells like perfume. Sort of like perfume. His lips are wet—icky, and his face against hers hurts. He fusses with her dress, settles her on his lap. The damp wool gabardine of his uniform hurts her legs. The decorations on his jacket hurt her cheek. "You be nice," echoes, echoes, echoes. His fingers, exploring those places they aren't supposed to go. The fingers hurt. This man is hurting Franniemarie. Franniemarie does not cry out. Franniemarie is nice. The smell of damp wool gabardine fills her nostrils.

Over and over, the scene repeats itself. Sometimes with the thin blue-eyed man, sometimes with another. His eyes are brown. He is heavier. He is gentler and the smell of damp wool gabardine fills her nostrils—fills her nostrils with a smell that will live with her the rest of her life.

CHAPTER 25

Fishermen off the coast of new england say they are frequently hauling in barrels filled with poisonous waste.

"Shit, that's not news. They've been screaming about it for at least five years. Does our government do anything about it? Hell no, they're too busy 'saving the world for democracy."

"So what are you going to do about it?

"Ain't nothing anyone can do but bitch. Once I knew the son of one of those New England fisherman. Grasso said his old man had been unable to work in over two years, ever since he'd hauled in a leaking barrel that smelled so strong he became unconscious. The Coast Guard told them it was full of toxic waste. His dad went out everyday he could to fish, but most of the time he was too weak to haul in his nets. He was poisoned for sure and what did the government do? Nada. Just like me. Some days my walker and I can make it to the john. Some days we don't. You're witness to my condition."

Indeed, Cricket's struggle to regain his equilibrium and his strength as his body recuperated from the infection made him painfully aware of the effort Ace put into his own recovery each day, aware of his struggle against some malingering fatigue, his struggle against an ever present malaise.

"Ace?"

"What?"

"Bet this old man can beat you in a race to the end of the hall and back."

"What'll you wager?"

"Nip of my good whiskey?"

"You're on." Ace pushed himself up, then closed his eyes a moment before working his walker into a position in front of him."

Cricket squiggled himself onto his good side, slipped one leg off the bed, fished for his slipper with his toe and wondered what made him challenge his roommate so. *Is it for my roommate or for myself. No matter, it helps."*

Halfway back Ace's wife, carrying their child, turned onto their corridor. On seeing them Ace sped up, thump shuffle shuffle, thump shuffle shuffle, thump, until triumphantly he faced them. "Mary Beth, it's so damn good to see you. I'd hug you if I wouldn't fall down. I'd take Isaac. I'd lighten your load, if I could."

"It's okay, Peter. I've grown strong." She slowed her steps to match his.

Cricket passed them, gripped and shuffled his way to their room. Once there, he sat on the edge of his bed and maneuvered himself into a position facing the wall. He faced the wall to protect himself as much as to give them a feeling of privacy. *What would we have done if one of our children was born like that?* Isaac, with a gross hemangioma on his forehead and one leg inches shorter than the other, at one and a half he can crawl but he can't walk. Nearly blind, he is already wearing glasses.

"The good news is the doctor says he is bright. He can tell because he understands what I want, and the other day he laughed when the dog ran after a ball, slipped on the rug, and rolled over. Skipper had such a surprised look on his face. I laughed, too. Oh, Peter, the doctor says a sense of humor is a sign of intelligence. He likes mostly to sit on my lap and listen to me read and look at the pictures. The doctor says those are all good signs. He's pulling himself up and isn't as afraid of falling as he used to be." As if in agreement, Isaac gurgled and smacked his lips.

"And, Peter, he gave him a clean bill of health. We're so lucky. Peg's baby doesn't have a thyroid and she's blind. Marlene's is retarded, not much better than a vegetable and so deformed they don't have any hope for her." Breathlessly, she added, "And you darling, you are looking better than you have since before that war began."

In the silence that followed, Cricket could feel their kisses, their passion. He pushed himself deeper into his bed.

After his family left, Ace slithered out of bed. Hanging onto his walker he called out, "Cricket, Cricket, look you dumb fuck I know you're not sleeping, so turn your ass over. Did you hear that? Isaac has a clean bill of health."

"That's great news, Ace." Cricket worked his body into a position facing his roommate. "Now what we gotta do is get you up and running. You gotta be taking care of those two."

Despair flooded his roommate's face. "What's a man to do when he doesn't know one day from the next if he's going to be able to stand, sometimes even sit up for that matter."

"Know anything about computers?"

"Not much. But I'm good at cards. That's how I got the nickname 'Ace'.

"Are you good at math?"

"Hell, yes. How do you think I got good at cards?"

"Brooks keeps saying I should be keeping the farm records on a computer. I suspect he's right, but I can always think of a million excuses not to get one. You like computers?"

"Never thought about it, guess I like what they do."

"Well, start liking 'em a whole lot more. My son has a friend who troubleshoots for the computer illiterate. That's something you can do and still pace yourself—could work around your drag ass moments."

"Yeah, I could if I had a clue."

"Shit man, you gotta start somewhere. Then it's just one footfall at a time."

"Now it sounds like you're on a mission."

"I am." Cricket pulled the phone off the table and onto his bed. Dialing, he added, "You and I are going to start learning something new. Me just to use one, you to troubleshoot for us computer challenged yokels. I am on a mission, and don't you forget it."

CHAPTER 26

FIVE DAYS AFTER Franniemarie was admitted to the hospital, she was released. The nurse wheeled her to the exit. Yves offered his arm, and she took it. A crisp sea breeze accompanied them to the car. Franniemarie kept gulping it in, and it tingled her interior. She felt lightheaded, not from her physical illness but out of relief—the relief that comes from discovering grave inner truths and in so doing, finding yourself suddenly released—free.

Yves settled her into his truck, "You okay?"

"More okay than I've been since I was three. It seems strange now, that today's staff isn't wearing white. Neither are the hospital walls, yet that's how I saw them when I came in."

"You were pretty sick. You returned to a safe place, a place you experienced when you were a little child."

"You weren't surprised when I told you about the moments I relived in the hospital, were you?"

Yves smiled tenderly, "Not really."

"You knew I'd been abused?"

"I thought it was a possibility. Want to catch a bite before I take you home?"

"What I'd really like is to go to Portland and find some patio furniture for my new deck, that and some plants. Besides, it's too early for lunch."

"Whoa! Lady, you're supposed to take it easy for a bit."

"I could take it easier on a lounge chair on my deck. Tempe tattled. She said you put up the planters on the east and south sides and a clear wind shield on the ocean side. I can't wait to get the furniture for it and settle in."

"We could probably find something you'd like in Lincoln City."

"Lincoln City, here we come."

Late afternoon, Yves practically carried Franniemarie up the stairs and put her into bed. While she slept, he hauled up the furniture: three metal chairs and a lounger with cushions, three small tables, and five giant pottery pots. After tamping potting material into her containers and setting her two tomato plants, he went to the kitchen, heated soup and carved off a couple of thick slices of whole wheat bread.

Brushing her hair back, Franniemarie straggled in. "Something smells good."

"Morning, Sleepyhead. Want to take your supper on the deck?" Without waiting for a reply, Yves placed the food on a tray. "Lead away."

"Oh, Yves. It's wonderful. It's way beyond anything I ever imagined."

"I take it you like it?" Yves set supper on a small table.

In answer, Franniemarie wrapped her hand around his biceps, then facing him she slid her arms around his neck and kissed him—kissed him again and again and again.

Yves gently disentangled them. "Sweetheart, you need to eat."

Breathless, she sat down.

"Wine. Would you like a glass of wine?"

"I would. And you?"

"I would."

With grave deliberation, Franniemarie took her glass from Yves. Watching him, she took a sip. "I like your hands. Sometimes when I fall asleep, I do so with my tongue tracing an image of your long, slender, strong, fingers. And your hair, now caught in a ponytail, but when I see you before I fall asleep it's unclasped and fallen around your shoulders. When I was young I thought I was liberated. I thought my revulsion toward crew cuts and clean shaven faces was just a hippie preference. Today, I'm amused by my ignorance. I slept with anyone I didn't find repulsive because I couldn't say no. Because I could say no to some, I thought I was making choices and that made me liberated. I was a woman as free as any man to sleep with anyone I chose."

"Would you prefer me with a beard?"

"No. I prefer you just as you are." Franniemarie finished her soup. "You're the first man I've wanted, not because I wanted him to want me, but because I wanted him."

Yves' fingers began caressing hers. She picked up his hand and slowly savored his finger-tips. Then she was in his arms, his strong lithe body carrying her to the bedroom and laying her gently on the bed. When she started to rush the love-making Yves said, "Easy, Sweetheart, this is as much for you as for me." He uncovered her secret places, making her pant and strain until she released. Only then did he allow his own.

In the morning, Franniemarie watched him sleeping. Watched and ached to touch his face, trail her fingers across his cheek bones, along his jaw. Yves opened his eyes, gently drew her to him. Soon his hair was framing his face as he hovered over her and she knew pure sexual joy.

Late for work, Yves left Franniemarie in bed.

And Franniemarie felt positively chatoyant, her body polished opalescent by the act of love. Lazy memories of the past twenty-four hours purred through her, then took a turn to the image of her father—a picture of her father in his navy garb. She became aware of a breath she'd been holding all of her life. The uniforms were all olive drab not navy blue. She exhaled a tremulous shiver and felt altogether good.

Stretching, she left the bed and slipped on a bathrobe. Rummaging in her cardboard box, near the bottom she found the last of her aunt's journals. It had been weeks since she'd done reading of any kind. On a tray she placed a glass of milk, a banana, and an apricot Danish. It was a glorious day with the sun painting white caps silver on an extremely blue ocean.

"I'll never do business with Huffeldt again, that's for sure. Edward Graunstadt hasn't the sense to pull in his ears. He's worse than Mrs. Ellington. And he has the nerve to greet me with a broad smile. That silly, long-eared braying animal! I'm ashamed for anyone to know I ever met Edward Graunstadt. A certain ridiculous attorney still thinks he's going to be treated like what he isn't, a decent person. Next time he gets funny with some woman, I hope she'll call the police. He who filches my good name steals more than great riches, and he who annoys me with improper advances makes me feel as if my own little town were a nasty jungle of savagery. Saw Mr. Grieg yesterday and pretended not to because I hoped he wouldn't notice me with my hair in pins. Vanitas, vanitatis est omnia vanitas."

Why am I reading this drivel? I found my road back; I don't need to find hers. I don't need her to show me the way. What I need to do is take a good look at the showroom and garage. That's what I need to do. However, first things first, do the dishes. Get dressed.

The showroom windows were filthy and the room smelled of dust and disuse. Worse, the garage smelled of oil and the floors were caked in dirt. Franniemarie threw open all the doors. The roll-up doors between the showroom and the garage went up in a cloud of dust. *Mistake! Should have washed them first. At least vacuumed them off. Only, I don't have a vacuum. Better call Willis and let him know I'm ready to go back to work.*

Before she could get to a phone Willis drove up. "What in tarnation do you think you're doing, young lady? Just out of the hospital and here you are in the middle of what I can see by the light of your eye is the beginning of another project."

"Know what I want to do with this place?"

"I'd wager I'm about to find out."

"I want to start putting the garage in order in preparation for the potting studio. This room is going to be an art gallery, a place where we can also hold literary readings. Tell you what, if you'll measure these rooms, I'll put on a pot of coffee and we could make our plans on the patio."

"Don't you think we should redo the stairwell first?"

"I'm of a mood to tackle this now."

"We can't finish the office until we do the stairwell."

"Please, Willis, humor me."

What seemed to Willis to be a sudden whim, wasn't. The project had been hovering in the back of her mind since she first saw the place. Since the day she overheard the two fellows at the Triad fussing about needing space to set up a pottery. Quicker than a sneaker wave, Franniemarie had the pottery laid out in her mind, and had made a list of her gallery needs. Picture molding, a variety of rectangles and cubes made of chipboard and painted the same shade of white as the walls. The floors were thirteen-inch, square black and white tiles. *The tiles will scrub up just fine. All I'll need is a couple of picnic benches. I'll paint the pottery sort of a creamy clay color, the color of the beach when the sand is dry.*

"I want the pottery to be ready for Mark and John when their wheels and bricks come in."

"Franniemarie, have you a clue as to how a kiln is built?"

"Nope. John and Mark do. For now, we only need to get this place cleaned out and painted. We need to seal down three of the bay doors. I think it might be best to leave the fourth one functional. If you can get the materials for that project and what you need for mending the glass block windows on the south end of the building, I'll pick up the paint."

Willis had no more than pulled out when Franniemarie had a bucket in hand, determined to wash the windows. Once started, she couldn't quit. By the time Yves returned, she'd not only washed all the windows, but she'd prepped the gallery for painting. She was spreading out the drop-cloths when he arrived.

"For God's sake, Frannie—what in hell do you think you're doing?"

In a rush, she told him of her plans, the first he'd heard of them. Mid-sentence, he held up his hand. "Stop, Frannie. Just stop."

"But I…"

Yves put his finger to her lips. "Shusssssss. Wash up. We're going to go out to eat and we're going to talk."

"Japanese?"

"Japanese it will be."

Yves poured the plum wine with an air of gravity that was also both firm and gentle. Raising his glass, he said, "To Franniemarie Martin, the woman I love."

Franniemarie thought she'd faint. However, before she touched the glass to her lips he'd set his down and continued, "Above all, I want you to remember how deeply I love you because what I'm about to bring up may not seem loving. One of your traits—that is both charming and alarming—is your high energy. Unfortunately, I see it followed by great depression and much pain. That is not charming. And it is always distressing. Especially when it's happening to the person you love."

"Yves, I can't help the way I am. I've always been this way." Franniemarie choked back tears. "I spent a lifetime trying to be different with Cricket. I ran away so that just once I could wake up when my body wanted to—to sleep at its whim. I'd be free to get lost in my thought, to never need to explain my absences in thought or body to anyone."

Yves took her hand in his. "I understand. But can you understand the pain another might feel when you are either hurting or working yourself into a state where you will not be well?"

Franniemarie swallowed and nodded, "Oh, Yves! I thought this was going to be different. I thought you accepted me." When the waitress set their plates in front of them, she looked down to hide her tears.

"Please, Frannie, don't go there. There are options. Once, you told me you don't believe in compromises. What I'm asking is that you get help. No, listen to me. There are drugs out there for this sort of thing. You don't have to live on a roller-coaster. And, yes, you still will be you."

"And who, Yves, do you think I am?"

"I think you're a lovely, fascinating, creative lady who is possibly bi-polar."

"Manic-depressive."

"Same thing. How long have you known?"

"Since college. I had a breakdown. Hadn't slept in five days, started hallucinating, and everything turned ugly. Spent three weeks in a psych ward on 400 milligrams of thorazine a day. When they turned me loose, they said that was all they could do for me and they'd expect me to be back three, four times a year for the rest of my life. I've never been back."

"Might I add, I think you're one tough lady."

Franniemarie looked puzzled.

"Not many can keep themselves together for a year, not to mention the best part of a lifetime. How did you do it?"

"Meditating, Writing poetry. Not talking about it. And about twenty years ago, when the depression was really bad, our family doctor put me on Prozac. That helped smooth me out, at least the down side. I left home without my meds."

"Today they have better options."

"So you want me to change?"

"I want you to get help. Give it a try. If it doesn't work, you come back to where you are now."

"Without you?"

"Not unless that's what you want."

Quietly, they began to eat. Yves broke the silence. "Would you mind if Fang came to live with us? I feel guilty leaving him alone so much of the time. He's really not much trou …"

"I'd be honored to have Fang guarding my place. However, if you're moving in I must warn you, TV is not allowed in my house. On the other hand Mission oak is, and, if that wonderful set you have in your living room is yours, it's welcome. Besides, then Tempe will have a better place to sleep than the floor."

"Are you going to eat that shrimp or…"

"Don't you dare!" Franniemarie returned her poised chopsticks to her plate.

CHAPTER 27

Brooks came in carrying an armload of computer boxes. "Are you guys in luck! Big sale on at "Eake's Office and Supply." I just brought you guys a couple of laptops and a printer. Figured it'd save space and the two of you could share for now. Bob Fletcher will be coming over three nights a week from seven to eight. He teaches computer science at Kearney State. He's an easygoing guy. I know you're going to like him. Plus, he's not charging an arm and a leg."

Like little kids, they soon had the boxes all torn to hell and the room looking like Christmas.

Margie, of the fine ass, poked her head in, "I see you have new toys. What I want to know is, where are you kids planning to eat?"

Cricket and Ace looked at each other. Cricket spoke first. "I think it's time we started eating in the dining room."

"You do understand you have to dress to eat there."

"Sounds like as good an excuse as any." Ace sounded determined, if not sure.

"You know," she added, "wouldn't hurt if you shaved more than once every three or four days either."

"That a requirement?" Ace challenged.

"No. You're allowed to be slobs." Margie turned heel and bounced her assets out.

"Dad, I got Lilianna's number."

"Your mom there?"

"Got an answering machine. She hasn't called back."

"Then she's there."

"How do you know that?"

"Okay. I haven't seen you in two weeks. If I know you, your call went through soon after. By the way, how'd you get her number?"

"Went through your old phone bills. Called the only number listed for San Francisco."

"Right," Cricket already had his laptop plugged in and turned on. "Lilianna would have called back if she weren't there. You might have to go get her."

"Dad! I can't get away now. You know that."

"So, wait till she comes home."

"It's been damn near four months. This looks less and less like a time out to me."

"Just like your mother, no patience." Cricket toyed with the keyboard. "Brooks, did you know we have a secret court? Right here in the US of A."

"You've been cooped up too long."

"Really. It was set up by Nixon."

"No, it wasn't." Ace interrupted. "Nixon claimed he had the right to conduct unilateral searches, in the name of national security, of course. Congress wanted some sort of legal process and review. Congress set up the secret courts."

Cricket yawned. "Whatever. Our Constitution says the government has to have probable cause to search or seize. This Foreign Intelligence Surveillance Act, set up by those bozos, allows secret searches for any reason. Now these yahoos can enter your house, wiretap your phone—your computer, even your house—and you'll never know they are there 'cause they don't even have to tell you they're doing it."

"Dad. That doesn't help with Mom."

"Don't you see? There are bigger things out there than us missing Mom."

"Geesus Dad, You're outta your ever-loving mind. Man, how long you gonna be in this place."

"Doc says a couple more weeks. I'm getting stronger and faster every day. You better watch out." Cricket's mood became somber. "And, Brooks, keep calling Lilianna. Maybe leave a message that I'm not dead. Okay."

"Yeah. That's the best I can do for now."

CHAPTER 28

FRANNIEMARIE FOUND A psychiatrist working at Samaritan Hospital in Lincoln City. Actually, she found two listed in the directory. At first, she was afraid to make an appointment. Afraid she would lose herself, her creativity, her energy. She was more afraid she'd lose Yves. A part of her knew that wouldn't happen. Another part knew it was an issue of trust—trust and caring, acknowledgment of caring. After thoughtful deliberation, she chose the woman, and she was glad she had. Dr. Asher was cheerful, bright, and decisive. Franniemarie left the session with assurance she would yet be the person she'd come to know and accept, a prescription for Lithium, and an appointment for the following Tuesday.

As she set down the groceries, her aunt's last journal caught her eye. *I should finish reading it. I owe her that.*

"I'm hard in the way things that have survived a long siege are hard. I don't mean the kind of hardness Aunt Fern means, I'm hard in a way Aunt Fern doesn't know about, and in a way she never will. I'm hard and I'm old in the way of unprotected women who are at the mercy of gossip and have been in isolation for so many years they no longer have emotions in common with other women. The things most women feel have been burned out of me for keeps and those things I feel, they don't. I don't want a career and I don't want a marriage. I like to write stories, but I don't like pressure. I just want to diddle."

Hard, hard, hard, schmard. I get paranoid, too, but damn, when she goes on like this it bores me. And it makes me see how absurd my behavior is. Like why should she, me, give a damn. Let the bastards talk. Hell! Give them loads to talk about or get the hell outta Dodge. I did. Here, nobody knows, nobody cares, and that includes me.

Franniemarie's rant turned into rage. *It was wrong. So damn wrong! How can anyone commit dastardly crimes against children? Dostoevsky knew it. But Mother never knew Dostoevsky. I can't even confront her. If I did, she'd say she didn't know what I was talking about. She'd say I was out of my mind. The damn bitch would then start in on me, soon I'd be defending myself, then I'd be crying in frustration and the frustration would turn to pain.* And the pain morphed into a memory. "Mom, were there any medical conditions in my father's family that I should know about?"

"Did you know your father died dancing in the arms of another woman?"

"I thought you told me he was killed switching for the Union Pacific."

"Why would I say something like that?"

"I don't know, but once you did."

"You don't know shit, Franniemarie, you're a liar, a liar and a thief."

"I'm not a liar, and I'm not a thief."

"Like hell, you stole ten dollars from me."

"I didn't."

Yves found his sweetheart curled into fetal position in a lawn chair, rocking and sobbing, rocking and sobbing, and shaking with rage. Wordlessly, he wrapped her in his arms and carried her to the grand Mission rocker in the living room.

Slowly the sobs receded. "Yves, my mother is one of the most evil persons in this world. Like her sister, she spins a world filled with trivia, evil, and has no concept of responsibility. Even more scary is the thought that I am no different. Yves, I was a lousy parent to Brooks."

"Well, that proves you're not one of them."

"How can you know that?"

"If you were then you wouldn't be questioning your past, your parenting, or lack of." Yves caressed her hair until her sobs turned to hiccups.

"Thank you. Thank you for giving me that."

"I gave you nothing, I was only the messenger."

"Oh, shoot!"

"Please don't. We have to get those groceries put away and make supper."

"I want to go to the caves."

"I just got back. Why don't you go to the caves while I fix us a bite to eat?"

The caves were dark and cool and the sound that echoed off their walls came wavering low, then screeching high alternating nasal and bull frog deep and ending on a B flat reverberation that left her joyous in the acceptance that she was not one of them.

Over supper she confessed to Yves that she'd never told Cricket about her promiscuous past, and that with him she'd always lived a lie.

Between bites, Yves said, "I'm more interested in the why?"

"Oh, he'd never have understood."

"Sounds like you never gave him the chance."

"I know. I couldn't take it if he rejected me. He was so normal, so solid. He was my anchor."

"But you left."

"Only because he's dead. Only because I wanted to be free. To be me. To wake up when my body wanted to. To sleep at its whim. Free to get lost in my thoughts—to never need to explain my absences in thought or body to anyone. To live a life where everything that goes wrong is not my fault. I was always excusing myself, making apologies, apologies for living in order to remain acceptable. Yves, I only want to be in a space where it is okay to be the person I am, faults and all. That's why it's so good to be here. To be here with the man I love, the man who knows me better than I do."

CHAPTER 29

Tired and out of sorts, Lilianna carted her camera and tripod into the house. Today the sun crossed her, and the weather report wasn't good for tomorrow. The phone rang and she left it unanswered. "This is Brooks Hanks, Franniemarie's son. We're trying to locate her, and I was wondering if she'd been to see you. If she's with you could you have her call me? Thanks."

Great, now I have to worry about the rest of her family. No, I promised I wouldn't tell them she was here and she isn't. Besides he didn't leave a number. Lilianna dipped a spoon into a jar of crunchy peanut butter and began sucking on it. *I wish I knew where she was. There's so much I'd like to tell her.* Ripping open her mail became one more dissatisfaction in a long day of disappointment, nothing but bills. *Well, what did I expect? A letter from Frannie?*

Time to cut the lonely line. Lilianna picked up the phone. "Rachael! How'd you and Davida like to come to supper?

Yeah, I do mean now. Oh shit, I forgot all about it. Meet you there at six."

Quickly, Lilianna changed into her favorite black jeans, black silk turtleneck and an open weave, airy, knitted shrug that reminded her of dust motes. Her garb created a perfect backdrop for her heavy silver jewelry. *Bubbles may be ex, but there's no way I'd miss her opening at the Paper Tiger. Besides, everyone who's anyone will be there.*

As usual, Bubble's work amazed her. The bronze figures were haunting, and her animals equally so. *Or were they haunted?* Lilianna wasn't sure which. Clarice introduced her to the curator who turned out to be a fan of Lilianna's work. "You imbue your buildings with persona we never knew they had," she said.

Clarice asked, "Did you know she also does ocean?"

"Ocean?"

"Yeah that. I think building photos mixed with ocean pieces would be a stopper."

Giddy with delight, Lilianna schmoozed till the last of the guests left, all except for the curator Alice, Clarice, and Davida. Together they packed trays of leftover munchies, trashed the empty glasses, and swept the floors. Alice confessed that her next show had been cancelled. Her artist had some major surgery and was not going to be ready. In fact, she'd heard that his lover was taking him to Spain for recovery. "He's totally screwed up my advertising. May he roast in Spain!"

"This just might be your opportunity to do a Lilianna Tourneau show. I can see it now, Lilianna Tourneau photographer of architecture and sea," Davida sipped her wine.

Alice thought about that for three beats too long, "Would you be interested?"

"Yes," Lilianna's reply came three beats too soon.

"I'm familiar with your architectural work. It's superb—however, not diverse enough to fill out a one-person show. Could you bring by some of those seascapes tomorrow?"

"What time?"

Alice looked at her calendar. "Let's try two-ish."

"Two-ish it will be."

The two-ish meeting went quite well, and the following weeks fairly swam past. Between assignments, Lilianna immersed herself developing, matting and framing her chosen pieces. While cutting glass for her favorite picture, a wave, that rose from the sea and transcended from its dark beginnings into translucence, dominated the picture. Cresting white, it brought her back to her moment with her mother, the moment Annamarie watched the sea sweep her father off the *Lyckodam*, the moment she, Lilianna, was given full identity. *Did Nannette kill Franniemarie's father?* The question nagged and nagged until she gave up and called her mother. Lilianna chose late evening in hopes that her mother would be deep into the drink, and she was not disappointed.

"Lilibaby, it's so good to hear from you." Annamarie answered the gossipy questions about friends and children with abandon, even sharing stories about friends of friends whom she, Annamarie, did not know. She poured herself another Brandy Alexander, and another.

"So about Nannette! I'm curious about Aunt Nannette. How did she kill her husband?"

"Nannette was a great storyteller. Matter of fact, she was the best actress in the family, not me. By the time she was twelve, she was always writing plays."

"I thought Aunt Dorien was the writer."

"We all wrote. We're talking Nannette now. The plays she wrote were always about murdering our father. You know how kids are, they all hate their parents. Anyway, in her plays the murderess always got away with murder because she always either got someone else to do it or she just worked with the natural circumstances at hand. If it is natural, who's going to blame whom? Now Dorien! She always wrote goody-goody save the world plays."

"And you?"

"Mine were run-a-way-from-home-become-famous-and-find-out-you're-really-a princess—better yet a queen, in your stories."

"Still, I ask, did Nannette kill Franniemarie's father?"

"Well, she was mad enough at him. You know, he didn't smoke or drink, but he loved the ladies, especially dancing with the ladies. Nannette always said he died dancing in the arms of another woman."

"So she didn't kill him."

"Not really. During the war, he was a switchman on the Union Pacific. It was a very dangerous job. I believe she said he was hit by a train or pushed into a train between a couple of cars. I don't remember which. Nor do I remember by whom. I wasn't there. And she always had so many men falling all over her. Anyway, he didn't die then. They took him to the hospital and gave him transfusions. It's my understanding that they didn't know about RH negative and positive and they gave him the wrong kind. He died of a blood clot. Either that or an overdose of the morphine he was on. But this is old news, did you know Solvieg's son?"

No I didn't, nor do I give a rat's ass. "What I really called about is this show I'm having at the Paper Tiger. I was hoping you could come."

Annamarie suggested she call her secretary in the morning.

Lilianna had no more gone back to framing her picture when the phone rang. She finished twisting the wire to the second screw and picked it up. "Brooks? Oh, yes, Brooks, Franniemarie's son. I'm so sorry, she's not here ... She was here, but that was months ago ... I haven't a clue where she is now. I wish I knew. Then I could invite her to a gallery opening coming up next month ... It's a show of my work ... You see, we got into this tiff and she left and ... So Cricket is going to be okay. That's good news ... If I hear from her ... Yes. If I hear from her I'll have her call?"

CHAPTER 30

W ILLIS, MARK, AND John had the pottery nearly finished. Now Franniemarie was pushing to finish the stairwell before the grand opening. The show would be an eclectic mix: John and Mark's pottery of course, plus jewelry by Souther, a fellow architect of Tempe's acquaintance. Franniemarie was still trying to nail down something, someone for the wall space: watercolor, pastel, acrylic, oil, lithograph, photography—any two-dimensional media that caught her fancy.

When Tempe arrived the two of them spent the weekend searching for talent they could use in their gallery. Talent was not missing along the coast. The trip was like a walk on the beach, the jaspers, agates, and fossils were to be found, but nailing down the creators was another issue.

On Monday morning, Franniemarie kissed Yves goodbye. Too early to start calling potential artists, the place was clean, Willis didn't need her help, neither did Mark or John, and it was too cold to sit outside. Franniemarie concluded she had two choices; she could write a poem or she could finish reading her aunt's journals. Choosing the latter, she poured herself a cup of coffee and curled up in the big Mission rocker.

"I remember Dory, as a baby, had a tendency to think poorly of herself. I remember scolding her and disciplining her sharply for her faults and explaining that all children had these same faults and had to be taught this same way and she was to feel in no way ashamed of herself for doing what was normal for all children to do, but must learn not to do. I've always criticized her before people lest she get the idea that her little wrongdoings were too terrible to be brought into the light of day, lest she ever think only she possessed that particular fault. A naughty thing, yes, but a natural fault that everyone at some time had done and gotten over. That takes the dynamite out of it. The universality of similar experience destroys everything, but the desire to conform to a popularly accepted standard of suitable behavior. It makes the child realize that many people don't follow that standard because they are poorly trained."

Not a conclusion I'd have come to. Aunt Dorien tried so hard with so few tools to do right by her daughter. Ultimately, she failed. Had my sons lived, would I have failed them as well? Of course I would have. I didn't have any more answers to parenting than did my aunt. For all we do not want to, we parent much as we were parented. That Brooks lives is no credit to me.

By morning's end, she'd acquired a fabric artist and another who worked in pastels. With great satisfaction, she started a new cup of coffee. Footfalls on the stairwell brought Franniemarie out of her reverie. She opened to Joan. "Come in, come in. Good thing we searched the coast and identified some artists. I found a couple available, and who are dynamite."

"Where did you get this lovely Mission furniture?"

"It's Yves'."

"So we're an item now?"

"Could say that."

Fang, bad breath, coughing and all, came out of the bedroom. "And who's this?"

"Fang. He belongs to Yves—comes with the territory. "

Joan curled her lips. "Nasty little thing, isn't it?"

"Ah, give him a break, he *is* eighteen. Besides, sometimes I wake up with a cough and bad breath."

"Pray the territory is worth it."

"Believe me, it is. Yves has been wonderful. And he knows me better than I do."

"I'd call that scary."

Fang dug in a flower box built especially for the purpose, and did his duty. "I'd call that icky."

Franniemarie shrugged her shoulders. "Yves takes care of it—saves me from hauling him down the stairs. These last two weeks he's become too crippled to make it on his own."

"So you're going to marry?"

"I've been asked."

"And?"

"And it's not so simple. Look, I'm not ready to talk about it. It's not about Yves, it's about me."

"Geeze, Frannie, I never knew you to be cautious."

"Well, Joan, meet the new me."

"Something's working right. Your new digs are delightful. And this patio—it's wonderful. Kinda makes my place feel hemmed in. However, speaking of my place, I finished another batch of your rocks." Joan dug to the bottom of her great black leather purse and pulled out a paper bag of agates and jaspers.

Amidst ohs and ahs, Willis walked in. He soon joined the chorus, as Franniemarie added one polished rock at a time to her tall cylindrical vase and placed it on the table in the sun.

"I plan on starting that staircase today. I think I can rip her out before evening, but there's no way I'll get her back together today. Just so's you know, you're going to have to use the rope ladder off the patio at least for today and tomorrow. Longer if you're gonna freshen it up."

"Don't mind me. I was about to leave." Joan gathered her purse and stood. "Let me know when you set the wedding date."

"How about the gallery opening?"

"Ah, well. I suppose the important things must come first. However, I wouldn't wait too long. Strike while the iron's hot; don't let the big one get away and all that."

"Get outta here!" Franniemarie closed the door behind her old friend. Turning to Willis, she asked, "You need some help?"

"Na, I'm fine."

"You won't be ripping out the stairwell from the landing up are you?"

"Nope."

"In that case, wouldn't it work just as well if you left a ladder to the landing, at least for tonight?"

"Yep," with that, Willis was off to gather his tools.

Franniemarie rinsed the cups in the sink, retrieved her aunt's journal, sat on the patio and stared into space.

When Brooks was growing up, I didn't have much of a relationship with him. He was his daddy's boy. I never felt he was my child. I suspect that was my way of protecting myself from the inevitabilities of this world. Kids will grow up and either leave you, hate you, or worse—die. He isn't dead. He hasn't left. Perhaps he hates me. God knows he has every right. I told him Christina wasn't the right woman for him. I disapproved of the match so much I attended the wedding in body only. They knew it. Christina is so cold, so distant. I called her the Ice Princess. What more should I have expected, after all. If he thought of me at all he probably would have labeled me the Ice Queen. Now I wish I could just visit with him. I can't make it right, but I can be different.

I could call him. Pretend I don't know Cricket is dead. I should call him. The estate, such as it is, will be a nightmare without me. The place rightfully belongs to him. If Cricket isn't dead, then that solves that. Either way, I could lie and say I was mad and only went to see Lilianna, we had an argument and one thing just led to another. Actually, that's sort of how it did happen.

I wish I hadn't left Lilianna the way I did. I'd love to have her meet Yves, to come to the opening. She'd like Yves.

Franniemarie found her cousin's number and dialed. *The worst that could happen would be she'd hang up on me. Not that I'd blame her.*

"Lilianna? It's Franniemarie" In a surprised rush, she ran on, "I'm so sorry I left you the way I did. Please let me tell you who I was then … No that's not quite right … You do? … No it wasn't you. It was me … Yes, I really did want to give you a gift … I want to explain. I do that sort of thing all the time. Lilianna, I'm bi-polar. And as Lew Palladio would say, 'She hasn't a lick of good sense'. But I didn't understand bi-polar then. I do now. What I'm trying to say is, then I thought you were the one who was being unreasonable, but now I understand it was me … You don't? … Oh, Lilianna, so much has happened since I last saw you and it seems like years instead of months. I want to invite you to a gallery opening … It's my gallery … No, I haven't thought of a name yet … Yes, it needs a name … It will be 'FANG'S CHOICE'." Franniemarie surprised herself. "I'm glad you like it. And I have so much to tell … You have an opening, too? When? But of course … At least your opening is after mine. Are you ready? … Good, I'm not yet, but believe me I will be. And I have this person I … Brooks called? … What did you tell him? … Good! … Cricket's alive? … I'm glad he's alive, but it complicates the hell outta my life. Christ, I'm in love with the man of my dreams. Please don't tell them where I am. Not just yet, I have to digest this, I have to figure out what I'm doing … You still don't know if my mother killed my father. Lilianna, it doesn't matter. We all know she was capable of it. On the other hand, life might have done the job for her. It doesn't matter because I'm cleaned of her." Franniemarie hung up after promising that either she and Yves or Tempe would pick her up at the Portland Airport. She placed the phone in its cradle and compulsively went back to her aunt's journal.

"I don't live in my subconscious mind. I've always been able to say to myself, There must be some good explanation, some virtuous … explanation. I have never needed to forget anything."

Auntie, dear Auntie, if you only knew.

"The things I really like, I liked best when I was small—the things I liked the least, I like the least now. And I am a procrastinator. I always was. Then, when I finally get to it, I make a clean sweep, do everything, then start all over letting things slip. Things slip when I paint, sew, visit, or study. And everything slips while I try to find out where I went wrong or something has upset my life."

On that empty note, Dorien's journal was finished. Franniemarie rummaged in a bottom kitchen drawer and pulled out a suede bound journal with gold edges, and began:

A SEASON FOR KNOWING

It was that kind of no nonsense snow—
it comes down slow and steady and says, "I
mean business. The business of getting on with
the stuff of changing seasons—the stuff that
turns minds, dreams, fall, into winter.
And she was that kind of gardener who
wouldn't take can't for an answer—always
raising those plants that couldn't be grown in her
climate—always denying the dross of her existence.
When hypnotic snow began to build a curtain
between her garden and the mountain, between the dark
green lavender, standing lovely against the grey stone
fence, and acceptance—she grabbed her scissors,
cradled the cherished lavender in her heavy arms and
reluctantly but decisively cut it down.
And after, when she gathered in wood enough to last
the time it takes nature to knit the earth a jacket,
cosseted before her fire, she dared the thought,
"I've violated this fine flower—cut it down
before its time."
For over thirty years she hid the knowing,
fiercely proud that she was something special,
as if in clear seeing she would not survive. And
now she knew, and now she was ashamed,

cheapened in this understanding, the fabric
she'd been built of had been woven in the same
trite weft of nearly every woman. We've all
been molested, raped, abused—violation
is the norm, the commonality, the Coral Ware
of our existence, denigrating our desire
to be Sevres, at least Bavarian,
or maybe Spode. Oh,
for God's sake! Not
some paper plate!

*****

Yves poured wine. Franniemarie, Joan, and Lilianna
waltzed the crowd kibitzing with the featured artists, patrons,
and, of course, all the artists' friends, the locals, and the
tourists. Tempe handled the transactions. Mark and John
showed off their pottery. For this moment all was clean, the
rolling carts, racks, and shelving, the wedging table, reclaim
bins, the test tiles on the line together created a rhythm that
begged a portrait as if they held an innocent expectation of a
future. The electric kiln waited for the green ware and outside
the brick kiln stood majestic, a harbinger of times to come.

The gala was a smashing success.

*****

Yves and Franniemarie took Lilianna to the airport to
catch an early morning flight to San Francisco. Following the
ocean to Lincoln City, they watched the sun rise on the water.
Lilianna marveled at the changing picturesque pastoral scene

as they journeyed inland to Portland. "I should know better than to travel without my camera. Whatever was I thinking?"

They parted with promises to attend her opening, and promises that next time they'd spend more time together. Then she was gone.

In the still of her absence, Yves asked Franniemarie if she'd like to go to "Powell's Book Store".

"Yes, oh, yes! I want to get a book of poetry by this poet, Zarzyski."

On that note, the climate was changed and they spent the rest of the day lost in Powell's. Franniemarie bought several volumes of poetry in addition to the Zarzyski. Late afternoon, Yves took her back by way of Corvallis. She spent the first leg of the trip reading poetry to him.

Once through Corvallis, they were headed west, into the sunset—headed home.

"Now that the gallery is launched, I think it's time you decided what you're going to do about your marital status. It's not fair to any of us to dally longer."

Franniemarie stared out the window. *I know where I want this to end. I want to be with Yves, write—perhaps to carve in jasper. To live in the wonderful space we have created, But how do I tell my family? Do I just file for a divorce and take it from there? Do I call Cricket and say it's over for me? That's harsh.*"

"Penny for your thoughts."

Franniemarie looked up, then quickly down. The sun was blindingly bright. "Wondering about the best way to break it to them. I'm not going to talk to Cricket. At least not now. I think I'll talk to Brooks. Take it from … Oh, My God!"

The crash came so fast, so hard the car spun before the force of the impact, and propelled it off the road, flipping it over. Franniemarie never heard the sirens.

CHAPTER 31

"Yves, Yves." FRANNIEMARIE vomited into a basin.

"Ms. Martin, you have a concussion."

The words did not register. "Yves, please Yves. Yves, where are you?" Again. she lost conscience.

While one ER team ministered to Franniemarie, another pronounced Yves dead. The police worked to track down relatives. The DMV gave them the phone number recorded when her car was registered. Joan answered. "Franniemarie has moved to Newport … She has no family… I'll be there." Joan grabbed her purse, reminded herself to stay calm, to drive carefully, and headed to Newport, destination Samaritan Hospital.

"Ms. Martin is in stable condition. She has a concussion and there is a gross hematoma on her left arm. Considering the accident, the car is totally mangled, her condition is phenomenal. She's going to be fine. Unfortunately, Mr. Montagne died of head trauma and a broken neck. His death was instant. Ms. Martin is one lucky woman."

Just how fine will she be when she knows her Yves is gone? Joan wondered. Sick to her stomach, she called Mark and John. They agreed to run the gallery till Franniemarie was able to return. Next, she called Templeton. *Brooks, I should call Brooks. Damn, I haven't a clue how to get ahold of him. Franniemarie never even mentioned where she and Cricket lived—had lived. Only Nebraska.*

When Templeton arrived, they held each other, silently weeping, neither able to process the tragedy, neither able to sort out how, when the swelling in her brain receded, they were going to tell Franniemarie that Yves was dead.

Staff offered them dinner, but they declined. Staff brought them drinks and yogurt. They shared stories about their friend. Both agreed that calling her mother, even if they could track her down, would be a bad idea. Templeton wondered if they should contact Cricket. Joan was surprised that Cricket was alive, more surprised that they were yet married. Joan was hurt that Franniemarie had not found fit to share that portion of her life with her.

"I think she didn't want you to have to lie for her," Templeton comforted. "Since hardly anyone knew me, it was unlikely I'd ever have to."

Templeton tossed her yogurt cup into the wastebasket and volunteered, "Someone should call Willis. I could do that and ask him to let me in to search for family members. She probably has their numbers written in the phone book. You good for staying?"

Joan nodded.

When Templeton returned, she brought with her the phone numbers for Yves' mother, as well as those of Lilianna, and Brooks.

The police contacted Mrs. Montagne. Templeton called Lilianna, Joan called Brooks.

When Franniemarie woke, her two friends stood on either side of her bed. Joan reached up to take the hand held above her head by pillows in deference to the hematoma. Templeton, standing waist level, held her right hand.

"Yves. Where is Yves?"

Neither Templeton nor Joan could speak for their tears and swollen throats.

"He's dead, isn't he? He's dead."

They nodded.

Franniemarie began to keen. Joan's and Templeton's voices joined hers. A nurse closed the door.

*****

Franniemarie stood at the foot of her bed and wept. With baby steps she worked her way to its head, picked up Yves' pillow and clasped it to her chest. Burying her face in it, she inhaled the scent of his hair, a trace of his aftershave. She gathered Grand's comforter and took it along with the pillow to the lounge chair and there, inhaling the lasting scent of Yves, the comforting smell of salt water, the rhythmic sounds of the waves, rocked herself into sleep.

First light of dawn found her heading down to the caves. Inside she cried out, "Yves, help! Please help! I cannot go on without you." Then she fell to keening, and the keening turned into a sound mantra that left her in a space that understood that only she could help herself. That is the way it is—that is the way it has always been. She was marked to know herself, to become whole—to become one with all that is.

Back in her kitchen, she toasted a slice of bread and washed it down with milk; then, with shaking hands, she dialed Brooks.

"... physically? I'm okay. Brooks, I was a dreadful mother ... It matters to me ... It's not all right. We can't just dismiss a lifetime, your lifetime ... Yes, I know you had Dad, and later Christina ... I wasn't starting in on Christina ... Brooks, I hardly know her... That's just my point ... For God's sake, hear me out. I want to give her a chance. I want to know her ... Like me, huh? ... No. I just found it interesting. I can't go back. Not just now ... It's not that simple ... Brooks, I met a man ... Yes, we had an affair ... No ... No ... No. Brooks, he's dead ... No ... Yes. No ... "Franniemarie held back tears. "It's not that simple ... Here I have a life ... I have a place of my own and a gallery to run ... Yes, a gallery ..."

In the end she promised to talk to Cricket. She told him she was both surprised and unburdened to know he was alive. She did not add that she had purposefully left him for dead, nor that she was glad to be free to submit her medical bills to their insurance.

Before the day was out, Yves' mother came knocking at her door. Brushing Franniemarie aside, she went straight for the point. "I've come to collect my son's things." She had already picked up his wallet and the keys to his truck. Silently, Franniemarie gathered his clothes. Mrs. Montagne found Fang, "positively disgusting," and wanted no part of him. As to the Mission furniture, she sniffed, "A bit plebeian for my tastes," and on that note removed herself. *No wonder Yves knew me so well. He fully understood what I was running from.*

Below the patio, John was painting the brick kiln shelves in preparation for tomorrow's firing. Franniemarie watched while steeling herself for confrontation with Cricket. *Or is it some kind of confrontation with myself?*

That evening she poured herself a stiff shot of Knob Creek, settled into the Mission rocker, and called Cricket.

To her surprise, he seemed genuinely happy to hear from her. *I can't seem to get beyond the fact I left him for dead. I can't seem to grasp that everyone is not privy to my mind, past and present.* She started to tell him how it was with her when she left.

He stopped her. "Not now Frannie. I want to see you. There will be plenty of time to talk when I get there."

Get there! No. I'm not ready.

"Brooks told me how it is with you. I understand. I'll come to see you. You know Frannie," he hurried on, "I've never been to the ocean. There's a lot of the country I've never seen. I'm not up to farming yet, but I can travel if I take it slow. Don't say no. Give me directions, and I can be there in ten days."

"Ten days. That's when I was planning to leave to go to Lilianna's opening. She's an architectural photographer, and she has a show in San Francisco. That would be a few days after you arrived. I'm planning to go. This just won't …"

"Franniemarie, you're assuming I wouldn't enjoy the show, wouldn't want to see San Francisco. You're forgetting all the good times we had in college. Remember Chicago and Old Town North? Listening to Ramblin' Jack Elliott and that other fellow… what's his name?"

"Braheny, John Braheny."

"Yeah, him. Frannie, I'll take you to San Francisco. It'll be like old times. I can be with you in less than ten days."

Ain't got no use for your red apple juice, got me a honey-baby now, got me a honey-baby now. Braheny's rich, melodic tenor shivered through her mind. *That's when Cricket started calling me Franniebaby.*

*****

About midday, Cricket arrived in his trusty Chevy truck. He'd hardly gotten out when, flabbergasted, he started in, "You haven't replaced your car yet? You can't be living out here all alone and no car."

"But Cricket, I don't even know where to begin. I'm not sure what I want. "

"Going through Lincoln City, I saw a Chevy dealer. We wouldn't go wrong to start there."

"But Cricket, I was planning to take you to the beach."

"First things, first. Hop in. We're going to get you some wheels." Before Franniemarie could protest, Cricket had already dragged his lame leg back to the truck and had hoisted it into the cab. Reaching across the seat, he popped open the door and ordered her to jump in.

"You wouldn't believe how Brooks is managing the farm. Not just Pru Ellen's farm, but ours as well. He's a pistol." Cricket shook his head.

With a start, Franniemarie realized he was totally bald. *He must have been going bald for years but I never noticed. How can that be?*

"And Pru Ellen. You wouldn't believe her. Well, either her or Val. Those two came home from their cruise just full of piss and vinegar. All ready to sign on to another trip, this time to the Virgin Islands."

Franniemarie stared at Cricket. *I lost any desire for him when he cut his hair short and started shaving. In fact, I found*

*him repulsive. At least sexually repulsive. Now that he's bald, that's
gone. Or is it, now that I know why I developed an aversion to
clean faces and short hair, he is no longer repulsive? Not attractive,
but certainly not repulsive.*

"Penny for your thoughts."

"Why don't you grow your beard again?"

Cricket shrugged, "Could I guess? Don't have to worry
about getting it tangled in the machinery anymore." He ran his
sturdy, square hand down his cheek. "Would make mornings
easier. You think it'd look good?"

"If it doesn't, you can always shave it off."

Five car lots later, they ran across a used Chevy that caught
Franniemarie's fancy. It was only two years old, under 30,000
miles and a rich forest green. That was it for Franniemarie.
Cricket was not ready, but he was resigned. He knew his
Franniebaby, and she was done.

Once home Franniemarie started to offer Cricket a beer.
He surprised her saying, "I'll have same's you."

She poured each a glass of burgundy, set the take-out
lasagna from Don Petre's in the microwave, and heated the
French bread in the oven. "I'd like to eat on the patio deck."

Again Cricket surprised her, "Suits me fine."

*When did he ever agree to eat outdoors? Certainly not even
when he was courting.*

They ate a simple green salad with a vinaigrette dressing
and sipped their wine. Cricket broke the discomfort of their
silence. "Franniemarie, we've never really talked."

She held her breath.

"What I want you to know is this, I've always known about
the river of men that ran through your life before you met
me. I didn't know why, but I did know it was painful to you

and I didn't know how to talk about it. Also, I didn't see the point in it. It stopped with me and that was all that counted."

Franniemarie cried tears of sorrow, tears of relief, tears purifying poisons that ran in her blood.

"Did Brooks tell you about Yves."

"That you loved each other, that he understood you, that you lived together and that he died." Cricket took his napkin and reached across the small table to brush away her tears.

Franniemarie changed the subject. "And you, Cricket. Brooks told me about the ruptured spleen, the crushed hip, the long stay in the rest home. It must have been hell. I mean you've always been so active. I swear if you were ever still, you were either eating or sleeping."

Laughing, she exchanged salad plates for lasagna and returned to the deck.

"Wasn't easy. Funny thing is what saved me. I was put in with this bleeding heart liberal and forced to listen to NPR for over three months. I tell you that gave me something to chew on. In the end, I grew fond of him."

By the time they retired, he to her bed, she to the Mission daven-o, Cricket had spun the tale of himself and Ace. In his telling, it became a kind of love affair in its own right. A loathing turned to understanding, and turned to love.

Early morning, hours before low tide, Franniemarie took Cricket to Ona Beach. On a long walk north past Lost Creek Trail she told him about Yves and spared no detail. When she finished, for the longest time Cricket walked in silence. Gravely he broke the silence, "You know me. I haven't much imagination. I've lived a steady life, the only ups and downs being sick cows and the markets. I have no marvelous tales of love and loss to share. But I need to tell you this, I've never been so lonely as these last months without you."

Cricket took her in his arms and held her close until perfect strangers came running past yelling, "Sneaker! Sneaker!"

Franniemarie grabbed his hand and together they ran just ahead of the wave. Breathless and laughing, as the errant wave receded, she explained why one has to watch out for sneaker waves; they can be huge, they can knock you down and in certain circumstances can pull you under. A bit further, they were skipping over great flat-topped black rocks, some covered with slippery, mossy greenery. In the waters between the rocks, they found a couple of agates and one lovely fossilized clam shell.

"You find these treasures every day?"

"Every day I come to the beach."

"No wonder you're so fascinated."

"And you haven't even seen the caves."

On the walk back, his leg began to throb. She adjusted her stride to his slower pace and told him the story of the caves, of her hospitalization with pneumonia, the kindness of Joan, and Tempe, the sorrow she was feeling in the loss of Yves and the painful unlocking of those secrets from which her mind had tried so hard and long to protect her.

Cricket told her how he was helping Ace through community college.

Franniemarie took his hand and squeezed it in approval.

Mornings, the following week, she took him to the Oregon Coast Aquarium, Agate Beach (where they found no agates), Devil's Punch Bowl and Boiler Bay. Then south to Cape Perpetua, where they took a fairly long hike—Cricket frequently resting his tired leg without complaint, the Heceta

Head Lighthouse, and the Sea Lion Caves. Afternoons, Franniemarie manned the gallery. Sometimes Cricket took Fang for a walk, other times he napped, or read, or visited with Franniemarie. Each day he grew visibly stronger.

On Friday night, Tempe and Joan came for supper. The deck was cool and lovely. Franniemarie's vegetables were beginning to vine and trail down the sides of her boxes. The shrimp salad and homemade biscuits were a hit. Best of all, the conversation was easy.

Franniemarie and Cricket announced they'd go down to Lilianna's opening, that she'd fly back from San Francisco provided Tempe agreed to pick her up in Portland. John and Mark had already agreed to watch both Fang and the Gallery. Templeton's affirmation insured the success of the adventure.

Indeed, I had forgotten how much fun we had in our first years together.

On the way down to San Francisco, they visited the redwood forests. In the silent hush of the giants, they held each other close but they did not kiss.

Lilianna's opening was well attended, and they were comfortable to be there. Franniemarie delighted in introducing Cricket to Bubbles and Clarice, Rachael and Davida. For a moment, they were an exotic couple from that never-never land of Nebraska, and Cricket's beard gave him a distinctive air that was not lost on Franniemarie.

On the way to the airport, Cricket suggested they meet again in Arizona, just for a vacation. They'd visit the Grand Canyon, the Havasupai Indian Reservation and, who knew, perhaps they'd even go to Las Vegas. She'd fly into Flagstaff where he'd pick her up.

Franniemarie sucked in her breath. She remembered a passage from her aunt, '*One of the first things Gill said, after our honeymoon, was that he was so glad to be married because now he could relax and stop courting me.*' Cricket's been so like the man I met and married. Courtship comes easy to some.

Franniemarie said, "You know, I do have a business to run. I'll keep it in mind, but at this time of my life, my business comes first."

They promised to keep in touch.

In parting, Cricket gently kissed her fingertips.

THE END

A niece sets out on a quest to better understand an enigmatic aunt in this novel.

When readers first encounter Franniemarie Hanks, she is plagued with problems and uncertainties. For one, she's engaged in a combustible relationship with her husband, Cricket. "I could kill him," she muses, "might be worth it to never hear another country western whine." Her one source of sanity is drawn from staring out into Nebraska's prairie—an uncluttered expanse of possibility …. When Franniemarie receives a call from the Oakland Welfare Department regarding her Aunt Dorien, who has been branded as "strictly loony tunes" … it appears like yet more bad news. What in fact transpires is a journey of self-discovery. Franniemarie … "pedal to metal" into the Nebraska landscape, eager to learn more about her aunt, her family … She quickly discovers that Aunt Dorien has been committed but also that she was a prolific writer, albeit never … Franniemarie is delighted to discover Aunt Dorien's undiscovered talent and begins piecing together family memories. Many classic road novels, like Kerouac's On the Road, employ a male protagonist. Here, a daring heroine seizes the trajectory of the road, and the … refreshing result is a tender exploration of the self. On her heart-rending odyssey, Franniemarie faces up to her own fraught past; yet finding solace in a creative endeavor, namely the art of writing, also becomes a key theme. Elliott (Songs of Bernie Bjorn, 2016, etc.), who's also an accomplished poet, appears to have effortless access to a wealth of rich, beautiful imagery: "In the park, the flowering acacia bleeds scarlet, thru every break in foliage, a scarlet banner raised especially for me." She also displays a shrewd understanding of the role of writing in catharsis and memory. The result is a rare thing: a clever, well-crafted novel that has both an absorbing storyline and the artful poignancy of an elegantly composed collection of poetry.

An emotionally intuitive and impeccably written tale focusing on a female adventurer.

—Kirkus Reviews (starred review)